TEXAS PROUD

TEXAS PROUD

DIANA PALMER

MILLS & BOON

First published in Great Britain 2020
by Mills & Boon, an imprint of HarperCollins*Publishers*
1 London Bridge Street, London, SE1 9GF

Large Print edition 2020

© 2020 Diana Palmer

ISBN: 978-0-263-08529-7

MIX
Paper from
responsible sources
FSC **FSC** C007454

This book is produced from independently certified FSC™ paper to ensure responsible forest management. For more information visit www.harpercollins.co.uk/green.

Printed and bound in Great Britain
by CPI Group (UK) Ltd, Croydon, CR0 4YY

In loving memory of
Glenda Dalton Boling (1945–2019)
of Homer, Georgia.

You were my cousin, my friend, my
favorite bookseller, my hostess for
over twenty years of book signings
with my friend Jan Walker. You left a
hole in the world with your passing,
Glenda. And all of us who loved you
will miss you, as long as we live.

Chapter One

Her name was Bernadette Epperson, but everybody she knew in Jacobsville, Texas, called her Bernie. She was Blake Kemp's new paralegal, and she shared the office with Olivia Richards, who was also a paralegal. They had replaced former employees, one who'd married and moved away, the other who'd gone to work in San Antonio for the DA there.

They were an interesting contrast: Olivia, the tall, willowy brunette, and Bernie, the slender blonde with long, thick platinum blond hair. They'd known each other since grammar school and they were friends. It made for a relaxed, happy office atmosphere.

Ordinarily, one paralegal would have been adequate for the Jacobs County district attorney's office. But the DA, Blake Kemp, had hired Olivia to also work as a part-time paralegal. That was because Olivia covered for her friend at the office when Bernie had flares of rheumatoid arthritis. It was one of the more painful forms of arthritis, and when she had attacks it meant walking with a cane and taking more anti-inflammatories, along with the dangerous drugs she took to help keep the disease from worsening. It also meant no social life to speak of. Bernie would have liked having a fellow of her own, but single men knew about her and nobody seemed willing to take on Bernie, along with a progressive disease that could one day make her disabled.

There were new treatments, of course. Some of them involved weekly shots that halted the progression of the disease. But those shots were incredibly expensive, and even with a reduced price offered by kindly charitable foundations, they were still out of her price range. So it was methotrexate and prednisone and folic acid. And trying not to brood about the whole thing.

She was on her way to her room at Mrs.

Brown's boardinghouse. It was raining, and the rain was cold. It was October and cool. Not the best time to forget her raincoat, but she'd been in a hurry and late for work, so it was still hanging in her closet at home. Ah, well, she thought philosophically, at least she had a nice thick sweater over her thin blouse. She laughed hysterically to herself. The sweater was a sponge. She felt water rolling down over her flat stomach under her clothes.

She laughed so hard that she didn't see a raised portion of the sidewalk. It caught her toe and she tripped. She fell into the road just as a big black limousine came along. Her cane went flying and she hit the pavement on her belly. She was fortunate enough to catch herself on her forearms, but the impact winded her. Luckily for her, the driver saw her in time to stop from running over her. It was dark and only the streetlights showed, blurry light through the curtains of rain.

A man got out. She saw his shoes. Big feet. Expensive shoes, like some of the visiting district attorneys who showed up to talk to her boss. Slacks that were made of wool. She could tell, because she used wool to knit with.

"You okay?" a deep, velvety voice asked.

"Yes," she panted. "Just...winded."

She rolled over and sat up.

A tall man, built like a wrestler, with broad shoulders and a leonine head, squatted down, staring at her with deep-set brown eyes in an olive complexion. His jet-black hair was threaded with just a little silver, and it was thick and wavy around his head. A lock of it fell onto his forehead as he bent over her. He had high cheekbones and the sort of mouth that was seen in action movies with he-men. He was gorgeous. She couldn't help staring. She couldn't remember ever having a man send her speechless just by looking at her.

"Nice timing," he mused. "Saw the limo coming, did we? And jumped right out in front of it, too."

She was too shaken to think of a comeback, although she should have. She checked her palms. They were a little scraped but not bleeding.

"I tripped."

"Did you really?"

That damned sarcastic, mocking smile made her very angry. "Could you find my cane, please?" she asked.

"Cane?"

She heard his voice change. She hated that note in it. "It went flying when I hit the raised part of the sidewalk. It's over that way." She indicated the sidewalk. "On the other side, probably. It's red enamel. With dragons on it."

"With dragons. Mmm-hmm."

A car door opened. Another man came around the front of the car. He was older than Bernie but younger than the man squatting down next to her. He was wearing a suit.

"What's that about dragons?" the man asked, faintly amused.

"Her cane. That way, she says." He pointed.

The other man made a sound in his throat.

"Look anyway," the big man told him.

"All right, I'm going." There was a pause while Bernie sat in the road getting wetter by the minute.

"Well, I'll be…!"

The other man came back, holding the cane. He was scowling. "Where the devil did you get something like that?" he asked as he handed it down to her.

"Internet," she said. The pain was getting worse. Much worse. She needed a heavy dose of anti-inflammatories, and a bed and a heating pad.

She swallowed hard. "Please don't...stare when I get up. There's only one way I can do it, and it's embarrassing." She got on all fours and pushed herself up with difficulty, holding on to the cane for support. She lifted her head to the rain and got her breath back. "Thanks for not running over me," she said heavily.

The big man had stood up when she did. He was scowling. "What's the matter with you? Sprain?"

She looked up. It was a long way. "Rheumatoid arthritis."

"Arthritis? At your age?" the man asked, surprised.

She drew herself up angrily. "Rheumatoid," she emphasized. "It's systemic. An autoimmune disease. Only one percent of people in the world have it, although it's the most common autoimmune disease. Now if you don't mind, I have to get home before I drown."

"We'll drive you," the big man offered belatedly.

"Frankly, I'd rather drown, thanks." She turned, very slowly, and managed to get going without too much visible effort. But walking was laborious, and she was gritting her teeth before she'd gotten five steps.

"Oh, hell."

She heard the soft curse before she felt herself suddenly picked up like a sack of potatoes and carried back toward the limousine.

The other man was holding the door open.

"You put me down!" she grumbled, trying to struggle. She winced, because movement hurt.

"When I get you home," he said. "Where's home?"

He put her into the limousine and climbed in beside her. The other man closed the door and got in behind the wheel.

"I'll get the seat wet," she protested.

"It's leather. It will clean. Where's home?"

She drew in a breath. She was in so much pain that she couldn't even protest anymore. "Mrs. Brown's boardinghouse. Two blocks down and to the right. It's a big Victorian house with a white fence around it and a room-to-rent sign," she added.

The driver nodded, started the engine and took off.

The big man was still watching her. She was

clutching the cane with a little hand that had gone white from the pressure she was using.

He studied her, his eyes on the thick plait of platinum blond hair down her back. Her clothes were plastered to her. Nice body, a little small-breasted and long legs. She had green eyes. Very pale green. Pretty bow mouth. Wide-spaced eyes under thick black eyelashes. Not beautiful. But attractive.

"Who are you?" he asked belatedly.

"My name is Bernadette," she said.

"Sweet," he mused. "There was a song about Saint Bernadette," he recalled.

She flushed. "My mother loved it. That's why she gave me the name."

"I'm Michael. Michael Fiore, but most people call me Mikey." He watched her face, but there was no recognition. She didn't know the name. Surprising. He'd been a resident of Jacobsville a few years back, when his cousin, Paul Fiore of the San Antonio FBI office, was investigating a case that involved Sari Grayling, who later became Paul's wife. Sari and her sister, Meredith, had been targeted by a hit man, courtesy of a man whose mother was killed by the Graylings' late father. Mikey had made some friends here.

"Nice to meet you," she managed. She grimaced.

"Hurts pretty bad, huh?" he asked, his dark eyes narrowing. He looked up. Santelli was pulling into a parking spot just in front of a Victorian house with a room-to-rent sign. "Is this it?" he asked.

She looked up through the window. She nodded. "Thanks so much..."

"Stay put," he said.

He went out the other door that Santi was holding open for him, around the car and opened her door. He reached in and picked her up, cane and purse and all.

"Come knock on the door for me, Santi," he told his companion.

Bernie tried to protest, but the big man kept walking. He smelled of cigar smoke and expensive cologne, and the feel of his big arms around her made her feel odd. Trembly. Nervous. Very nervous. She had one arm around his broad shoulders to hold on, her hand spread beside his neck. He was warm and comforting. It had been a long time since she'd been held by anyone, and it had never felt like this.

Santi knocked on the door.

Bernie could have told him that he could just walk in, but he wasn't from here, so he didn't know.

Plump Mrs. Brown opened the door, still wearing her apron because she offered supper to her roomers. She stopped dead, with her mouth open, as she saw Bernie being carried by a stranger.

"I fell," Bernie explained. "He was kind enough to stop and bring me home…"

"Oh, dear, should you go see Dr. Coltrain?" she said worriedly.

"I'm fine, really, just a little bruised dignity to speak of," she assured the landlady. "You can put me down," she said to Mikey.

"Where's her room?" Mikey asked politely. He smiled at the older woman, and she flushed and laughed nervously.

"It's right down here. She can't climb the stairs, so she has a room near the front…"

She led the way. He put Bernie down in a chair beside her bed.

"You need a hot bath, dear, and some coffee," Mrs. Brown fussed.

There was a bathroom between Bernie's room and the empty room next door.

"Can you manage?" the big man asked gently.

She nodded. "I'm okay. Really. Thanks."

He shrugged broad shoulders. He frowned. "You shouldn't be walking so far."

"Tell her, tell her," Mrs. Brown fretted. "She walks four blocks to and from work every single day!"

"Dr. Coltrain says exercise is good for me," she retorted.

"Exercise. Not torture," Mrs. Brown muttered.

The big man was thinking. "We'll see you again," he said quietly.

She nodded. "Thanks."

He cocked his head. His eyes narrowed. "First impressions aren't always accurate."

Her eyebrows arched. "Gosh, was that an apology?"

He scowled. "I don't apologize. Ever."

"That didn't hurt, that didn't hurt, that didn't hurt," she mimicked a comedian who'd said that very thing in a movie. She grinned. Probably he didn't have a clue what she was talking about.

He threw back his head and roared. *"Police Academy,"* he said, naming the movie.

Her jaw fell.

"Yeah. That guy was me, at his age," he confessed. "Take a bath. And don't fall in."

She made a face at him.

His dark eyes twinkled. "See you, kid."

He walked out before she could correct the impression.

He stopped at the front door. "That room to let," he asked Mrs. Brown. "Is it still available?"

"Why, yes," she said, flushing again. She laughed. "You'd be very welcome. We have three ladies living here, but..."

"I'm easy to please," he said. "And I won't be any trouble. I hate hotels."

She smiled. "So do I. My husband was in rodeo. We spent years on the road. I got so sick of room keys..."

He laughed. "That's me. Okay. If you don't mind, I'll have my stuff here later today."

"I don't mind at all."

"How much in advance?" he asked, producing his wallet.

She told him. He handed her several bills.

"I don't rob banks, if that's what you're thinking," he said with a wry smile. "I'm a businessman. I live in New Jersey, and I own a hotel in Vegas. Which is why I hate staying in them."

"Oh! You have business here, then?"

He nodded solemnly. "Business," he agreed. "I'll be around for a while."

"It will be nice to have the room rented," she confessed. "It's been vacant for a long time. My last tenant got married."

"I'll see you later, then." He hesitated, looking back toward the room where he'd left Bernadette. "She'll be okay, you think?"

"Yes. She might look fragile, but Bernie's tough. She's had to be."

"Bernie?" His eyes widened.

She laughed. "That's what we call her. We've known Bernadette all her life."

"Small towns." He smiled. "I grew up in one, myself. Far from here." He pulled out a business card and handed it to her. "The lower number is my cell phone. If she needs anything tonight, you call me, okay? I can come and drive her to the hospital if she needs to be seen."

Mrs. Brown was surprised at that concern from a stranger. "You have a kind heart."

He shrugged. "Not always. See you."

He went out, motioning for Santi to follow

him. They got in the limo and drove off. Mrs. Brown watched it go with real interest. She wondered who the outsider was.

Mikey was all too aware of the driver's irritation. "They told me to keep an eye on you all the time," he told Mikey.

"Yeah, well, I'm not sharing a room with you, no matter what the hell they told you. Besides," he added, settling back into his seat, "Cash Grier's got one of his men shadowing me with a sniper kit."

"It's a small town," Santi began.

"A small town with half the retired mercs in America," Mikey cut in. "And my cousin lives right down the road. Remember him? Senior FBI agent Paul Fiore? Lives in Jacobsville, works out of San Antonio, worth millions?"

"Oh. Him. Right."

"Besides, I know the sniper Grier's got watching me." He chuckled. "He doesn't miss. Ever. And they snagged *The Avengers* to watch when the sniper's asleep."

"The Avengers?" Santi roared. "That's a comic book!"

"Rogers and Barton. They're called the Avengers because Captain America's name in the series is Rogers, and Hawkeye's is Barton. Get it?"

"Yeah."

"I know how bad Mario Cotillo wants me, Santi," Mikey said quietly. "I'm the only thing standing between Tony Garza and a murder-one conviction, because I know Tony didn't do it and I can prove it. Tony's in hiding, too, in an even safer place than me."

"Where?" Santi asked.

Mikey laughed coarsely. "Sure, like I'm going to tell you."

Santi stiffened. "I'm no snitch," he said, offended.

"Anybody can hack a cell phone or the elaborate two-way radio we got in this car, and listen to us when we talk," Mikey said with visible impatience. "Use your brain, okay?"

"I do!"

"Well, you must be keeping it in a safe place when you're not using it," Mikey muttered under his breath, but not so that Santi could hear him. The guy was good muscle and a capable driver. It wouldn't do to upset him too much. Not now, anyway.

Mikey leaned back with a long sigh and thought

of the woman he'd met tonight. He was sorry he'd misjudged her, but plenty of women had thrown themselves into his path. He was extremely wealthy. He had money in Swiss banks that the feds couldn't touch. And while he'd been accused of a few crimes, including murder, he'd never even been indicted. His record was pretty clean. Well, for a guy in his profession. He was a crime boss back in Jersey, where Tony Garza was the big boss. Tony owned half the rackets around Newark. But Tony had some major new competition, an outsider who saw himself as the next Capone. He'd targeted Tony at once, planned to take him down on a fake murder charge with the help of a friend who worked in the federal attorney's office. It had backfired. Tony also had friends there. So did Mikey. But Mikey had been with Tony in a bar when the murder had taken place and by chance, Mikey had a photo of himself and Tony with a date stamp on his cell phone. He'd sent copies to Paulie and Cash Grier and a friend down in the Bahamas. Before the feds could jump Tony, who might have been dealt with handily and at once before it even came to trial, Mikey and Tony had both skipped town.

The next obvious play by Cotillo would be to put out contracts on Mikey and Tony. Mikey smiled. He knew most of the heavy hitters in the business. So did Tony. It wouldn't work, but Cotillo didn't know that. Yet. Meanwhile, Mikey and Tony were playing a waiting game. Both had feds on the job protecting them. Mikey wasn't telling Santi that, however. He didn't trust anybody really, except his cousin Paul. The fewer people who knew, the safer he was going to be.

Not that life held such attractions for him these days. He had all the money he'd ever need. He had a fearsome reputation, which gave him plenty of protection back home in New Jersey. But he was alone. He was a lonely man. He'd asked a woman to share his life only once, and she'd laughed. He was good in bed and he bought her pretty things, but she wasn't going to get married to a known gangster. She had her reputation to think of. After all, she was a debutante, from one of the most prominent families in Maryland. Marry a hood? Ha! Fat chance.

It had broken his heart. Even now, years and years after it happened, it was a sore spot. He was more than his reputation. He was fair and honest, and he never hurt anybody without a damned good reason. Mostly, he went after people who hurt people he cared about.

Well, there was also the odd job for Tony when he was younger. But those days were mostly behind him. He could still handle a sniper kit when he needed to. It was just that he didn't have the same need for notoriety that had once ruled his life.

Nobody needed him. Funny, the main reason he'd enjoyed the debutante was that she'd pretended to be helpless and clingy. He'd enjoyed that. Since his grandmother's death, there had been nobody who cared about him except Paul, and nobody who needed him at all. Briefly, he'd helped his cousin protect a young woman from Jacobsville, Merrie Grayling, before she married the Wyoming rancher. But that had been sort of an accessory thing. He'd liked her very much, yet as a sort of adoptive baby sister, nothing romantic. It had been nice, helping Paulie with that little chore, especially since he knew the contract killer who'd been assigned to get Merrie. He had known how to get the hit called off—actually, by getting Merrie, an artist of great talent, to do a portrait of Tony. The contract killer had ended badly, but that happened sometimes.

Most sane people didn't go against Tony, who'd told the guy to call off the hit.

But all that had been three years ago. Life moved on. Now here was Mikey, in hiding from a newcomer in Jersey, trying to protect his friend Tony.

He thought again about the young woman who'd fallen in front of the limo. He felt bad that he'd misjudged her. She was pretty. What had she called herself—Bernadette? He smiled. He'd been to France, to the grotto where Saint Bernadette had dug into a mudhole, found a clear spring and seen the apparition she referred to as the Immaculate Conception, and he'd seen Bernadette in her coffin. She looked no older than when she'd died, a century and more ago, a beautiful young woman. He wondered if her namesake even knew who Saint Bernadette was. He wondered why she'd been given that name.

So many questions. Well, he was going to be staying in the same rooming house, so he'd probably get the chance to talk to her, to ask her about her family. She was nice. She didn't like pity, although she had a devastating medical condition, and she had a temper. He smiled, remembering that thick plait of blond hair down her back. He loved long hair. It must be hard to keep, for someone with her limitations.

His little Greek grandmother had been arthritic. He recalled her gnarled hands and the times when she hadn't been able to get out of bed. Mikey had carried her from room to room when she had special company, or outside when she wanted to sit in the sun. He couldn't remember what sort of arthritis she'd had, but it was in the family bible, along with plenty of other family information. He kept the bible in a safe-deposit box back in Jersey, along with precious photographs of people long dead. There had been one of the debutante. But he'd burned that one.

The car was eating up the miles to San Antonio, where Mikey had left his luggage in a hotel under an assumed name. He'd send Santi in to pick it up and pay the bill, just in case, while he waited outside in the parking lot. You couldn't be too careful. He needed to send a text to Paulie, as well, but that could wait until he was back in Jacobsville. He should ask Paulie about hackers and what they could find out, and how. He still wasn't up on modern methods of surveillance.

He leaned back against the seat with a long sigh. Bernadette. He smiled to himself.

Bernadette took a hot bath, and it did help ease some of the discomfort. Mrs. Brown had been kind enough to add a handhold on the side of the tub so that Bernadette would find it easier to get in and out of the tub. She took showers, however, not baths. It was so much quicker to stand up. Besides, the bathroom was used by all the boarders on the ground floor, although there had been just Bernadette for several weeks, and poor Mrs. Brown had enough to do without having to scrub the tub all the time. She did have a daily woman who came in to help with the heavy chores. But Bernadette was fastidious and it bothered her, the idea of baths when at least one of the former boarders had been male and liked lots of musk-smelling bath oil. For women, especially, baths in a less than spotlessly clean tub could lead to infections. Bernie had enough to worry about without those. So, she took showers.

She dressed in her pajama bottoms and one of the soft, thick T-shirts that she wore with it.

There was a tap at the door and Mrs. Brown

came in with a cup of tea in a beautiful ceramic cup on its delicate saucer. "Chamomile tea," she said with a smile. "It will help you sleep, sweetheart."

"You're spoiling me," Bernadette complained softly. "You have enough to do without adding me to your burdens."

"You're no burden," Mrs. Brown said gently. "You keep your room spotless, you never mess anything up, and I have yet to have to pick up after you anywhere." She sighed. "I wish we could say the same for the two nice women on the second floor, and don't you dare tell them I said that!"

Bernadette laughed. "I won't. You know I don't gossip."

"Of course you don't." She put the cup and saucer on the bedside table. "What a nice man who brought you home," she added with a speculative glance that Bernadette missed. "He's renting a room here, too!"

Bernadette caught her breath. "He is?" she stammered, and flushed a little.

Mrs. Brown chuckled. "He is. The one on the other side of the bathroom, but that won't be a problem. I'll make sure he knows to knock first when he needs to use it."

"Okay, then." She sipped tea and smiled with her eyes closed. "This is so good!"

"I put honey in it, instead of sugar, and just a hint of cinnamon."

Bernadette looked up at the older woman. "You know, he thought I'd fallen in front of his car on purpose."

"You fell? You didn't tell me!"

She sipped her tea. "The sidewalk was slippery and my toe hit a brick that was just a little out of place. I went flying into the street. Lucky for me that his driver had good brakes." She frowned. "It was a limousine."

"I noticed," Mrs. Brown said with a wry smile. "He was wearing a very expensive suit, as well. I think I recognized him. He looks like Paul Fiore's cousin."

"I heard about that," Bernadette said, "when I was working as a receptionist for a group of attorneys, before I got my paralegal certification from night school and Mr. Kemp hired me. I never saw him, but people talked about him. He was helping protect Merrie Grayling, wasn't he?"

"That was the gossip. Goodness, imagine having contract killers stalking two local girls in the same family!" She shook her head. "I had it from the Grayling girls' housekeeper, Mandy Swilling. She said the girls' father had killed a local woman for selling him out to the feds on racketeering charges, and the woman's son put out contracts on both Grayling's daughters, to get even. He thought their father loved them so much that it would really hurt him." She sighed. "Well, the man was dead by then, and the woman's son was charged with conspiracy to commit murder. They say he'll be in prison for a long time, even though he did try to help them find the killers."

"Good enough for him," Bernie said. "Murder is a nasty business."

"That's another thing. They say that Mr. Fiore's cousin Mikey is mixed up with organized crime."

"His cousin?"

"The man who carried you inside the house tonight," Mrs. Brown replied.

Bernie sat with the cup suspended in one hand. "Oh. Him." She laughed. She hadn't really been paying attention.

"Him." She laughed. "But I don't believe it. He's so nice. He was really concerned about you."

"Not when I first fell, he wasn't," Bernie said, wrinkling her nose. "He thought I did it on purpose to get his attention." She hesitated. "Well, you know, he is drop-dead gorgeous. When I first saw him, I could hardly even get my breath," she confessed. "It was like being hit in the stomach. I've never seen a real live man who looked like that. He could be in movies." She flushed. "Well, he's good-looking, I mean."

"I suppose some women do find excuses to attract men like that," Mrs. Brown said in his defense.

"I suppose. He changed his mind when he saw the cane, though." Her face grew sad. "When I was in high school, there was this really nice boy. I thought he was going to ask me to the senior prom. I was so excited. One of my girl-friends said he was talking about me to someone else, although she didn't hear what he said." She looked down into the now-empty cup. "Then another friend told me the truth. He said that I wasn't bad to look at, but he didn't want to take a disabled girl to a dance." She smiled sadly, aware of Mrs. Brown's angry expression. "After that, I sort of gave up on dating."

"There must have been nicer boys," she replied.

"Oh, there were. But there were prettier girls who didn't walk with canes." She put down the cup and saucer. "I didn't need the cane all the time, of course. But when I had flares, I'd just fall if I made a misstep." She shook her head. "No man is going to want a woman who may end up an invalid one day. So I go to work and save all I can, and hope that by the time I need to give up and apply for disability, I'll have enough to tide me over until I can get it." She made a face. "Gosh, wouldn't it be nice not to have health issues?"

"It would. And I'm sorry that you do. But, Bernie, a man who loves you won't care if you have them." She added, "Any more than you'd care if he had them."

Bernie smiled. "You're a nice woman. I'm so lucky to live here. And thank you for the tea."

"You're very welcome. You get some sleep. Tomorrow's Saturday, so you can sleep in for a change."

"A nice change." She grimaced. "But I don't want you to wait breakfast for me…!"

"I'll put it on a plate in the fridge and you can heat it up in the microwave," said Mrs. Brown. "So stop worrying about things."

Bernie laughed. "Okay. Thanks again."

"You're very welcome." She hesitated at the door. 'What a very good thing that we don't have many young women living here, except you."

"Why?"

"Well, that nice man who brought you in is really good-looking, and we don't want a line forming at his door, now do we?" she teased.

Bernie blushed, but Mrs. Brown had closed the door before she saw it.

Chapter Two

Mikey waited for Santi in a parking spot near the front door of the San Antonio hotel. He hoped it wouldn't take too long. The streets were busy, even at this time of night, and some of the people milling around were wearing gang colors and had multiple tats. He knew about the Los Serpientes gang. Although they were technically based in Houston, they had a presence here in San Antonio. Paulie had told him about them. They looked out for children and old people. Amazing. Kind of like the Yakuza in Japan.

Japan was a great place to visit. Mikey had gone there for several weeks after his tour of duty in the Middle East. He'd needed to wind down and get over some of the things he'd seen and done there. He'd been with a group of military overseas that included two men from here, Rogers and Barton, who'd been protecting the Grayling girls from contract killers. He hadn't served directly with them, but Cag Hart and the local DA, Blake Kemp, had been overseas at the same time. From Afghanistan to Iraq, he'd carried a rifle and served his country. The memories weren't good, but he had others he lived with. He just added the more recent ones to them.

He'd been surprised to find his company commander involved with Merrie Grayling. The Wyoming rancher, Ren Colter, had been the company commander of his sniper unit overseas. In fact, the Grayling girls' protectors, Rogers and Barton, had also been part of his group. What a homecoming that had been. Not a really great one, because Mikey had gotten in trouble scrounging materials for a brothel. But his commanding officer had gotten him out of trouble with Ren, because Mikey had the greatest luck in the world at poker. He never lost. It was one reason he was so rich. Of course, he couldn't get into casinos anymore. He didn't cheat. He didn't have to. But that luck had gotten him barred all over the world, even in Monte Carlo. He chuckled. It was sort of a mark of honor, being barred from those places. So he didn't mind that much. He had all the money he'd ever need until he died an old man, so who cared?

The car trunk opened suddenly. Mikey's hand had gone automatically under his jacket to the .45 he'd put there before Santi went into the hotel. He kept it in a secure compartment under the seat, custom-made. He hadn't needed it in Jacobsville, but this was unknown territory, and it was dangerous not to go heeled. He had a concealed carry permit, but for Jersey, not here. He supposed he'd have to go see the sheriff in Jacobs County and get one for Texas. That would be Hayes Carson. He knew the sheriff from three years ago. They got on.

Santi opened the door and got in behind the wheel. "All the bags are in the trunk, chief," he told his boss. "We need to stop anywhere else before we head south?"

"Not unless you're hungry."

"I could eat."

"Well, there's a nice restaurant in a better part of town. Let's go looking." He glanced out through the tinted windows at a young man who was giving the limo a real hard look. "I'm not overjoyed with the clientele hereabouts."

"Me, neither."

"So, let's go. We'll drive around and see if we can find someplace Italian. I think Paulie said a new place had just opened recently. Carlo's. Put it in the computer."

Santi fed it into the onboard GPS. "Got it, chief. Only three blocks away."

"Okay! Head out."

They were well into their plates of spaghetti when Mikey noticed a couple of customers in suits giving them a cursory inspection.

"Feds," Mikey said under his breath. "At the second table over. Don't look," he added.

"Know them?"

"Nope," Mikey said.

"FBI, you think?"

Mikey chuckled. "If they were, Paulie would have mentioned that I had a tail here in the city."

"Then who?"

"If I were guessing, US Marshals," he replied. "The big dark one looks vaguely familiar, but I can't quite place him. He was working with Paulie during the time I spent in Jacobsville three years ago."

"Marshals?" Santi asked, and he shifted restlessly.

"Relax. They aren't planning to toss our butts in jail. There's this thing called due process," Mikey said imperturbably. "We'll have fewer worries down in Jacobs County. Jacobsville is so small that any stranger sticks out. Besides, we've got shadows of our own."

"Good ones?"

"You bet," Mikey replied with a smug grin. "So eat your supper and I'll move into my new temporary home."

"I don't like being down the road in a motel," Santi muttered. "Even with all the other guys watching your back."

"Well, I'm not sharing the room," Mikey said flatly. "It's barely big enough for me and all my stuff, without trying to fit you into it. No room for another bed, anyway."

"I guess you got a point."

"Of course I do. Besides, it's not like I'm going to get hit until they track me down here."

"The limo is going to attract attention," Santi said worriedly.

"Yeah, well, no more attention than the gossip will, but there's not a place in the world I'd be safer. Strangers stick out here. Remember, I told you about Cash Grier's wife being tracked here by a contract killer, and what happened to him?"

Santi chuckled. "Yeah. Grier's wife hit him so hard with an iron skillet that he ran to the cops for protection."

"Exactly. Nobody messes with Tippy Grier. What a knockout. A movie star, and she's married to the police chief and has two kids. I never thought Grier could settle down in a small town. He didn't seem the sort."

"That's what everybody says." Santi paused. "I feel bad about that poor girl we almost hit," he added, surprisingly, because he wasn't sentimental. "She was nice, and we thought she was trying to play us."

"We come by our suspicious natures honestly," Mikey reminded him. "But, yeah, she was nice. Needs looking after," he said quietly. "Not that she seems the kind of woman who'd let anybody look after her."

"I noticed that."

Mikey glanced at his watch. "We'd better go." He signaled to a waiter for the check.

Bernadette was reading in bed. The pain was pretty bad, a combination of the rain and the fall. She needed something to take her mind off it, so she pulled out her cell phone, on which she kept dozens of books. Many were romance novels. She realized that her condition would keep most men away, and it was nice to daydream about having a kind man sweep her off her feet.

She couldn't stop thinking about the big dark-haired man who'd done that earlier in the evening. He was kin to Paul Fiore, who was married to Sari Grayling. Bernie worked with Sari in the local DA's office. She wondered if she could get away with asking her anything about the man, who'd been very kind to her after mistaking her for some kind of con woman.

She shouldn't be thinking about him. A man that handsome probably had women hanging on to his ankles everywhere he walked. He was apparently rich, as well. There was another woman in her office, the receptionist, Jessie Tennison, a gorgeous brunette in her late twenties, who was crazy about men and openly solicited any

rich one who came into the office. Mr. Kemp,
the DA, had already called her down about it
once. A second offense would cost her the job,
he'd added. Her position didn't include sexual
harassment of clients.

What a new world it was, Bernie mused, when
a woman could be accused of what was often
seen as a man's offense. But, then, her coworker
was very pretty. She was just ambitious. She
had a failed marriage behind her. Gossip was
that her ex-husband had been wealthy but had
a gambling habit and lost it all on one draw of a
card. Nobody knew, because the woman didn't
talk about herself. Well, not to the women in
the office.

A sudden commotion caught her attention.
There was movement in the hall. Some bump-
ing and a familiar deep male voice. Her heart
jumped. That was the man who'd brought her
home earlier. She knew his voice already. It was
hard to miss, with that definite New Jersey accent. She knew about that because of Paul Fiore.
He had one just like it.

There was more noise, then a door closing.
More footsteps. Voices. The front door opening
and closing, and then a car driving away.

Mrs. Brown knocked at Bernie's door and then slipped in, closing it behind her. "Sorry about the noise. Mr. Fiore's just moving in," she added with an affectionate smile.

Bernie tried not to show the delight she felt. "Is he going to stay long? Did he say?"

"Not really," she said. "His driver is staying at a motel down the road." She laughed. "Mr. Fiore said no way was he sharing that room with another man, especially not one as big as his driver."

Bernie laughed softly. "I guess not."

"So you'll need to knock before you go into the bathroom, like I mentioned earlier," Mrs. Brown continued. "Just in case. I told Mr. Fiore again that he'd need to do the same thing, since you're sharing." She looked worried. Bernie was flushed. "I'm so sorry. If I had a room with a bathroom free, I'd—"

"Those are upstairs," Bernie interrupted gently, "and we both know that I have a problem with stairs." She sighed and shook her head. "The rain and the walk and the fall pretty much did me in today. You were right. I should have gotten a cab. It isn't that expensive, and I don't spend much of what I make, except on books."

That was true. Her rent included all utilities and even the cable that gave her television access— not that she watched much TV.

"I know that walking is supposed to be good for you," the older woman replied. "But not when you're having a flare." She drew in a breath. "Bernie, if you wrote the company that makes that injectable medicine, they might…"

"I already did," Bernie said softly. "They offered me a discount, but even so, it's almost a thousand dollars a month. There's no way I could afford that, discount or not. Besides," she said philosophically, "it might not work for me. Sometimes it doesn't. It's a gamble."

"I guess so." Mrs. Brown looked sad. "Maybe someday they'll find a cure."

"Maybe they will."

"Well, I'll let you get back to your book," she teased, because she knew about the late-night reading habit. "Need anything from the kitchen before I turn out the lights?"

"Not a thing. I have my water right here." She indicated two bottles of water that she kept by her bedside.

"You could have some ice in a glass to go with it."

Bernie shook her head. "It would just melt. But thank you, Mrs. Brown. You're so good to me."

The older woman beamed. "I'm happy to have you here. You're the only resident I've ever had who never complained about anything. You'll spoil me."

"That's *my* line," Bernie teased, and she laughed. It made her look pretty.

"Sleep well."

"You, too."

Mrs. Brown went out and closed the door.

Bernie thought about that injectable medicine. Her rheumatologist in San Antonio had told her about it, encouraged her to try to get it. At Bernie's age, it might retard the progress of the disease, a disease that could lead to all sorts of complications, the worst of which was deformity in the hands and feet. Not only that, but RA was systemic. It could cause a lot of issues in other parts of the body, as well.

Chance, Bernie thought, would be a fine thing. She'd have to be very well-to-do in order to afford something so expensive as those shots. Well, meanwhile she had her other meds, and they worked well enough most of the time. It wasn't every day that she fell in a cold rain almost in front of somebody's fancy limousine. She smiled to herself and went back to her book.

Breakfast the next morning would have been interesting, Bernie thought to herself as she ate hers from a tray her kindly landlady had provided. But she couldn't get up. A weather system had moved in, dropping even more rain, and Bernie's poor body was still trying to cope with yesterday's fall. What a good thing it was Saturday. She'd have had a time getting to work.

Just as she finished the last drop of her coffee, there was a perfunctory knock and the man who'd rescued her walked in.

She pulled the sheet up over her breasts. The gown covered her nicely, but she'd never had a man in her bedroom in her life, except for her late father and her doctor. She flushed.

Mikey grinned from ear to ear. He loved that reaction. The women in his life were brassy and easy and unshockable. Here was a violet under a staircase, undiscovered, who blushed because a man saw her in her nightgown.

"Mrs. Brown said you might like a second cup of coffee," he said gently, approaching the bed with a cup and saucer.

"Oh, I, yes, I...thank you." She couldn't even talk normally. She was furious with herself, especially when her hands shook a little as she took the cup and saucer from him. He lifted the empty one from the tray, so she'd have someplace to put the new one.

He cocked his head and looked at her, fascinated. Her long blond hair was in a braid, a little frizzled from being slept on. She was wearing a cotton gown, and he could see the straps with their eyelet trim. It reminded him of his grandmother, who'd never liked artificial fabric.

"You aren't feeling so good today, are you?" he asked. "Need me to run you over to the doctor?"

The flush grew. "Oh. Thank you. No, I'm... well, it's sort of normal. When it rains, it hurts more. And I fell." She bit her lip because he looked so guilty. "It wasn't your fault, or your driver's," she added quickly. "I'm clumsy. My toe hit a brick on the sidewalk that was just a little raised and it caused me to lose my balance. That's why I use the cane on bad days. I'm clumsy even on flat surfaces..."

"My grandmother had arthritis," he said softly. "Her little hands and feet were gnarled like tree roots." He wasn't watching, so he didn't notice the discomfort in Bernie's face—her poor feet weren't very pretty, either. "I used to carry her in and out of the house when she had bad spells. She loved to sit in the sun." His dark eyes were sad. "She weighed barely eighty pounds, but she was like a little pit bull. Even the big guys were afraid of her."

"The big guys?" she asked, lost in his soft eyes.

He shrugged. "In the family," he said.

She frowned. She didn't understand.

"You really are a little violet under a stair," he mused to himself. "The family is what insiders call the mob," he explained. "The big guys are the dons, the men who run things. I'm from New Jersey. Most of my family was involved in organized crime. Well, except Paulie," he added with a chuckle. "He was always the odd guy out."

She smiled. "He's married to Sari Grayling, who works in our office."

He nodded. "Sweet woman. Her sister is one hel—heck of an artist," he said, amending the word he'd meant to use.

"She truly is. They had her do a portrait of

our local college president, who was retiring. It looked just like him."

He chuckled. "The one she painted three years ago saved her life. Her father whacked a woman whose son hired contract men to go after Grayling's daughters. Merrie painted the big don from back home, and he called off the hit." He didn't add how Tony Garza had called it off.

"We heard about all that. I wasn't working for the district attorney's office at the time. I was working for a local attorney who moved his practice to San Antonio. But we all knew," she added. "Everybody talked about it. He actually gave her away at her wedding, didn't he?"

He nodded. "Tony's wife died young. He never had kids, never remarried." He grinned. "He tells everybody he's Merrie's dad. Gets a reaction, let me tell you, especially when he mentions that her brother-in-law is a fed."

She sipped coffee, fascinated by him.

It was mutual. He smiled very slowly, his heart doing odd things in his chest. It had been many years since he'd felt such tenderness for anything female, except his grandmother.

"Do you have family?" he asked suddenly.

Her face clouded. "Not anymore," she said softly, without elaborating.

"Me, neither," he replied. "Except for Paulie. We're first cousins."

"Mr. Fiore's nice," she said.

He nodded. He was thinking about Tony, in hiding and waiting for developments that would save him from life in prison. Mikey had the proof that could save him. But he had to stay alive long enough to present it. Here, in Jacobsville, was his best bet. He'd agreed, knowing how many ex-mercs and ex-military lived here.

But as he stared at this sweet, kind young woman, he thought about the danger he might be putting her in. Even in a foolproof situation, there could be snags. After all, the contract killer who'd been after Merrie actually got onto Ren Colter's property in Wyoming and had her bedroom staked out before she came back to her sister and brother-in-law.

Bernie cocked her head. "Something's worrying you."

He started. "How do you know?"

She drew in a slow breath and averted her eyes. "People think I'm strange."

He moved a step closer to the bed. "How so?"

She shifted restlessly. "I...well, I sort of know things about people." She flushed.

He nodded. "Like Merrie. She has that sort of perception. She painted a picture of me that nailed me to a T, and she'd never even met me."

She looked up. "Oh. Then you're not...intimidated by strange things."

He chuckled. "Nothing intimidates me, kid," he teased.

She smiled.

"So. You think something's worrying me." One brown eye narrowed. "What, exactly?"

She drew in a long breath and stared into his eyes. "Somebody wants to keep you from telling something you know," she said after a minute, and saw the shock hit his face.

"Damn."

"And it worries you that somebody might hurt anybody around you."

"Need to get a crystal ball and a kerchief and set up shop," he teased gently. "You're absolutely on the money. But that's between you and me, okay? The fewer people who know things, the fewer can talk about them."

She nodded. "I don't talk about things I know,

as a rule. I work for the DA's office. Gossip isn't encouraged."

He chuckled. "I guess not."

Her coffee was now stone-cold, but she sipped it, for something to do.

He stared at her with conflicting emotions. She was unique, he thought. He'd never met anybody in his life like her.

She stared back. Her heart was almost smothering her with its wild beat. She was grateful that she had the covers pulled up, so he couldn't see her gown fluttering with her heartbeat.

There was another quick knock and Mrs. Brown came in. "Finished, dear?" she asked as she went to pick up the tray. "You can just set that on here, Mr. Fiore," she told Mikey with a smile. "I'll…"

He put it on the tray and then took the tray from her. "You're too delicate to be lifting heavy weights," he said with a grin. "I'll carry it for you."

"Oh, Mr. Fiore," she laughed, and blushed like a girl. "If you need anything, you just call me, Bernie, ok?"

"I will. Thanks. Both of you," she added.

Mrs. Brown smiled. As Mikey went through the door, he turned and winked at her.

That wink kept her heart fluttering all day, and it kept her awake most of the night.

She was able to go to the table for breakfast the next morning, even if she moved with a little difficulty. Her medicines worked slowly, but at least they did work. She had prednisone to take with the worst attacks, and it helped tremendously.

"You look better today," Mrs. Brown said. "Going to church?"

"Yes," she replied with a smile. "I'm hitching a ride with the Farwalkers."

Mikey frowned. "The Farwalkers? Wait a minute. Farwalker. Carson Farwalker. He's one of the doctors here. I remember."

Bernie laughed. "Yes. He's married to Carlie Blair. Her dad is pastor of the local Methodist church. I don't have a car, so they come by to get me most Sundays for services. Sometimes it's just Carlie and their little boy, Jacob, if Carson's on call."

He didn't mention that he knew that pastor,

Jake Blair. He also knew things about the man's past that he wasn't sharing.

"My whole family was Catholic," he said. "Well, not Paulie. But then, he always went his own way."

"The Ruiz family here is Catholic," she said. "He's a Texas Ranger. His wife is a nurse. She works in San Antonio, too, so they commute. They're very nice people."

"I never met Ruiz, but I heard about him. Ranch the size of a small state, they say."

Bernie grinned. "Yes. It is rather large, but they aren't social people, if you get my meaning."

"Goodness, no," Miss Pirkle, one of the tenants said with a smile. "Your cousin and his family are like that, too, Mr. Fiore," she added, her thin face animated as she spoke. "Down-to-earth. Good people."

"Thanks," he said.

"We have a lot of moneyed families in Jacobsville and Comanche Wells," old Mrs. Bartwell interjected with a smile. "Most of them earned their wealth the hard way, especially the Ballengers. They started out with nothing. Now

Calhoun is a United States senator and Justin
runs their huge feed lot here."

"That's a real rags-to-riches story," Miss Pirkle
agreed. "Their sons are nice, too. Imagine, two
brothers, three children apiece, and not a girl in
the bunch," she added on a laugh.

"I wouldn't mind a little girl," Mikey said, surprising himself. He didn't dare look at Bernie,
who'd inspired the comment. He could almost
picture her in a little frilly dress at the age of five
or six. She would have been a pretty child. He
hadn't thought about children in a long time, not
since his ex-fiancée had noted that she wasn't
marrying some famous criminal. It had broken
Mikey's heart. Women were treacherous.

"Children are sweet," Bernie said softly as she
finished her bacon and eggs. "The Griers come
into our office a lot with their daughter, Tris, and
their son, Marcus. I love seeing their children."

"The police chief," Mikey said, nodding. He
chuckled. "Not your average small-town cop."

"Not at all," Bernie agreed, tongue-in-cheek.

"That's true," Miss Pirkle said. "He was a
Texas Ranger!"

Bernie caught Mikey's eyes and held them. He
got the message. Their elderly breakfast com-

panion didn't know about the chief's past. Just as well to keep it quiet.

"Are you from here, too?" Mikey asked Miss Pirkle.

"No. I'm from Houston," she replied, her blue eyes smiling. "I came here with my mother about two years ago, just before I lost her." She took a breath and forced a smile. "I loved the town so much that I decided I'd just stay. I don't really have anybody back in Houston now."

"I'm not from here, either," Mrs. Bartwell said. "I'm a northern transplant. New York State."

"Thought I recognized that accent," Mikey teased.

Mrs. Bartwell chuckled. "I have a great-niece who lives in Chicago with her grandmother. Old money. Very old. They have ancestors who died in the French Revolution."

"My goodness!" Miss Pirkle exclaimed, all ears.

"My sister and I haven't spoken in twenty years," she added. "We had a minor disagreement that led to a terrible fight. My husband died of cancer and we had no children. My great-niece's mother was from Jacobsville. She was a Jacobs, in fact."

"Impressive," Bernie said with a grin. "Was she kin to Big John?"

"Yes, distantly."

"Big John?" Mikey asked curiously.

"Big John Jacobs," Bernie replied, because she knew the history by heart. "He was a share-cropper back in Georgia before the Union Army burned down his farm and killed most of his family, thinking they were slave owners. They weren't. They were poor, like the black family he saved from real slave owners. One of the Union officers was going to have him shot, but the black family got between him and the Army man and made him listen to the truth. They saved his life. He came here just after the Civil War with them. He didn't even have a proper house, so he and their families lived in one big shack together. He hired on some Comanche men and a good many cowboys from Mexico and started ranching with Texas longhorns. He made people uncomfortable because he wasn't a racist in a time when many people were. He married an heiress, convinced her father to build a railroad spur to the ranch, near present Ja-cobsville, so that he could ship his cattle north. Made a fortune at it."

"What a story," Mikey chuckled.

"And all true," Miss Pirkle said. "There's a statue of Big John on the town square. One of his direct descendants is married to Justin Ballenger, who owns one of the biggest feed lots in Texas."

"All this talk of great men makes me weak in the knees," Mikey teased.

"Do you have illustrious ancestors, Mr. Fiore?" Mrs. Brown asked with a mischievous grin.

"Nah," he said. "If I do, I don't know about it. My grandmother was the only illustrious person I ever knew."

"Was she famous?" Mrs. Bartwell asked.

"Well, she was famous back in Jersey," he mused. "Got mad at a don and chased him around the room with a salami."

There were confused looks.

"Mafia folks," he explained.

"Oh! Like in *The Sopranos*, that used to be on television!" Miss Pirkle said. "I never missed an episode!"

"Sort of like that," he said. "More like Marlon Brando in *The Godfather*," he said, chuckling. "Afterwards, he sent her a big present every

Christmas and even came to her funeral. She was fierce."

"Was she Italian?" Mrs. Brown asked.

He laughed. "She was Greek. Everybody else in my whole family was Italian except for her. She was a tiny little thing, but ferocious. I was terrified of her when I was a kid. So was Paulie. Our folks didn't have much time for us," he added, not explaining why, "so she pretty much raised us."

"I never knew either of my grandmothers," Bernie said as she sipped coffee.

Mikey was studying her closely. "Where were your grandparents from?" he asked.

She closed up like a flower. She forced a smile. "I'm not really sure," she lied. "My father and mother were from Jacobsville, though, and we lived here from the time I was old enough to remember things. I have to get ready for church. It was delicious, Mrs. Brown," she added.

"Thank you, dear," Mrs. Brown said, and grimaced a little. She knew about Bernie's past. Not many other local people did. She could almost feel Bernie's anguish. Not Mr. Fiore's fault for bringing it up. He didn't know. "Want a second cup of coffee to take with you while you dress?"

"If I drink two, I can fly around the room and land on the curtain rods," Bernie teased. "I'm hyper enough as it is. But thanks."

She glanced at Mikey, puzzled by the look on his face. She smiled at the others and went back to her room.

Jake Blair was a conundrum, Bernie thought as she walked in line out the front door to shake hands with him after the very nice sermon. He seemed to be very conventional, just like a minister was expected to be. But he drove a red Shelby Cobra Mustang with a souped-up engine, and there were whispers about his past. The same sort of whispers that followed Jacobsville's police chief, Cash Grier, wherever he went.

Bernie gripped her dragon cane tightly and glanced at the toddler in Dr. Carson Farwalker's arms as he and Carlie walked beside her.

"Imagine you two with a child." Bernie sighed as she went from one face to the other.

Carlie grinned. "Imagine us married!" she corrected with a loving look at her husband, which was returned. "They were taking bets at the police station the day we got married about when he'd do a flit."

"They're having a long wait, don't you think?" Carson chuckled.

"Very long," she agreed. "Imagine, we used to fight each other in World of Warcraft on battle-grounds and we never knew it. Not until my life was in danger and Dad had you watching me."

"I watched you a lot more than he told me to," Carson teased.

She laughed.

They'd moved up to Jake by now and he was giving them an amused grin. "There's my boy!" he said softly, and held his arms out for Jacob, who was named after him."

"Gimpa." The little boy laughed and hugged the tall man.

Jake hugged him close. "If anybody had told me ten years ago that I'd go all mushy over a grandchild, I guess I'd have laughed."

"If anybody had told me ten years ago that I'd be practicing medicine in a small Texas town, I'd have fainted," Carson chuckled.

"I like having family," Jake said, and smiled at

his daughter and son-in-law. "I never belonged anyplace in my life until now."

"Me, neither," Bernie said softly.

Jake looked at her kindly, and she knew that he'd heard the rumors. She just smiled. He was her minister, after all. Someday maybe she'd be able to talk about it. Mrs. Brown knew, but she was a clam. Not a lot of other people had any idea about Bernie's background because she'd lived for a few years, with her parents, in Floresville before coming back here with her father just before he died. She didn't like to think about those days. Not at all.

Jake looked behind his family at the few remaining, obviously impatient worshippers and handed his grandson back to Carson. "Ah, well, I'll see you all at the house later. I'm holding up progress," he added, and looked behind Carson at a man who actually flushed.

"Not a problem, Preacher," the man said. "It's just that the line's already forming for lunch at Barbara's Café…"

"Say no more," Jake chuckled. "Actually, I'm heading there myself. I can burn water."

"You can cook," Carlie chided.

"Only when I want to. And I don't want to,"

he confided with a grin. He kissed her cheek and shook hands with Carson. "I'll see you all for supper. You bringing it?"

"Of course," Carlie replied with a grin. "We know you can't boil water!"

He just laughed.

Bernie walked into the boardinghouse a little tired, but happy from the few hours of socializing with friends.

She wasn't looking where she was going, her mind still on the Farwalkers' little boy, whom she had sat beside in the back seat and cooed at all the way home. She ran right into Mikey and almost fell.

Chapter Three

Mikey just stared at her, smiling faintly as he caught her by both shoulders and spared her a fall. She did look pretty, with her long, platinum blond hair loose around her shoulders, wearing a pink dress in some soft material that displayed her nice figure without making it look indecent. He thought of all the women he'd known who paraded around in dresses cut up to the thigh and slashed to the waist in front. He compared them with Bernie, and found that he greatly preferred her to those glitzy women in his past.

"Thanks," she said, a husky note in her voice as she looked up at him with fascinated pale green eyes. It was a long way. He was husky for his height, and his head was leonine, broad, with a straight nose and chiseled lips and a square chin. He looked like a movie star. She'd never even seen a man so handsome.

"Deep thoughts?" he asked softly.

She caught her breath. "Sorry. I was just thinking how handsome you are." She flushed. "Oh, gosh," she groaned as that slipped out.

"It's okay," he teased. "I'm used to ladies swooning over me. No problem."

That broke the ice and she laughed.

He loved the way she looked when she laughed. Her whole face became radiant. Color bloomed on her cheeks. Her green eyes sparkled. Amazing, that a woman with her disability could laugh at all. But, then, his little grandmother had been the same. She never complained. She just accepted her lot in life and got on with living.

"You never complain, do you?" he asked suddenly.

"Well…not really," she stammered. "There's this saying that the boss has on the wall at work, a quote from Saint Francis of Assisi…"

"'God grant me the serenity to accept the things I cannot change; courage to change the things I can; and wisdom to know the differ-ence,'" he quoted.

She smiled. "You know it."

He shrugged. "My grandmother dragged me to mass every single Sunday until I was old enough to refuse to go. She had a plaque with that quote on it. I learned it by heart."

"It's nice."

"I guess."

He let her go belatedly. "You okay?"

"I'm fine. I wasn't paying attention to where I was going. Sorry I ran into you."

"Feel free to do it whenever you like," he said, and his dark eyes twinkled. "You fall down, kid, I'll pick you up every time."

She flushed. "Thanks. I'd do the same for you, if I could." She eyed his height. Her head came up to just past his shoulder. He probably weighed twice what she did, and the expensive suit he was wearing didn't disguise the muscular body under it. "I don't imagine I could pick you up, though."

He laughed. "Don't sweat it. I'll see you later."

She nodded.

He went around her and out the door, just as she heard a car pull up at the curb. His driver, no doubt. She wondered where he was going on a Sunday. But, then, that was really not her business.

It was the next morning before Bernie saw Mikey again, at the breakfast table. He was quiet and he looked very somber. He felt somber. Somebody had tracked Tony to the Bahamas and Marcus Carrera had called in some markers to keep him safe. Tony had used one of his throwaway phones to call Mikey—on the number Mikey had sent through a confederate.

Carrera, he recalled, was not a man to mess with. Once a big boss up north, the man had done a complete flip and gone legit. He was worth millions. He'd married a small-town Texas girl some years ago and they had two sons. The wife was actually from Jacobsville, a girl who used to do clothing repairs at the local dry cleaner's. Her father was as rich as Tony. Her mother had pretended to be her sister, but the truth came out when Carrera was threatened and his future wife saved him. Mikey knew Carrera's in-laws, but distantly. At least Tony was safe. But if they'd tracked him down, they probably had a good idea where Mikey was. It wouldn't take much work to discover that Mikey had been down here in Jacobsville three years ago to help out his cousin Paulie. That being said, however, it was still the safest place he could be. He had as much protection as he needed, from both sides of the law.

He looked around at the women at the table. His eyes lingered on Bernadette. He didn't want to put her in the line of fire. This had been a bad idea, getting a room at a boardinghouse. Or had it?

"Deep thoughts, Mr. Fiore?" Mrs. Brown teased. "You're very quiet."

He laughed self-consciously when he felt eyes on him. "Yeah. I was thinking about a friend of mine who's been in some trouble recently."

"We've all been there," Miss Pirkle said warmly. "I guess friends become like family after a time, don't they? We worry about them just as we would about kinfolk."

"And that's a fact," he agreed.

"My best friend drowned in a neighbor's swimming pool, when my family lived briefly in Floresville," Bernie commented.

"Did you see it?" Mikey asked.

She looked down at her plate. Her whole face clenched. "Yes. I didn't get to her in time."

"Listen, kid, sometimes things just happen. Like they're meant to happen. I'm not a religious man, but I believe life has a plan. Every life."

Bernie looked up at him. Her face relaxed a little. She drew in a long breath. "Yes. I think that, too." She smiled.

He smiled back.

The smiles lasted just a second too long to be casual. Mrs. Brown broke the silence by putting her cup noisily in the saucer without glancing at her boarders. It amused her, the streetwise Northerner and the shy Texas girl, finding each other fascinating. Mrs. Brown's husband had died years ago, leaving her with a big house outside town and a fistful of bills she couldn't pay. Opening her home to lodgers had made the difference. With her increased income, she was able to buy this house in town and turn it into a new boardinghouse. The sale of the first house had financed the purchase and remodeling of this one. The new location had been perfect for her boarders who worked in Jacobsville. She found that she had a natural aptitude for deal-ing with people, and it kept her bills paid and left her comfortably situated financially. But romance had been missing from her life. Now she was watching it unfold, with delight.

Mikey glanced at his wrist, at the very expensive thin gold watch he wore. "I have to run. I'm meeting Paulie up in San Antonio, but I'll be home in time for dinner," he told Mrs. Brown. He got up and leaned toward her. "What are we having?"

"Lasagna," she said with a grin. "And yes, I do know how to make it. Mandy Swilling taught me."

"You angel!" he said, and chuckled. "I'll definitely be back on time. See you all later."

They all called goodbyes. Bernie flushed when he turned at the doorway and glanced back at her with dark, soft eyes and a smile.

She felt good enough to walk the four blocks to work and she hardly needed the cane. Her life had taken a turn. She was happy for the first time in recent memory. Just the thought of Mikey Fiore made her tingle all over and glow inside.

That was noticed by the people she worked with, especially the new girl, Jessie Tennison.

Jessie was older than Bernadette's twenty-four years. She had to be at least twenty-seven. She'd been married and was now divorced, with no children. She had a roving eye for rich men. It had already gotten her in trouble with their boss, Mr. Kemp, the district attorney. That hadn't seemed to stop her. She wore very revealing clothing—she'd been called down about that, too—and she wasn't friendly to the women in the office.

Bernie put down her purse, folded her cane and took off her jacket before she sat down.

"I don't see why you work," Jessie said offhandedly, looking down her long nose at Bernie with a cold blue-eyed stare. "I'd just get on government relief and stay home."

"I don't need handouts. I work for my living," Bernie said. She smiled at the tall brunette, but not with any warmth.

Jessie shrugged. "Suit yourself. I'm going over to the courthouse on my break to talk to my friend Billie," she added, slipping into a long coat.

Bernie almost bit her tongue off to keep from mentioning that their breaks were only ten minutes long and it would take Jessie that long just to walk to the courthouse. The district attorney's office had been in the courthouse, but this year they'd moved to a new county building where they had more room. The increased space had delighted the office staff, which had grown considerably. Their new office was closer to Mrs. Brown's boardinghouse and Barbara's Café, but farther from the courthouse.

She didn't say it, but her coworker Olivia did. "Who's in the courthouse today, Jessie?" she asked with a blank expression. "Some really rich upper-class man who might need a companion...?"

"You...!" Jessie began just as Mr. Kemp's office door opened. She smiled at him, all sweetness. "I'm going to the courthouse on my break to see my friend Billie for just a minute, Mr. Kemp. Is that all right with you?" she added with a cold glance at her coworker.

"If it's absolutely necessary," he replied tersely. He wasn't pleased with his new employee. In fact, he was beginning to think he'd made a big mistake. A glowing recommendation from a San Antonio attorney had gotten Jessie the job, mainly because there were no other applicants. Competent receptionists with several years' ex-

perience weren't thick on the ground around Jacobsville.

"It really is," she said, and looked as if it wasn't
the whole truth. "I have a friend in the hospital
in San Antonio. Billie's been to see him," she
added quickly.

"Okay. Try not to take too long." He paused
and looked at her for a long time. "You get a
ten-minute break. Not an hour."

"Oh, yes, sir." She was all sugary sweetness
as she walked out the door in a cloud of cloy-
ing perfume.

Bernie's coworker fanned the air with a file
folder, making a face.

Not five minutes later, assistant DA Glory
Ramirez walked in the door and made a face.
"Who's been filming a perfume commercial in
here?" she asked.

"Somebody who's mad at me, probably," Sari
Fiore, their second assistant DA, laughed as she
came in behind Glory. "Perfume gives me a migraine."

"I'll turn the air conditioner on long enough
to suck it out of the building," Mr. Kemp volunteered.

"Ask her to wash it all off. I dare you," Sari said to the boss.

He laughed and went back into his office. The phone rang. Sari picked it up, nodded, spoke into the receiver and pressed a button. It was for Mr. Kemp. She hung up.

"Where's Jessie?" Sari asked curtly. "The phone is her job, not ours."

"There's some rich guy at the courthouse," Olivia told her. "She had a call from her friend Billie, who works as a temporary assistant in the Clerk of Court's office. I guess that was what it was about, although she said she was going to ask about a sick friend."

"She can't do that on the phone?" Sari asked, aghast.

"Well, she can't see the rich guy over the phone," Olivia said demurely and with a wicked smile.

"Jessie's a pill," Glory added. "I wonder how she ever got past the boss to hire on here. She's definitely not like any legal receptionist I've ever known."

"She's big-city, not small-town," Sari said. "She's got an accent like that lawyer from Manhattan who was down here last month."

"I noticed," Glory replied. "How are you feeling, Bernie?"

Bernie flushed and grinned. "I'm doing fine."

"Oh?" Sari teased. "We heard about your new boarder at Mrs. Brown's."

Bernie went scarlet.

"That was mean," Glory told Sari.

"Sorry," Sari said, but she was still grinning. "Isn't Mikey a doll?" she added. "He could pose for commercials."

"I noticed," Bernie said. "He's very good-looking."

"We heard about the fall. You okay?"

Bernie gasped. "Does he tell you guys everything?"

"Well, not everything. Just when he feels guilty about something." She smiled gently. "He felt really bad that he'd misjudged you. But it's not surprising. He's had women jump in front of his car before."

"My goodness!" Bernie exclaimed, fascinated.

"He is very rich," Glory pointed out. "And some women are less than scrupulous."

"Very true," Bernie said. "But I'm not."

"He noticed," Sari replied, tongue in cheek. "He said you remind him of his grandmother."

Bernie's eyes widened to saucers, and she looked absolutely horrified.

"No!" Sari said quickly. "He didn't mean he thought you were old. He said you had the same kind heart and the same sharp tongue she did. He was tickled when you compared him to that guy in the *Police Academy* movie." Her blue eyes sparkled as she looked at Bernie. "Paul said he really was like that guy, too."

Bernie laughed. "He's a lot of fun around the boardinghouse. He makes our two older ladies very flustered. Mrs. Brown, too."

"He's a dish. But he's not really a ladies' man, despite the appearance," Sari added. "In fact, he doesn't like most women. He had a hard experience some years back. I guess it affected him."

"We've all had hard experiences," Glory remarked. She shook her head. "If anybody had ever told me I'd marry Rodrigo…!"

"If anybody had ever told me that I'd finally marry Paul…" Sari countered, and they both laughed.

Both women had had a hard path to the altar, with some painful experiences along the way. Now they were happy. Glory and Rodrigo had a son, but Paul and Sari hadn't started a family.

Despite being filthy rich, they were both career oriented. Paul was FBI at the San Antonio office and Sari was an assistant DA here in Jacobs County. Children were definitely in their future, Sari often said, but not just at the moment.

Bernie would have loved a child. It would have been difficult for her with her physical issues, but that wouldn't deter her if she ever found a man who loved her enough to marry her. She thought briefly of Mikey and her heart fluttered, but she knew she wasn't beautiful or cultured enough to appeal to a man so sophisticated. And if he'd reached his present age, which had to be somewhere in his thirties, unmarried, he was unlikely to be thinking of marrying anybody in the future. What a depressing thought, she realized, and how silly of her to be thinking of it in the first place. He was only here temporarily. He belonged up north.

She sat very still, aware of conversation around her and not hearing it. Mikey belonged up north. But he was in Jacobsville for no apparent reason, and he'd taken a room at a boardinghouse, which meant he was staying for a while. Why?

She knew he was worried about the people around him in the boardinghouse. Had he made somebody really mad, and they were after him? Was he in Jacobsville because he was safe here? She'd heard just a snippet of gossip from Mrs. Brown, that Mr. Fiore was being watched by one of Eb Scott's men. Nobody knew why. But Eb's men were mercenaries, experienced in combat. Bernie hoped that Mikey wasn't being hunted.

What an odd word to think of, she mused as she pulled up the computer program she used in her work. Hunted. She'd guessed that Mikey was worried about somebody else. Her heart jumped. Was it a woman, perhaps? No. Sari said he was sour on women. A man? Somebody from his past with a grudge? He knew a lot about organized crime. Maybe it was somebody he'd come across in his job, because Mrs. Brown said he told her he owned a hotel in Las Vegas. He must, she thought, be very rich indeed if he owned property in that expensive place.

She was well into research on a new case precedent for the boss when Jessie breezed back in, wafting her expense perfume everywhere.

Sari glared at her. "Jessie, I've told you that heavy perfume brings on migraines. I'd hate to have to speak to Mr. Kemp about it."

"Oh, I'm sorry!" Jessie said at once, feigning surprise. "I won't wear so much from now on."

"Thanks." Sari gave her a look she didn't see and went back to work.

"Well, was he there, your rich mark?" Olivia drawled.

Jessie glared at her. "I don't have a rich mark."

"Some wealthy gentleman?" Olivia probed further.

Jessie took off her coat and sat down at her desk. "I don't know. He was riding in a black limousine. He's from New Jersey."

Bernie's heart dropped to her feet. She only knew one rich man in Jacobsville who rode around in a black limousine. It had to be Mikey. Jessie was beautiful and sophisticated, probably the sort of woman Mikey would really go for. Jessie was an oddity in Jacobsville, where most women weren't streetwise. The older woman probably charmed him.

While she was thinking, Jessie's cold eyes stabbed into her face. "He said he's living at Mrs. Brown's boardinghouse. That's where you live, isn't it, Bernadette?"

"Yes," Bernie said shortly.

Jessie laughed, her scrutiny almost insulting.

"Well, you won't be any sort of competition, will you? I mean, no sane man is going to want to take on a woman who can't stand up without a cane—"

"That's enough," Mr. Kemp said shortly from his open office door, and he looked even more formidable than usual. "You get one more warning, Jessie, then you're on your way back to San Antonio. You do not disparage coworkers. Ever."

Jessie actually flushed. She hadn't realized the boss could hear her. She'd have to be a lot more careful. There weren't any other jobs available in Jacobsville right now, and she couldn't afford to lose this one.

"I'm very sorry, Mr. Kemp," she began.

"Bernie's the one who's owed an apology."

"Yes, sir." Jessie turned to Bernie. "I'm sorry. That was wrong of me."

"Okay," Bernie said, but she didn't really look at the other woman.

Mr. Kemp hesitated for just a minute before he went back into his office.

"Careless, Jessie," Olivia said in a biting undertone. "Better make sure the boss isn't listening when you start making rude comments about one of us."

Jessie looked as if she might explode. The phone rang and saved her from making her situation any worse.

At lunchtime, Olivia and Bernie went to Barbara's Café to eat. Glory and Sari went home, where Glory had a babysitter and she could visit with her son while she ate. Sari had lunch with Mandy Swilling, the Grayling housekeeper. Jessie was stuck in the office until the others returned, thanks to Mr. Kemp who insisted that somebody had to answer the phone while he was out of the office. Jessie was almost smoking when the other women went out the door.

"Jessie's a pain," Olivia said curtly.

Bernie's pale green eyes sparkled as she dug into her chef's salad. "You really made her mad."

"Well, nobody else says anything," the other woman defended herself. Her voice softened. "Least of all you, Bernie. You're the sweetest woman I've ever known, except for my late grandmother. You could find one kind thing to say about the devil," she teased.

Bernie laughed softly. "I guess so."

"At least Sari finally said something about the

heavy perfume. I know it gives her fits. She's prone to migraines from just the stress of her job. Jessie doesn't care what she does or says unless the boss loses his temper." She frowned. "What's she doing down here?" she added with a frown. "I mean, she worked in San Antonio, where salaries are a lot higher. She doesn't know anybody in Jacobsville."

"The boss said she wanted a slower pace," Bernie replied.

"Sure. Like she has any stress. Unless answering the phone gives you ulcers," Olivia said drily. "Or bending over the desk to show as much cleavage as possible when a wealthy client comes in."

"Oh, shame on you!" Bernie said, laughing.

"I know. I'm bad. But Jessie's worse. She met your fellow boardinghouse occupant, too," Olivia added with a pointed glance at Bernie's flushed face. "She'll be after him soon. Nobody here rides around in a limo except Paul's cousin Mikey. Sari used to, but she mostly just drives now that all the threats to her and her sister are gone."

"He's here for a reason, too," Bernie said.

"A guess, or that intuition that makes most people nervous?" Olivia teased.

Bernie laughed. "Maybe a bit of both."

"Or maybe not." Olivia glanced up and then down again. "Any idea about what he might be doing today?"

Bernie's heart jumped and she felt it flutter. Incredible, that she knew absolutely where he was, without even looking. "He's coming in the door."

She hadn't looked up. She did now, and there he was, in a dark suit with a patterned blue tie, looking around until he spotted Bernie. He grinned as he went to the counter and placed his order, paying for it before he joined Olivia and Bernie at their table.

"Room for one more?" he asked with a grin at both women. "I don't really know anybody else in here, and I'm shy."

"Oh, sure you are," Olivia said with a wry smile. She wiped her mouth. "I have to get back before Jessie turns purple and says we're starving her. You stay and finish your salad, Bernie," she added as she stood up. "You have a half hour before you have to come back."

"Jessie. That the underdressed brunette who works in your office?" he asked.

They nodded.

"Don't tell her I'm here, okay?" he asked Olivia. He shook his head. "I know how deer feel in hunting season."

They both laughed.

"I won't. I promise," Olivia said. She winked at Bernie and went to carry her tray back.

Mikey looked at Bernie slowly, taking in the blond braid and the nice gray suit she was wearing with a pink camisole. "You look pretty," he said softly.

She flushed and laughed self-consciously. "Thanks."

"You're a breath of spring compared to the women I know," he added quietly, watching her. "Brassy, overbearing women don't do a thing for me these days. I guess I'm jaded."

She smiled shyly. "You're very handsome and you're wealthy. I guess women do chase you. Even movie stars and rich women."

He pursed his lips. "They used to. It's the other stuff that puts them off."

Her thin eyebrows lifted. "The other stuff?" she asked.

He shrugged. "My connections."

She still wasn't getting it. While she tried to, Barbara brought his steak and salad and black coffee, and put it down in front of him.

"I hope it's done right," she told Mikey. "My cook tends to get meat a little overdone. One of our customers actually carried his back into the kitchen and proceeded to show him how to cook it properly."

"Jon Blackhawk," Bernie guessed.

"How did you know?" Barbara asked.

"He's the only gourmet chef I know, and he's Paul's boss at the FBI office in San Antonio. They were both down here recently on a case. And nobody eats anywhere else in Jacobsville except here," she teased.

Barbara chuckled. "Exactly. It didn't come to blows, but it was close. My temporary cook's from New Jersey," she added.

Mikey's ears perked up. He glanced at Barbara.

She made a face. "His people are heavily federal, if you get my meaning. His brother works for the US Marshals Service in San Antonio, and he's a former policeman where he came from. He's retired."

"Oh." Mikey relaxed, just a little.

"I was going to add… Goodness, excuse me," she said, suddenly flustered as she went back to the counter.

Bernie's eyes followed her, and she grinned to herself as she watched a husky man in a police uniform smile at Barbara as she went to wait on him.

"Okay, what's that little smirk all about?" Mikey teased.

"That guy at the counter. That's Fred Baldwin. He worked as a policeman here for a while, then at a local ranch. Now he's back on the police force. He's sweet on Barbara and vice versa."

Mikey glanced in that direction and laughed softly. "I can see what you mean."

"Her son's a lieutenant of detectives with San Antonio PD," Bernie added.

He nodded. "I met him, last time I was here. Nice guy."

"Her daughter-in-law's father is the head of the CIA," she added.

"I heard that, too. Her son's dad is a head of state, down in South America."

"He does have some interesting connections," Bernie agreed.

* * *

Mikey finished his steak. "What's there to do around here at night?" he asked.

She pursed her lips. "Well, people go to concerts at the local high school on the weekends sometimes. Other people drive in the Line."

"What the hell...heck's the Line?" he amended.

"A bunch of people drive around in a line. Teenagers, married people, even old people sometimes. They have a leader, and they go all around the county, one after the other, sometimes even up to San Antonio and back."

He shook his head. "The things I miss, living in a city." His dark eyes met hers. "How about movies?"

"Jack Morris and his son just opened a drive-in theater outside town," she said. "He even built a snack bar with restrooms. He says he's bringing back the 1950s all by himself. It's pretty successful, too."

"What's playing right now?"

She named the movie, an action one about commandoes.

He smiled. "You like movies like that?" he asked.

"Well, yes," she confessed.

He chuckled. "I thought you had an adventurous nature. Mrs. Brown told me about those books you read in bed. She said you have some on outfits like the British SAS and the French Foreign Legion."

She blushed. "My goodness!"

"So, how about a movie Friday night?" he asked. "I'll have Santi rent a smaller car, one that won't get so much attention from the populace."

Her heart skipped a beat and ran wild. "You want to take me out, on a date?"

"Of course I do," he said softly.

She thought she might faint. "But I… I have all sorts of health issues…"

"Bernadette, you have a kind heart," he said quietly, his dark eyes soft on her face. "None of the other stuff matters. Least of all an illness you can't help." He grinned. "I won't ask you to go mountain climbing with me. I promise."

She laughed. "That's a deal, then."

He shook his head. "Why would you think you're untouchable?"

"A local boy told me that when I was in high school. He said he didn't want to get mixed up with a handicapped girl."

"Idiot," he muttered.

She smiled at him. "Thanks."

"How long ago?"

She blinked. "How long ago was it?"

He shifted. "Clumsy way to put it. How old are you?" he added. His dark eyes twinkled. "Past the age of consent?" he probed.

She closed up and looked uncomfortable.

He put a big, warm hand over hers on the table. "I don't proposition women I haven't even dated yet," he said softly. "And you aren't the sort of girl who'd ever get such a proposition from me. Honest."

She caught her breath. He was so unexpected. "I'm twenty-four. Almost twenty-five."

He was shocked and looked it. "You don't look your age, kid."

She beamed. "Thanks."

He laughed and curled his fingers around hers, enjoying the sensations that ran through him. Judging by the flush, she was feeling something similar.

"Careful," she said under her breath as more people came in the front door.

"Careful, why? Somebody with a gun looking our way?" he asked, and not entirely facetiously.

"Gossip."

He scowled. "What?"

"Gossip," she repeated. "If people see you standing close together or holding hands, they start talking about you, especially if you're local and unmarried. You'll get talked about."

"Like I care," he teased.

She felt as if she could float. "Really?"

His teeth were perfect and very white. She noticed, because he didn't seem to smile much. "I don't mind gossip. Do you?"

She hesitated. But, really, nobody here was likely to gossip about her to him, at least. Not many people knew about her parents or, especially, her grandparents. "No," she said after a minute. "I don't mind, either."

"Just as well. I have no plans to stop holding hands with you," he said. "It feels nice."

"It feels very nice," she said.

He had Santi drive her back to her office. He even got out, helped her from the car and walked her to the door.

"That woman in the courthouse said she works here. That right?" he asked.

She made a face and nodded.

"Then I won't come in. Phew," he added. "She could start a perfume shop on what she was wearing."

"She could in there, too," she said.

He laughed. "Well, I'll see you back at Mrs. Brown's later. If it starts raining, you call me and I'll come pick you up."

She looked hesitant.

"Oh. Right." He pulled out his wallet, extracted a business card and handed it to her. "Cell phone. At the bottom. You can call me or you can text me. Texting is better. I hate talking on the damned phone."

She laughed. "So do I."

"Okay, then. See you later, kid."

"See you."

He got back in the car. She went into her office and closed the door behind her.

Jessie was watching. Her face was livid. She'd tried to cadge a ride back to the office in that nice limo and been refused. It made her furious that little miss sunshine there had managed it. And she was late back to work, to boot!

Chapter Four

Bernie didn't have to look to feel Jessie's fury, but she sat down at her desk without even glancing toward the front desk. Apparently Jessie wasn't going to push her luck by attacking Bernie, though. She settled down at her desk and busied herself typing up letters for the boss while she answered the phone.

It wasn't hard to avoid her at quitting time. Jessie was always the first one out the door, just in case the phone rang and somebody had to answer it. She was never on time in the mornings, either, something resented by all her coworkers.

"Phew," Bernie said with heartfelt thanks

when Jessie was out of sight. "I thought my number was up when we got back from lunch."

"Jessie won't quit," Olivia said quietly. "She's got that nice rich visitor in her sights and she'll do anything to get his attention. You watch out," she added.

Bernie sighed. "I guess she'll really hit the ceiling when she finds out I'm going to a movie with him."

"Movie?" Sari asked, all ears.

"When?" Glory asked.

She laughed. "Friday night. He's taking me to the drive-in."

"Ooh," Sari mused. "Heavy stuff."

Bernie blushed. "He's so good-looking. Honestly, I feel dowdy compared to Jessie."

"He didn't like Jessie, though, did he?" Olivia reminded her. "He told me not to mention he was having lunch with us when I went back to the office. He wasn't impressed by her. In fact," she added with a chuckle, "he said he knew how deer felt during hunting season."

"Wouldn't that get her goat?" Sari teased. "I wasn't kidding about Mikey," she added to Bernie. "He really isn't a ladies' man."

"He could be in movies," Bernie said.

"Yes, he could," Glory agreed. "I wonder." She glanced at Sari. "Didn't anybody ever try to get him to audition for a movie?"

"In fact, Paul says he was pursued by a Hollywood agent who saw him in Newark. He just smiled and walked away. He's shy, although that never comes across. He puts on a good act," Sari added.

"He's good with people," Bernie told them as they went out and locked the door, Mr. Kemp having gone home from a day in court already. "The ladies at the boardinghouse think he's just awesome."

"And what a lucky thing that Mrs. Brown only had one vacancy," Sari said. "Or Jessie would be over there like a flash."

"I still can't figure what she's doing down here," Glory said. "She's a bad fit for our office, and she doesn't mix with anybody in town except her friend Billie at the county clerk's office." She frowned. "In fact, Billie hasn't been here long, either, and she's a city girl from back east somewhere. They're both of them out of step with local people."

"Do they room together?" Bernie asked.

"Yes, at some motel out of town. That's got to

be expensive, too, since none of our local hotels serve meals."

"Which one do they stay at?" Glory asked.

"The one where all the movie stars live when they're in town filming," Sari told her. "The one with whirlpool baths and feather pillows and mini bars."

"Ouch," Glory laughed. "That's the most expensive place in town. Jessie doesn't make enough here to afford such luxury."

"Well, she and Billie share," Sari said. "I guess they share meal expenses, too. Jessie would never manage it alone."

"Don't mention your upcoming date in the office," Glory cautioned Bernie.

"I might not need to," Bernie said, waving Olivia goodbye as she drove off in her car. "We were sort of holding hands in Barbara's Café," she confessed.

Sari whistled.

Bernie looked at her curiously.

"And Mikey knows about small towns, too," she mused. "Apparently he doesn't mind people knowing that he likes you."

Bernie flushed. "Really? You think he does?"

"Paul does," Sari said. "And he knows Mikey a lot better than the rest of us do."

"Wow," Bernie said softly.

"There's my ride. My boys," Glory gushed, waving to Rodrigo at the wheel of their car and their little boy in the back seat. "See you tomorrow!"

"Have a good night," Bernie called. Glory waved as she got into the car and fastened her seat belt. Rodrigo waved at the women on his way past.

"There's just one thing," Sari said gently, turning to Bernie when they were alone. "Mikey's down here for a reason, and it's a dangerous one. I can't talk about it. But you should know that there's a risk in going around with him."

"I do know," Bernie replied. "I don't care."

"So it's like that already." Sari smiled. "I'd feel the same way if Paul was like Mikey. You know that Mikey's past isn't spotless?" she added a little worriedly.

"You mean, about his hotel business?"

Sari didn't know what to say. She felt uncomfortable telling tales. Well, better to let sleeping dogs lie. "It was a long time ago," she lied, smiling. "He'll tell you himself when he's ready."

"I don't care about his past," Bernie said softly, and she smiled. "I've never been so happy in my whole life."

"Judging by how much he smiles lately, neither has Mikey," Sari laughed. "Paul said he was the most somber man you've ever seen until lately. They grew up together."

Bernie nodded. "Their grandmother raised them. Mikey loved her."

"Yes, he did. Paul and Mikey had a rough childhood. Their grandmother was all they had. Well, and each other, although neither of them would admit it."

"They seem to get along well, from what Mikey says."

"They do now. It wasn't always that way." She glanced toward the curb. Paul was sitting at the wheel of their Jaguar. He waved. "Well, I'll go home. Can we drop you off?" she added.

Bernie laughed. "I'm doing really good today, and Dr. Coltrain says I need the exercise when I can get it. But thanks."

"No problem. Anytime. See you tomorrow."

Bernie waved them off and walked the four blocks to Mrs. Brown's boardinghouse. She felt as if her feet didn't even touch the sidewalk. Life was sweet.

* * *

She got through the rest of the week relatively unscathed by Jessie, although she received a lot of irritated looks when a couple of local people coming into the office mentioned that Bernie had been seen holding hands with Mikey at Barbara's Café. But apparently Jessie still thought Bernie was no competition for her. She did mention, loudly, that she was going to spend more time at Barbara's herself.

"And good luck to her," Sari laughed when Jessie left ahead of them all, as usual, at the end of the day. "Mikey's been in San Antonio for the past two days."

Bernie smiled with obvious relief. She hadn't seen him since their lunch at the café. He'd been out of town apparently. She'd wondered if he was leaving town. She'd hoped he'd say goodbye first, but his absence at the boardinghouse had worried her. Mrs. Brown only said that he had business to take care of, but she hadn't said how long it might take him to conduct it. Bernie figured it was something to do with the hotel he owned. It must take a lot of work to coordinate something so big, and he must have a lot of employees who had to be looked after as well.

"You didn't know," Sari guessed when she noted Bernie's expression.

"Well, no. He just told Mrs. Brown that he had business to take care of. We didn't know where he was."

"He and Paul have something going on together," Sari said, without mentioning what, although she knew. It was top-secret stuff, nothing she could tell even her worried coworker about.

"I hoped he wouldn't leave town without saying goodbye," Bernie replied.

"Are you kidding? He's taking you to a movie, remember?" Sari teased. "How could he leave town?"

Bernie laughed. "I guess he wouldn't, at that." She was beaming. "You know, I've only ever been on a few dates in my life." She hesitated and looked at Sari worriedly. "Mikey's sophisticated, you know? And I'm just a small-town girl with old-fashioned ideas about stuff."

"So was Della Carrera before she married Marcus here in town," she reminded the other woman. "Nobody's more sophisticated than Marcus Carrera."

Bernie smiled. "I guess not." She frowned.

"Mr. Carrera was big in the mob, wasn't he?" she added absently.

"He was. He went legitimate, though. He was actually working with the FBI to shut down a crooked crime figure who planned to open a casino near Marcus's."

"I heard something about that." Bernie shook her head. "I don't understand how people ever get involved with organized crime. It seems a shameful way to earn a living."

"That it is," Sari said, but became reserved. Bernie didn't know about Mikey and she didn't feel comfortable blowing his cover. "Well, I'm off. See you tomorrow!"

"Have a good night."

"You, too."

Bernie watched them drive away and started back to Mrs. Brown's. She could hardly contain her excitement about the coming date with Mikey.

Mikey, meanwhile, had been in conference with Paul, Jon Blackhawk and a US Marshal in San Antonio, while the three of them hashed out what they knew and what they didn't know about Cotillo. Mikey had stayed at a safe house with the marshal while they discussed the case and what they were going to do about the threat.

"I don't want the women in my boardinghouse hurt," Mikey said during one long session. "Just being around me could put them in danger."

"They won't be," Paul replied. "You've got more protection than you realize."

"Yeah, well, Merrie Colter had plenty of protection, too, and she ended up in the hospital when that contract man was after her," Mikey pointed out.

"No plan is foolproof," Jon Blackhawk, assistant SAC at the San Antonio FBI office agreed. "But we've got most of our bases covered. And, frankly, no place is going to be perfectly safe. If you leave your boardinghouse, the women who live there could still be in danger if the contract man decides they might know where you were."

Mikey felt sick to his stomach, although nothing showed in that poker face. "I suppose that's true," he said heavily.

"I've never lost a person I was protecting yet," US Marshal McLeod interjected. He was tall and husky like Mikey, but he had pale gray eyes in a face like stone and a .357 Magnum in a leather holster at his waist.

"You and that damned cannon," Paul muttered. "Why don't you move into the twenty-first century, McLeod, and sport a piece that didn't come out of the eighties?"

"It's a fine gun," McLeod said quietly. "It belonged to my father. He was killed in the line of duty, working for our local sheriff's office back home."

"Sorry," Paul said sheepishly.

McLeod shrugged. "No problem."

"I hope you got earplugs when you have to shoot that thing," Mikey mused.

"I got some, but if I take time to put them in, I'll be wearing them on the other side of the dirt."

Mikey chuckled. "Good point."

"Where's your piece?" Paul asked suspiciously.

"My piece?" Mikey opened his suit coat. "I don't carry a gun, Paulie. You know that."

"I know that you'd better get a Texas permit for that big .45 you keep in your car, before Cash Grier knows you don't have one," Paul said with a smirk.

Mikey sighed. "I was just thinking about that the other day. So. Where's Cotillo?"

There was a round of sighs. "Well, he was

in Newark," McLeod said. "I checked with our office there, but he's out of sight now. Nobody knows where he went. We have people checking," he added. "One of our guys has a Confidential Informant who's close to him. We'll find him."

"It's his contract killer we need to find," Paul interrupted. "If he offs Mikey, we have no case, and Tony Garza will go down like a sack of beans for murder one."

"Speaking just for myself, I'd prefer to live a few more years," Mikey mused.

"Especially since you have a hot date tomorrow night, I hear?" Paul said with an unholy grin.

Mikey embarrassed himself by flushing. The tint was noticeable even with his olive complexion.

"Hot date?" Jon asked.

Mikey cleared his throat. "She's a nice girl. Works as a paralegal for the district attorney's office in Jacobsville."

"Bernie," Paul said.

There were curious looks.

"Bernadette," Mikey muttered. "It's short for Bernadette."

"Pretty name," Jon said.

"She's a sweetheart," Paul told them. "Takes a real load off the district attorney, and the other women who work in the office love her, especially my wife." He glanced at Mikey. "Which begs the question, why don't you ever bring her over to the house to eat? You know Mandy wouldn't mind cooking extra."

Mikey shifted his feet. "It's early days yet. I just asked her to a movie."

"A drive-in, at that," Paul mentioned with a grin.

"You've got a drive-in theater in Jacobsville?" Jon exclaimed. "They went out in the fifties, didn't they?"

"In the sixties, mostly, but we've got a local guy who's trying to bring them back. He even built a small café on the premises with restrooms and pizza. So far, he's a raging success."

"My dad talked about going to drive-ins," McLeod mused. "He said it was the only place he could kiss my mother without half-a-dozen people watching. Big family," he added.

"I can't place that accent, McLeod," Paul said. "You sound Southern, but it's not really a Texas accent."

"North Carolina," McLeod said. "My people go back five generations there in the mountains. The first were Highlanders from Argyll in Scotland."

"Mine came from Greece and Italy," Paul said. "Well, mine and Mikey's," he added with a glance at his cousin.

"Mine met the boat yours came over on," Jon said with a straight face. He was part Lakota Sioux.

There was a round of laughter.

"I have some Cherokee blood in my family," McLeod volunteered. "My great-grandmother was Bird Clan. But we're mostly Scots."

"Can you play the pipes?" Jon asked curiously.

McLeod shrugged. "Enough to make the neighbors uncomfortable, anyway."

"I had a set of trap drums," Paul recalled wistfully. "We had some really loud, obnoxious neighbors upstairs when I lived in Newark, long before I moved here." He didn't add that at the time he'd had a wife and child who were killed by operatives of a man he put in prison. "I was terrible at playing, but it sure shut the upstairs neighbor up."

"You bad boy," Mikey teased.

"A man has to have a few weapons," he said drolly.

"Back to Cotillo," McLeod said. "We have someone watching you from our service down in Jacobsville. You don't need to know who, but we're on the job. I offered, but they shut me up immediately."

"They did? Why?" Mikey asked.

"They say my restaurant allowance is abused."

They all looked at him. He was substantial, but streamlined just the same.

A corner of his mouth pulled down. "They say I eat too much. Hey, I'm a big guy. It takes a lot of food. Besides, I hear some of the best food in Texas is at that café in Jacobsville."

"It is," Paul agreed. "Everybody eats there."

"So would I, if they'd let me. The boss said we needed somebody who liked salads and tofu."

Now they all really stared at him.

He glowered back. "She's a vegan," he said with spirit. "She gets upset if anybody mentions a steak."

"Tyranny," Paul teased.

"Anarchy," Mikey seconded.

"She should move back east, where she'll have plenty of company," Jon agreed. "I'm not giving up steaks, and I don't care if the SAC is a vegan or not."

"That's what I told her," McLeod replied. His black eyes sparkled. "Shut her up for ten minutes at least. But that's when she assigned me to him," he indicated Mikey. "She thinks it's a mean assignment." He chuckled. "I didn't try to change her mind."

"Good thing," Jon said. "I know your boss. She has a mean streak."

"She mustered out of the Army as a major," McLeod replied. "Honestly, I think she believes she's still in it."

"They make good agency heads," Jon said.

McLeod nodded. "But I'm still not eating tofu."

They all laughed.

"What about Cotillo?" Mikey asked after a minute.

"Why does that name sound so familiar?" Paul wondered. Then his face cleared. "Of course. It's that town across the border, you know, the one where an unnamed person that we all know offed the drug lord El Ladron and his buddies in a convoy." The unnamed person was Carson Farwalker, now a doctor in Jacobsville, who'd thrown several hand grenades under El Ladron's limo and was never charged.

"There's a cactus called ocotillo," Jon Blackhawk mused, "but that little town over the border was actually settled by an Italian family back in the late 1800s."

"Interesting," Mikey remarked. He sighed. "But the man is more worrisome than the town right now."

Faces became somber.

"When our CI finds out anything, I'll pass it on," McLeod said. "Meanwhile, he's got somebody watching Carrera down in the Bahamas." He indicated Jon.

Jon nodded. "Our field office has him under surveillance. And Carrera has some protection of his own, for himself and Tony Garza. You know, just because Carrera went straight doesn't mean he doesn't still have some pretty formidable ties to his old comrades. We understand he has two of them staying in the house with Della, his wife, and his two little boys."

"Two of the best," Mikey agreed. "I know them from the old days."

"Mikey," Paul said with real affection, "you never left the 'old days.'"

"Well," Mikey said with a sigh, "we are what we are, right, Paulie?"

"Right."

Bernie didn't really know how to dress for a drive-in movie, so she settled for pull-on navy blue slacks topped with a blue-checked button-up shirt and a long blue vest that came midthigh. She thought about putting her hair up in some complicated hairdo, but she left it long and soft around her shoulders. She'd toyed with having it cut. It was hard for a woman with disabilities to keep it clean and brushed, but she couldn't bear the thought of giving up the length. She had all sorts of pretty ribbons and ties to put her hair up with when she went to work. Even jeweled hairpins for special occasions. Not that there had been many of those, ever.

She glanced in the mirror and smiled at the excited, almost pretty girl in the mirror. She was going on a real date, with a man who made movie stars look ugly, and he liked her. She almost glowed.

There was a hard tap on the door. She got her coat and purse and opened the door. Mikey was wearing slacks and a designer shirt under a nice jacket. His shirt was blue, like hers.

He grinned at her. "Well, we seem to match."

"I noticed," she teased.

He gave her a thorough appraisal and felt his heart jump as he locked eyes with her. She was unique in his experience of women, which was extensive. She was so different from the aggressive, sensual women he'd liked in his youth. His tastes had changed over the years. Right now, Bernie was the sweetest thing in his life. He hoped he wasn't putting her in danger by being close to her.

"You ready to go?" he asked. "We must both be insane. A drive-in movie and it's just a week until Halloween! It's cold, even for south Texas!"

"I love drive-ins," she said softly. "And I don't care if it snows."

He chuckled. "Me, neither, kid." He took her hand in his and felt her catch her breath. He felt just the same. "Come on. I've got something a little less noticeable than the limo to go in."

A little less noticeable, she thought with surprise when she saw what he was driving. It was a luxury convertible, very pretty and probably very fast.

"Oh, my," she said.

"It goes like a bomb," he said, as he helped her inside the late-model Mercedes convertible. It was a deep blue color. The interior was leather, with wood trim on the steering wheel and the dash. She sank into luxury as she fastened her seat belt.

"Oh, my," she said again as he touched a control and her seat heated up and began to massage her back. "This is heavenly!" She closed her eyes and smiled. "Just heavenly!"

He chuckled. "I'm glad you like it. I go first-class, kid. Always have, even when I was young and full of pepper." He didn't like remembering exactly how he'd gone first-class. She made him feel guilty about the things he'd done in his pursuit of wealth. She didn't seem to covet wealth at all.

"I've never ridden in a car that had heated seats," she said excitedly. "And even a massage! It's just amazing!"

He smiled. He hadn't considered how uptown the car was to someone who probably rode around mostly in cabs that barely had heaters and air-conditioning. "Don't you drive?" he asked.

She felt the words all the way to her feet and averted her eyes so that he couldn't see the sadness in them. She couldn't have afforded a car. "I used to," she said softly. "Not anymore."

"You should go back to it," he replied as he pulled the car out into the street and accelerated. "I love to drive."

"This car must go very fast."

"It does. I'd demonstrate," he teased, "but you'd have to come bail me out of jail."

She laughed, the old fear and guilt subsiding. "I would, you know," she said softly. "Even if I had to sell everything I own."

He flushed.

"I mean, I'd find someone who could…" she began, all flustered because of what she'd blurted out. She was horribly embarrassed.

His big hand reached out for her small one and tangled with it. "Stop that," he chided gently. "You shouldn't feel guilty for enjoying somebody's company. Especially not mine." His hand contracted around hers. "I'm used to women who want what I've got," he added coldly.

"What you've got?" His fingers tangling gently with hers had her confused and shaky inside.

"Money, kid," he replied. "I've got enough in foreign banks to see me well into old age, even if I spend myself blind."

"Oh." Her hand stiffened in his.

He glanced at her and chuckled. "Now you think I suspect that you're only going out with me because I'm rich. Not you," he added in a deep, husky tone. "You're not the sort of woman who prefers things to people. I knew that right off. Proud as Lucifer, when you fell in front of the car and I made sarcastic remarks about how you'd fallen." He sighed sadly. "Worst mistake of my life, thinking you were like that. Believe me, I felt about two inches high when Santi found that cane you used."

She bit her lower lip. "I'm clumsy, sometimes," she said. "I fall over nothing when I'm having flares. I wish I was healthy," she added miserably.

"My little grandmother would sit and cry sometimes when the pain got really bad," he recalled quietly. "I'd fill a hot water bottle for her and read her stories in Greek to take her mind off it."

"You can speak Greek?" she asked.

"Greek, Italian, a little Spanish," he replied.

"I learned to read Greek characters," she said. "They're the Coptic alphabet, like Russian."

"Nice," he said, glancing at her with a smile. "Yes, they are. Hard for some people to learn, too."

"I love languages. I really only speak English and Spanish."

"Spanish?"

"Well, we deal with a lot of bilingual people, but some of the older people who come from countries south of ours don't understand English as well as their children. I can translate for them."

"Brainy," he teased.

"Not really. I had to study hard to learn the language, just like I had to study hard to learn to be a paralegal. I went to night school at our local community college," she added.

"I imagine that was hard," he said. "Working and going to school at the same time."

"It was," she confessed. "I wanted to learn the job, but I missed class sometimes. There was a nice woman who was studying it at the same time—Olivia, who works in our office—and she took notes so that I could catch up on what I missed. The professor was very understanding."

"You're a sweet kid," Mikey said softly. "I can imagine that most people bend rules for you."

She laughed. "Thanks." She glanced at him as they drove a little out of town to the wooded area that housed the new drive-in. "Did you go to school? I mean, after high school?"

"I got a couple of years of college when I was in the Army," he said. "Never graduated. I was too flighty to buckle down and do the work."

"What did you study?"

He chuckled. "Criminal justice. It seemed like a good idea at the time. I mean, considering what I did for a living."

She just stared at him, curious.

He felt his cheeks heat. He glanced at her. She didn't understand. "Didn't Sari talk about me at work?" he said.

"Just that you and her husband are first cousins and that you're close," she replied, and her eyes were innocent.

She wasn't putting on an act. She really didn't know what he'd been, what he still was. He hesitated to tell her. He loved the way she looked at him as if he had some quality that she'd never found in anyone else. She looked at him with affection, with respect. He couldn't remember another woman who'd cared about the man instead of the bank account. It made him humble.

He drew in a breath. "Well, Paulie and I are close," he agreed. His hand tightened around hers. "I meant, didn't you know about the trouble Isabel and Merrie had three years ago, when they were being stalked by a cleaner?"

"Oh, that," she said, nodding. "There was a lot of gossip about it," she added. "I don't remember much of what I heard, just that a man who was big in organized crime back east called off the hit man. She painted him." She laughed. "They said he walked her down the aisle when she married Paul. I didn't know her then, except I knew the family and that they were well-to-do. I never moved in those circles. I'm just ordinary."

"Honey, ordinary is the last thing you are," he said huskily as he pulled onto the dirt road that led to a drive-in with a huge white screen and a graveled lot with speakers on poles every few feet. "And we're here!"

He paid for their tickets and drove them through to a nice parking spot right in front of the screen. He looked at the ticket. "We've got a ten-minute wait," he said.

"What are we going to see?" she asked. "I didn't pay attention to the marquee."

He chuckled as he cut off the engine and turned to her. "You didn't notice?" he teased, black eyes sparkling as they met her pale ones.

"Not really," she confessed. "I was excited just to be going out with you." She flushed. "There are some very pretty single girls around Jacobsville, including Jessie, who works with us."

His fingers tangled softly with hers, caressing, arousing. "Jessie doesn't do a thing for me," he told her. "She's like the women I used to date back east. Brassy and out for everything they can get from a man."

"I guess so. We're not really like that here," she added. "Money is nice, but I have all I need. I'm not frivolous. My biggest expense is the drugstore. And the doctor," she said sadly.

"It doesn't matter," he said solemnly. "You're not of less value as a woman because you have a disability."

"Most local men thought I was," she replied. "I won't get better unless they come out with a miracle drug," she said. "There are shots I could take, but they're really expensive and there's no guarantee that they'd work. There's also infusion, where they shoot drugs into you with an IV and they last several weeks." She lowered her eyes to the big hand holding hers. It was strong and beautiful, as men's hands went. Long fingered, with perfectly manicured nails.

"I read about those shots," he replied. "Just before my grandmother died, I was researching new drugs that might help her. The pain got so damned bad that they had to give her opiates to cope with it." He made a face. "Then the government steps in and says that everybody's going to get addicted, so now you get an over-the-counter drug for pain even if you've got cancer," he added angrily. "Like that's going to help get illegal narcotics off the street! Hell, you can buy drugs, guns, anything you want in the back alley of any town in America, even small towns."

"You can?" she asked curiously.

"Of course you can. Even in prison."

"Wow."

He chuckled. "Kid, you really aren't worldly."

"I guess not," she said with a good-natured smile. "I don't have much of a social life. Well, I do have Twitter and Facebook, but I don't post very often. Mostly, I read what other people write. My goodness, I must be sheltered, because some of the things people post I wouldn't even tell to my best friend!"

"What sort of things?" he teased.

"I'm not saying," she replied.

He made a face. "That didn't hurt, that didn't hurt, that didn't hurt…" And he laughed, softly and with so much mischief that she burst out laughing, too.

He looked around. "Not so many people just yet. So." He caught a handful of her long, beautiful platinum hair and tugged her face under his. "Don't panic," he whispered as he bent his head. "This is just a test. I'm practicing mouth-to-mouth resuscitation, in case I ever have to save you…!"

Chapter Five

Bernie held her breath as she watched his firm, chiseled lips hover over hers. She could taste the coffee on his mouth, feel his breath as his face came closer, so that his dark eyes filled the world.

She clutched at his jacket, more overcome with emotion than she could have dreamed even a few weeks ago.

"I love your hair, Bernadette," he whispered as his hand contracted in it and his mouth slowly covered hers for the first time.

She gasped under the soft pressure, but she wasn't trying to get away. He gazed down at her. Her eyes were closed, her eyebrows drawn together. She looked as if she'd die if he didn't kiss her.

Which was exactly how he felt, himself. He settled his mouth over hers, gently because he could sense her attraction and her fear. It was hard to give control to another person. But it was a lesson she would have to learn. He was glad that she was learning it with him.

He guided her arms up around his neck as his lips became slowly more insistent, giving her time to absorb the newness of it, giving her time to let go of her restraint. It melted out of her as he drew her closer across the console, his lips opening now, pressing hers gently apart.

She heard his breath sigh out against her cheek, felt his arms enfolding her, protecting her. She moaned as the feeling became almost overpowering and her arms tightened around his neck.

"That's it, baby," he whispered. "Just like that. Don't hold back. I'll go slow, I promise."

And he did. He didn't force her or do anything to make her uncomfortable. His mouth slid finally against her cheek to rest at her ear. His heart was doing the hula in his chest. He could feel hers doing the same thing.

It was odd, to be chaste with her. Most women in his past would have been tearing his clothes off at this point, but Bernie was gentle and inexperienced. He could feel the need in her because he felt it, as well. It was new to want to protect and cherish someone. He felt as if he could fly.

"You taste like sugar candy," he whispered at her ear.

Her arms tightened and she laughed softly. She didn't know what to say.

His big hand smoothed the length of her hair. "I'm glad you left it down tonight," he murmured. "Just for me?"

"Just for you." Her voice sounded husky. She felt swollen all over. It was a delicious sensation, like going down on a roller coaster.

His face nuzzled hers. "I never expected something like this," he said in a deep, lazy tone. "I was going to stay in this little town for a while and bide my time, maybe find a poker game to get into or something. And here's this beautiful little violet, right in my boardinghouse."

"Me?" she stammered.

His hand slid under her hair. "You, Bernadette." His cheek slid against hers and his mouth covered hers again, but harder this time, hungrier.

She couldn't resist him. She didn't have the sophistication to even pretend that she didn't like what he was doing. Her fingers tangled in his thick, cool, wavy hair. She loved what he was doing to her. She couldn't hide it.

And he loved that about her. He loved that she felt the same attraction he did, and that she was innocent, untouched, vulnerable. She needed someone to take care of her. He needed someone to take care of. Since his grandmother's death, there had been nobody in his life to fill that need. Bernie's disability didn't put him off in the slightest. It made him feel protective.

Which made him slow down. He was taking things too far, too fast. He drew back very slowly, his dark eyes intent on her face, her eyes half-closed, her pretty mouth swollen, her body warm and soft in his arms. She radiated tenderness.

"It's been a long time since I felt like this," he whispered at her lips, brushing them with his own. "And even then, it wasn't so sweet."

She smiled against his mouth. "I've never felt anything like this," she confessed softly. "Not with anybody." She grimaced. "Not that there's ever been anybody, except a boy who kissed me at a party when I was sixteen." She sighed. "That was just before he said he liked me a lot but he didn't want to get involved with a crippled girl."

"You aren't crippled," he said shortly. "You have as brave a spirit as anybody I ever knew. You're strong and capable. You're a woman with a disability, not a disability that's female. If that makes sense."

"You mean, I have a disability but it doesn't define who I am," she translated.

He smiled. "Yeah. It's like that." He searched her pale green eyes. "I don't mind it. I told you about my grandmother, that she had it, too. Somebody who minds it isn't interested in you the right way. He's looking for somebody more…casual."

She knew what he meant. Her fingers went up to his face and traced it while she studied him with fascination. "I never knew anybody like you," she whispered.

"I never knew anybody like you," he replied, and he was serious. "I can't imagine how I missed seeing you when I was here before, three years ago."

"I heard about you back then. I was working for a firm of attorneys. But people just said you were helping your brother-in-law with some case," she added.

That might be a good thing. He wasn't sure how she'd feel if she knew the truth about him, about exactly why and how he'd helped the Grayling girls.

"You don't know much about me," he said after a minute.

"That's okay. You don't know much about me, either," she replied.

He grinned. "Don't tell me. You're a spy and you have a trench coat in your closet back in the boardinghouse."

"Don't you dare tell a soul," she chided. "They'd send people to sack me up and take me away."

"I'd never do that," he said softly, and he smiled. "Not in a million years."

In the back of his mind, he was hearing a song recorded by Meatloaf about doing anything for love. He sang softly, a little off-key.

She caught her breath. "It's one of my favorite songs," she confessed. "Did you see the video?"

"I did. I watch it on YouTube sometimes." He laughed. "It's one of my favorites, too. What other sort of music do you like?"

Just as she started to answer, there was a gentle rap on the window.

Startled, Mikey let go of Bernie and put her gently back into her own seat before he powered down the window.

Cash Grier was standing there with a very knowing smile on his face, in his uniform.

"I have not been speeding in your town, and I never even jaywalked," Mikey began. "Besides that, we are outside the city limits."

Cash chuckled. "That's not why I'm here."

Mikey just waited.

Cash grimaced. "We've had a development," he said. "Nothing major. But Paul wants to talk to you, at the house."

"We just got here," Mikey said, visibly disturbed. "Can't it wait?"

"Sorry. No, it can't. Paul said to bring Bernie with you," he added with a smile in her direction.

"Oh." Mikey brightened. He turned to her. "Okay with you?"

She grinned. "Okay with me."

"We'll catch the movie another time," Mikey promised. He turned back to Cash. "You headed that way, too?"

Cash nodded. "You'll have two other cars following behind you, as well."

"Following us?" Bernie asked, concerned.

Cash and Mikey exchanged a long look. Mikey shook his head, just a jerk, but Cash understood at once that he wasn't to tell Bernie anything. "It's something to do with a case Paul's working on," Cash told Bernie with an easy smile. "No worries."

"Okay," she said, and smiled shyly.

"We'll be right along." Mikey took the speaker off the window and put it on its stand, powering the window up afterward. "Sorry about this," he told Bernie.

"You're related to an FBI agent," she said. "And I don't mind. Really."

He caught her hand in his as he turned onto the road. "You're easy to be with," he said softly. "You don't complain, you don't fuss. Even when you probably should."

She laughed. "I love being with you. Anywhere at all."

"That's how I feel." He curled her fingers into his and drove the rest of the way to Paul's house in silence. He was worried, and couldn't let it show. It must be something big if Paulie wanted to interrupt a date. His cousin wasn't the sort to interfere unless it was warranted. Which led Mikey to worry about exactly what the new development was.

His first thought was that they'd found Tony in some sort of horrible condition. They knew that Cotillo had a contract out on him, and that he could probably figure out that Tony was in the Bahamas since he and Marcus Carrera were close. He hoped Tony was still alive, even though it put Mikey in more danger.

He glanced at Bernadette and felt his heart clench. He was already attached to her. He couldn't bear the thought of letting her get hurt because of him. And she still didn't know anything about him, really, or the danger he was in. He was putting her in danger. If someone came looking for him, they'd go after the weakest link. An hour in any restaurant or bar around, and they'd know that Mikey was dating this cute little paralegal who worked for the DA. Bernadette could be used against him. In fact, so could

Mrs. Brown and her other residents. Mikey had a weakness for motherly women, and people knew about it.

"You're worried," she said softly from beside him.

His head turned. His shocked expression said it all.

"You hide things very well," she continued. "You really do have a poker face. But it's inside you. I can feel it."

He let out a long breath and his fingers contracted. "You see deep, just like Paulie's sister-in-law."

"Merrie was always like that, even in school."

"You've lived here a long time, haven't you?"

"Well, off and on, yes. I was born here, but when I was little, my parents moved to Floresville. My dad worked on a cattle ranch there as a foreman." Her face closed up. "Dad and I moved back here when I was about ten years old."

He was reading between the lines. Something had happened in Floresville that still caused her pain after all that time. He wondered what it was. But he wasn't going to ask. Not yet. They had time.

"I lived all my life in Newark," he said.

"Yes, you told me. You said you own a hotel in Las Vegas," she added, fascinated. "It must be a lot of responsibility, taking care of something so big," she added.

He chuckled. "You have no idea. I didn't know what I was getting into. I had some spare cash and I thought it would be fun to own something big and elegant. It's not what it's cracked up to be. The labor problems alone are enough to send me to the nearest bar."

"I guess a lot of people work for you."

They did, but not in the hotel business. He employed a number of men who worked just a little outside the law on various projects for him. He wasn't about to go into that with her. He thought about the life he'd lived, the things he'd done to get rich. It had seemed so important at the time, as if nothing was more important than having things, having expensive things, having money. He'd come out of the armed forces with a lot of contacts and even more ideas, and he'd put them into practice in the years since then. Now, when he thought of Bernadette and what a straight arrow she was, he felt uncomfortable. What would she think of him when she knew what he was, what he'd been, what he'd done? Already, the thought of losing her trust was painful.

"You have to stop worrying about things you can't change," she said, reminding him of a conversation they'd had some time ago about that.

He chuckled. "That's the thing, kid. There's a lot of stuff I *can* change. I just don't know how to go about it without getting thrown in the slammer."

She laughed because she thought it was a joke.

He smiled. It wasn't a joke at all. He had men who could take on a contract killer with great success, but it would put him in bad stead with the FBI and the US Marshals Service, which was helping protect him. His hands were tied. He couldn't put Paulie on the firing line by acting on his own. Besides, if he helped put Cotillo away, it put him in a great bargaining position with Uncle Sam. He might need a favor one day. It was to his advantage not to use his usual methods of dealing with threats.

"If you get arrested, I can bake a nail file in a cake and come to see you," she said with a wicked little grin.

He sighed. "Honey, they don't have iron bars on the outside of cells anymore. They're all inside and all the doors lock along the way. You'd never get out that way."

She frowned. She'd never been in a real jail, but he seemed to know a lot about them. She reasoned that he'd probably been with his cousin to see somebody in jail on a case or something. It didn't worry her.

He glanced at her and smiled. She really didn't see the bad part of him. It was amazing—that she had such insight but didn't see wickedness in his actions. Probably she didn't look for it. Apparently, her own life had been a sheltered one.

The big house at Graylings was ablaze with lights when Mikey pulled up into the driveway. There were two black sedans and a black SUV. The sedans had government license plates.

"Feds," Mikey said with a sigh as he helped Bernie out of the car.

She glanced at the backs of the cars parked side by side. She smiled. "Government plates. I guess they think people won't know as long as they don't have flashing lights on top," she teased.

He chuckled. "Good one." He caught her hand in his as they walked up to the front door. He drew in a breath. "Listen, kid," he said as they reached it, "there are things going on that I can't tell you about."

"I don't mind," she said, and looked up at him with perfect trust. In fact, she was in so far over her head that she wouldn't have minded if he robbed banks for a living.

He smiled slowly. "You're almost too good to be true," he chuckled. "Don't you have any wicked, terrible things in your past?"

The door opened, but not before he saw the expression that washed across her face, quickly hidden when Sari Fiore opened the door and grinned at them, holding hands.

"Sorry to have to break up your date," she told Bernie, "but we didn't have a choice. You can keep me company while the men talk. Mandy's gone to bed with a headache, so I'm alone. Well, almost alone," she amended when three men walked into the hall.

"Hey, Mikey," Paul Fiore greeted his cousin.

"Hey, Paulie."

"You know McLeod already," he said to Mikey, indicating a big, dark man, "and this is Senior FBI Agent Jarrod Murdock from our San Antonio office."

"I heard about you," Mikey mused as he looked at tall, blond Murdock, an imposing man who never seemed to smile. "Didn't they threaten to dress up like a ninja and throw you in the back of a pickup if you made coffee again…?" he teased.

Murdock made a face. "Not my fault I can't make good coffee," he scoffed. "I wasn't raised to be a woman."

The two women present gave him a wide-eyed, shocked look.

He cleared his throat. "Well, men aren't built right to make coffee," he amended. "Our hands are too big." He added that last bit tongue in cheek. And he wasn't smiling, but his pale blue eyes were twinkling just the same.

"That's the only comment that saved you from a picket line outside your office," Sari said in a mock threatening tone.

"God forbid!" Murdock said. "They'd fire me for sure."

"Not really," Paul commented. "You're too good a shot. You and Rick Marquez's wife hold the record for the most perfect scores in the city in a single year."

"She missed one shot last month," Murdock

replied. He grinned. "Morning sickness. So I hold the record right now."

"She's pregnant?" Sari asked. "Oh, that's so nice! I hope it's a boy this time."

"They already have two girls," Bernie told Mikey with a smile.

"I like little girls," Mikey said. "Little boys, too. Kids are sweet."

"Not all of them," Agent McLeod said coldly with glittering silver eyes.

"Oh, that's right," Paul commented. "That family you were looking after had a kid who stayed in juvie hall most of his life. What was that he painted your car with?"

McLeod eyes narrowed. "Skull and crossbones."

"And you couldn't touch him, because he was in protective custody."

"Oh, I wouldn't say that," McLeod replied. "I had a long talk with his probation officer. He's getting visits at school, at home, at his part-time job…"

"You vicious man," Sari chuckled.

"Maybe the skull and crossbones was more accurate than we know," Murdock commented.

"Watch it," McLeod said, "or I'll buy myself a ninja suit and a pickup truck."

They all burst out laughing.

"Well, come on into the study," Paul said to the men. He glanced at Sari.

"Bernie and I will be in the kitchen, discussing world politics," Sari replied.

Bernie looked up at Mikey with soft, pretty green eyes. "See you later."

He smiled slowly. "You will." He brought her fingers to his mouth and brushed them with it before he followed the men into the study.

Bernie had to be prompted to follow Sari into the kitchen. She was spellbound.

"If anybody had told me that Mikey would fall all over himself for a small-town Texas girl, I'd have fainted," Sari teased. "Honestly, you're all he talks about when he and Paul get together!"

Bernie flushed. "He's all I talk about at the boardinghouse. I've never met anybody like him. He's so…sophisticated and charming and sweet."

"Sweet?" Sari's eyes were popping.

Bernie laughed. "Well, he is."

"I suppose people bring out different qualities in other people," Sari said philosophically as she made coffee. "I owe Mikey a lot. So does my sister. He helped keep us alive."

"I heard that you were threatened, because of your father," Bernie said quietly. "Not the particulars, of course, just that Mikey helped your husband with the investigation."

"Mikey put us in touch with a gentleman who saved Merrie's life," Sari said, without going into any detail. "She was almost killed."

"I did hear about that. Some crazy man ran into her with a pickup truck, and then died in jail."

Sari nodded. She waited until the coffee perked and poured two cups of it. She put them on the table. She knew from the office that Bernie took hers black, just as Sari did.

Sari sat down across from her. "We lived through hard times," she recalled. "Our father was a madman. There were times when I thought he was going to kill us himself."

Bernie stared into her own coffee. "My grandfather had an unpredictable temper," she said. "You never knew which way he was going to jump. One time he'd laugh at something you said, and the next... Well, Mama and I had to be very careful what we said to him. So did my father."

"Your grandparents lived in Floresville, didn't they?" Sari asked gently.

Bernie's face clenched. She met the other woman's concerned blue eyes. "You know, don't you?" she asked.

Sari nodded. "From a former sheriff who moved here and had dealings with our office. But you know I don't gossip."

Bernie smiled. "Yes, I do." She put both hands around the coffee cup, feeling its warmth. "My grandfather wasn't a bad man. He just had an uncontrollable temper. But he could be danger- ous. And he was, one time too many." She gri- maced. "We lived out of town on a ranch, but gossip travels among country folk. After it hap- pened, Dad lost his job and wasn't given refer- ences, so we came back to Jacobsville. I was only ten. Dad and I were targeted once by one of the victim's relatives."

"I've been through the wars myself, you know. But I don't blame people for what their relatives do," she added firmly.

"Neither do I. But there was some gossip even here. Fortunately, there wasn't so much that Dad couldn't find work. He went to Duke Wright and got a job. He never got like Granddaddy. I used to think if only somebody had forced my grandfather to see a doctor and get on medication. If only we'd realized that he had mental health issues," she said huskily.

"*If.* There's a horrible word. *If only.*"

"Yes." Bernie nodded. She looked up. "You won't tell Mikey? I mean, I'll tell him eventually, but it's early days yet and—"

"Mikey has secrets, too," Sari interrupted. "He won't hold anything against you. He's more worried about what you'll think of him. He's...had some problems in his past."

Bernie cocked her head. "Can you tell me about them?"

"I think he should tell you," Sari replied. "I don't like to carry tales. He's not a bad man," she added firmly. "Everybody has shameful secrets. Some get told, some never do, some we carry inside us forever like festering wounds."

Bernie nodded. "That's like mine. Festering wounds. They blamed all of us, you see, not just my dad. They blamed Mama and me, as well."

"Bernie, you were just a kid. How could anyone have blamed you?"

"They said Mama made him mad in the first place," she explained. She closed her eyes. "I was just ten years old, I didn't have anything to do with it. Neither did Dad. But people died, and I live with the guilt."

"You shouldn't have to," Sari said curtly. "There was no possible way you could have stopped it."

"Losing my grandmother and my mother was the worst of it, especially for Dad," Bernie confessed softly.

She put a hand over Bernie's. "You can't live in the past. I'm having a hard time with that myself. My father killed a woman. He more than likely killed my own mother. I have to live with that, and so does Merrie. We have our own guilt, although I don't know what we could have done to stop it. We were terrified of our father, and he was so rich that nobody around here would go against him. He made threats and people did what he wanted them to." She sighed. "It was like a nightmare, especially when he was arrested. He tried to make me marry a foreign prince so that he'd have money for his defense attorney," she recalled bitterly. "He came at me with the belt and I screamed for help. He died with the belt in his hand. I thought I'd killed him."

"You'd never hurt a fly," Bernie returned gently. "Neither would Merrie. Your father was an evil man. That doesn't mean you'd ever be like him. You couldn't be."

Sari smiled. "Thanks. I mean it. Thanks very much."

"I guess we're all products of our childhoods," she commented. She searched Sari's blue eyes in their frame of red-gold hair. "What was Mikey's like, do you know? He said he grew up in Newark, and his grandmother raised him and your husband."

Sari smiled. "She did. She was Greek, very small and very loving, even though she was strict with them."

"What about their parents?"

"The less said the better," Sari said coolly. "I'm frankly amazed that they both turned out as well as they did."

Bernie sighed. "I know how that feels, except it was my grandfather, not my parents."

Sari nodded. She smiled. "I hope you're prepared for Monday. When Jessie finds out about the hot date, she's going to be a handful. Glory and I will run interference for you. And it isn't as if Mikey even likes her."

Bernie sighed. "That's a good thing. She's really beautiful."

"She is. But as our police chief likes to say, so are some snakes."

They both laughed.

In the office, things were less amusing. One of Cotillo's henchmen had actually managed to get inside Marcus Carrera's Bow Tie Casino in the Bahamas while Tony Garza was in his private study there. Only quick thinking by Carrera's bodyguard, Mr. Smith, who sensed something out of the ordinary, had saved the day. The henchman was arrested and held for trial.

"They found the henchman dead in his cell the next day, of course," Paul told his cousin.

"Of course." Mikey stuck his hands in his pockets. "It's a good bet that Cotillo knows where I am, as well. I've got no place else to go in the world where I'd have protection like this," he added.

"True enough," McLeod said. His gray eyes narrowed. "Once you testify, we have plans for you."

"They'd better be plans for two people, because I'm not leaving here without Bernadette."

The words came as a pleasant shock to his cousin, who'd only known Mikey to get serious about a woman once in his life, and that had ended badly.

McLeod chuckled. "We can arrange that."

"Okay, then."

"But we're going to have to up the protection," Paul said. "Eb Scott wanted to lend us the Avengers," he added, referring to Rogers and Barton, two of Scott's top men, "but they're on a top-secret mission overseas. He sent us Chet Billings instead. And we've got Agent Murdock here assigned to you as well."

"So long as he doesn't try to make coffee for me, we're square," Mikey said with a glance at the tall FBI agent.

Murdock just laughed.

"What about Carrera?" Mikey asked. "Is his family going to be under threat, as well?"

"He hired on some old friends," Paul said. "Several old friends, from back home."

Mikey knew what he meant, without explanation. "If I were Cotillo, I'd fold my tent and go back to Jersey."

"Not a chance," Paul said quietly. "He thinks he has what it takes to put Tony Garza down and take over his whole operation."

"Sounds to me like a man with a huge narcissistic complex," Murdock murmured.

"Or a man on a raging drug high," McLeod inserted.

"Maybe both," Paul replied. "People are getting involved in this who don't even have ties to Tony's business. They just don't like the idea of an untried, arrogant newcomer trucking into their territory and trying to set everybody aside who's been in the business for generations."

"I know several low-level bosses who hate Cotillo's guts and would love to move on him, There's even a rumor that one of the bigger New York families wants him out," Mikey said. "But Tony's the only one with the power to put him away. If Cotillo hadn't tried to frame him on that murder one charge, Cotillo would be running south as fast as his fat little legs would carry him."

"We've got the video you made," Paul told Mikey. "It's even got the time stamp."

"Sure," Mikey replied with a wry smile.

"But the defense could swear that it was photoshopped, that I lied to save my friend."

"Not if you testify," McLeod replied. "You're the best insurance we've got that Cotillo can't bring his murderous operation into Jersey. Listen, nobody thinks you and Tony sing with the angels, okay?" he added. "But there are levels of criminals. Cotillo is a cutthroat with no conscience, who's only in it for the money. He'll kill anybody who gets in his way. Tony has more class than that. And you," he said to Mikey, "never hurt a person unless they hurt somebody you cared about."

Mikey flushed. "Cut it out," he muttered. "You'll ruin my image."

Paul chuckled. "He's right, though," he told his cousin. "Merrie said that after she'd painted you."

"Hell of a painting," Mikey replied. "And she didn't even know me."

"What painting?" McLeod asked.

"Wait a sec." Paul pulled out his cell phone and turned to the photo app. He thumbed through it and showed it to McLeod. It was the painting

Merrie had done of Mikey, which Paul had photographed before he sent it to his cousin.

"Damn," McLeod said, looking from the portrait to Mikey. "And she didn't know what you did for a living?"

Mikey shook his head. "She painted that from some snapshots Paul had. Well, from a couple of digital images, from his cell phone, like that one. I was amazed. She did Tony, too. Some artist!"

"Some artist, indeed." McLeod agreed.

"Back to the problem at hand," Paul said when he put down the phone. "We need to double security. And you need to find another way to hang out with Bernie. A safer way than a drive-in theater in the country."

Mikey muttered under his breath. "What, like having tea in her bedroom in the boardinghouse? That'll help her rep."

"You can bring her here," Paul said. "We have the best security in town."

"You mean it?" Mikey asked.

"You bet," Paul told him. "You can watch movies together in the sunroom." He pursed his lips. "Where Cash Grier isn't likely to tap on the window."

"Which brings to mind a question," Mikey said. "Why was Grier looking for me at a movie theater out of town? Not his jurisdiction, is it?"

Chapter Six

"Cash was home and Sheriff Carson wasn't answering his phone," Paul said, "to make a long story short. Our police chief volunteered. His kids were protesting bedtime, so he pretty much walked off and left Tippy and Rory with it," he added, naming Cash's wife and young brother-in-law.

"In which case, he might want to spend the night at a friend's house," Mikey chuckled, "if what I've heard about his missus is true. Did she really use an iron skillet on that guy who came in her back door with a .45?"

"Absolutely she did," Paul confirmed. "She's

still a celebrity for that, not to mention being a former model and movie star."

"And gorgeous," Agent Murdock said with a sigh. "Even two kids haven't changed that."

Paul chuckled. "Tell me about it. Not that I did bad myself in the wife department. My Sari would give all the movie stars a run for their money."

"She's a doll," Mikey agreed. He sighed. "Well, what are you guys doing about Cotillo while he's plotting to have me and Tony killed?"

"We think he has somebody locally," Paul said, suddenly somber. "We don't know who. There are several people who just started working in Jacobsville recently, some of them with pronounced northern accents, like mine and yours."

Mikey grimaced. "I think I met one of them. She works with Isabel in the DA's office. A woman named Jessie." He shook his head. "Apparently she likes rich men and she's predatory. She actually got my cell phone number and called to ask me out."

"I'll bet that went over well," Paul replied tongue in cheek, because he knew his cousin inside out. Mikey didn't like aggressive women.

"It didn't go over at all," Mikey replied. "I told her the number was private and I wasn't interested. Then I hung up and blocked her number."

"I never attract women who want to date me." Murdock sighed. "I guess you have to be handsome."

"There's nothing wrong with you, Murdock, except the way you make coffee," Paul said. "And I did save you from that visiting attorney who mentioned how the ficus plant needed fertilizer."

"Yes, he was looking right at me when he said it," Murdock said and sighed. "Not my fault. Nobody else in the office will even try it."

"I would, but I'm never at my desk long enough."

"I live on the damned telephone," Murdock said heavily. "I get picked every time the boss needs information that he has to get from people out of town. I spend most of the day tracking down contacts."

"You should apply for the SWAT team," Paul suggested. "You'd do well."

"I'd get somebody killed is what I'd do," Murdock returned. "I don't think fast enough for a job like that. I guess, all in all, information gathering is important work and I'm pretty good at finding people."

"He used to be a skip tracer for a detective in Houston," Paul told Mikey. "He was good."

"I still am," Murdock said with a grin. "I tracked down an escaped murderer just a few days ago by calling his mother and telling her I was an old Army buddy. She told me exactly where he was. Sweet lady. I felt really guilty."

"People break the law, they do time," Paul said. "That's the rules."

"Rules are for lesser mortals," Mikey said with a hollow laugh. "I never followed any in my life."

"Until now," Paul said, with twinkling black eyes. "Rules are what's keeping you alive."

"Well, that and Bernie, I guess," Mikey said, and a faint ruddy color ran along his high cheekbones. "We went to the drive-in earlier. We were having a great time until Grier tapped on the window."

"What movie did you see?" Agent Murdock asked.

Mikey cleared his throat. "It was some sort of action movie, I think. The title escapes me."

"I'll bet it does," Paul said under his breath.

"Isabel told me that Bernie poured coffee over ice when she went to get a cup, and then she toppled a bookcase, all in the same day. And she's not clumsy."

Mikey's eyes twinkled. "Well, well."

"She's a sweet woman," Paul said. "Sari's protective of her. That woman, Jessie, who works in the office, gives her a hard time."

"DA needs to take care of business and fire her," Mikey muttered.

"He's given her fair warning that she'll lose her job if she causes any more trouble," Paul replied. He put his hands in his pockets. "Back to the matter at hand, though. I phoned Marcus Carrera and asked him how things were going. He says Tony's getting restless. He doesn't like hiding from some cheap hood who wants to take over his territory. He's fuming that he didn't anticipate trouble from that quarter when the guy first moved in with his goons."

"If he comes back, he could die over here," Mikey said. "He knows that Cotillo will have people watching and waiting."

Paul nodded. "That's what I told Carrera. He said he'll talk some sense into Tony and make sure he stays put, no matter what it takes. He's got some old friends from his gangster days helping out. And he hired a group of mercs, one of whom used to live here—that Drake guy whose sister married the veterinarian, Bentley Rydel. Kell Drake, that was his name."

"That's some formidable backup," Mikey conceded. "I hope he won't have to stay there too long. But what about Cotillo?"

"We've got plans for him," Paul said. "I have friends in Jersey, too. They're doing some scouting for me. The agency turned one of our best field agents onto the case, and he's digging into Cotillo's background. With any luck, he'll find something we can use for leverage while we wait for Tony's trial to come up."

"Tony fled the country," Mikey said sadly. "That's going to go against him. Flight from prosecution."

"He didn't fly, he was flown—by us," Paul said with a grin. "So that's not a charge he'll be facing."

Mikey sighed. "His past isn't lily-white. Neither is mine. So far, Cotillo hasn't ever been charged with a crime, for all we know."

"That's right," Paul returned. "For all we know. That's why we're digging. There's a federal prosecutor also on the case, and using his own investigators to look at Cotillo and his associates. Eventually, somebody's going to talk."

"So long as they don't talk about me and Tony and what's in our pasts," Mikey said with a resigned breath. "I've been a bad man, Paulie. I hope it doesn't come back to bite me."

"Not that bad, and you don't have a single conviction," Paul told him.

"No," Mikey conceded with a sad smile. "But that doesn't mean I haven't deserved one."

Paul put a lean hand on Mikey's broad shoulder. "We go one day at a time and leave tomorrow to itself. Right?"

Mikey smiled. "Okay. Right. Well," he added, "I'd better take Bernie home. So much for the movies."

"We have movies on DVD and pay-per-view," Paul reminded him with a grin. "You can watch them together right here, where it's safe. And the door has a lock," he added with amused eyes when Mikey blushed.

Mikey told Bernie about it when he took her back to the boardinghouse, reluctantly. "I'm sorry we had to break it up tonight," he said gently. "But Paulie says we can watch pay-per-view at his place, whenever we want."

"I'd like that," she whispered as he drew her close.

"Me, too, baby." He kissed her hungrily and then put her gently away. "I'm going back over to the house for a while. But we'll make a new movie date later, okay?"

She beamed. "Okay!"

Later, over supper at the house, Mikey drank a second cup of black coffee. He was unusually quiet.

"What's biting you?" Paul asked.

He shrugged. "I was thinking about Cotillo and his stooges. You know, I never stopped having Santi drive me in the limo. I've been pretty visible here…"

"Disguises don't work with people like Cotillo," Paul replied. "Besides, this is one of the safest places in the world when somebody's hunting you. It saved Sari and Merrie."

"It did," Sari added to the conversation. "It will save you, too, and Tony, I hope. Merrie's very fond of him, you know."

Mikey smiled. "Baby Doll's fond of everybody. It's just the way she is."

"That's true."

"Why are you so morose?" Paul asked his cousin.

"I worry about taking Bernie out now that I know I'm being watched by Cotillo's hoods," he said, pushing his coffee cup around.

"We told you that you could bring her over here any time you like," Sari reminded him with a smile. "She's so sweet. I love working with her."

Mikey seemed to perk up a little. "You really meant that? You wouldn't mind?"

"Not at all," Sari replied. "There are plenty of places to walk within sight of the house. We have calves she can pet and cats in the barn, and there's also the sunroom." She cleared her throat and didn't dare look at Paul, because some momentous things had happened there before the two of them married.

Mikey chuckled. "Okay, then," he said. "Thanks."

"No problem," Paul told him, his dark eyes twinkling. "So. How about Saturday?"

"Saturday sounds fine," Mikey replied. "You guys are terrific."

"Thanks," Sari said.

"You're terrific, too, Mandy," Mikey added when the housekeeper came from the kitchen with a cake pan.

Mandy grinned. "Nice of you to say that, and I baked you a chocolate cake, too!"

Mikey hesitated, looked guilty. His face drew up. He didn't want to tell her.

"Mandy, he won't say, but he gets terrible migraine headaches," Paul told her gently. "Chocolate is one of his triggers."

"Oh, my goodness, I'm so sorry!" Mandy began.

"You're a sweetheart, and it's the thought that counts," Mikey told her with a smile. "I love chocolate. I just can't eat it."

"Well, I'll make you a nice vanilla pound cake tomorrow. How's that?" she teased.

"That, I'll eat, and thank you."

"It's no trouble at all. You helped keep my girls safe. I'll never forget you for it, not as long as I live."

Mikey flushed a little. "They're sweet girls, both of them." He glanced at Sari. "Sweet women," he amended.

Sari waved away the apology. "I don't get offended at every single word people come up with. Besides," she added with twinkling blue eyes, "I got called a whole new word in court by a man I was prosecuting for assault. The judge turned him every which way but loose."

Mikey chuckled. "Good for the judge."

"She's a great judge," Paul agreed. "I had to get a search warrant from her several years ago. We had a long talk about Sari's mother. The judge was friends with her."

"My mother was sweet, kind of like Bernie," Sari said. "She loved to plant flowers and grow things."

"My grandmother did, too," Paul said.

"Yeah, she always had an herb garden, and she grew tomatoes out in the backyard," Mikey added. "It was hard, losing her. She was the only real family Paulie and I ever had. Our parents weren't around much."

"Which was just as well," Paul said grimly.

Mikey nodded.

"Well, I've got some research to do," Sari said, rising. She bent to kiss Paul. "Don't eat my part of that cake," she warned. "I'll be back for it later."

"Would I do that?" Paul said with mock defensiveness.

"Of course you would," she replied. She chuckled as she left the room.

"Damn, you got lucky," Mikey said after she'd gone.

"I did. Maybe you got lucky, too," Paul said. "Everybody who knows Bernie loves her." He grimaced. "Shame what happened to her," he added.

"Yeah, the arthritis is pretty bad," Mikey agreed.

Paul frowned and had started to speak when his phone went off. He looked at the number and groaned, but he answered it. "Fiore," he said.

He listened, glanced at Mikey, grimaced again. "I see. Yeah, I'll make sure he knows. We'll double up down here. No worries. I wouldn't want to risk Carrera getting mad at me, either, but these guys aren't playing with a full deck, if you know what I mean. Sure. Okay. Thanks."

"Trouble?" Mikey asked.

Paul nodded. "Somebody made an attempt on Tony, a new one. He's in custody and they're hoping he'll sing like a bird when they extradite him back here."

"A break, maybe."

"Maybe. If they don't suicide him, like they did the other one."

"Yeah." Mikey drew in a breath. "You know, my life was going along so well up until now. I've got the hotel. I've got all the money I'll ever need. I was really thinking about a home and a family. I guess I lost sight of what I've been, what I've done." He looked up at Paul. "Maybe the universe is set up so that you get back what you give out, every time, in double measure. I don't mind for me. I just don't want to put her in the crosshairs. She's the sweetest woman I've ever met."

Paul didn't need prompting to know that his cousin was talking about Bernadette. There was a look on Mikey's face that his cousin hadn't seen in many years. "We've got all our bases covered," he told Mikey. "You have to remember, outsiders stand out here. There's already gossip about that woman Jessie in Isabel's office, and even Barbara's new cook at the café. Outsiders draw attention."

"Did you check out Jessie and the cook?" Mikey asked.

Paul gave him a sardonic glance. "What do you think?"

"Sorry."

"No worries. But we dug pretty deep. I think we'd have found anything obvious, like an arrest record. Well, unless the guy's working for one of the letter agencies," he added, referring to the federal intelligence and justice community.

"True."

"You going to bring Bernie over Saturday?" Paul asked.

Mikey chuckled. "What do you think?" he said, throwing his cousin's own words back at him, and they both laughed.

Bernie couldn't sleep. It had been raining all day and the pain was pretty bad. She had pain relievers, massive doses of ibuprofen for when all else failed, but she didn't like it. The medicine messed her stomach up, even when she took it with food. Besides that, there was a limited amount of time that she could take it. It was so powerful that it could cause major problems with the liver and kidneys if people used it for a long period of time without a break. She was afraid of that.

But this was one time when she had to have some relief. She could barely hold back the tears.

She got out of bed painfully and pulled on her white chenille robe. She was going to have to go and get a bottle of water out of the fridge. Mrs. Brown, bless her heart, kept it for her tenants, who were always welcome to anything to drink or any bedtime snacks they could find in her spotless kitchen.

Bernie walked very slowly into the kitchen and almost collided with Mikey, in burgundy silk pajama bottoms with a matching robe. His broad, hair-roughened chest was bare, with the robe open. He looked handsome and sensuous. Bernie's heart jumped wildly at just the sight of him.

Mikey smiled. He could see all that in her face. She was totally without artifice, he thought. An honest woman, who never hid what she felt.

"You look pretty with your hair down, honey," he said gently.

She did. Her long platinum hair waved around her shoulders and down almost to her waist in back. With her cheeks faintly flushed and her pale green eyes twinkling despite the pain, she was a dish.

She laughed self-consciously. "I was just

thinking how gorgeous *you* look," she confided with a bigger flush.

"What do you need?" he asked. He was holding a paper plate with crackers and sliced cheese on it, along with some slices of fresh pear.

"Just a bottle of water from the fridge and something to eat. I have to take one of the big pills. Pain's pretty bad," she said reluctantly.

"Here. Sit down. I'll get you some cheese and crackers."

"I can do that…"

"Don't fuss, honey," he said gently. He pulled out a chair and waited until she sat down. Then he fetched the water and sliced a little more cheese and put some more crackers on his paper plate. He sat down, too.

"The pears are nice," he said.

"I like fresh fruit," she said shyly.

They munched cheese in a pleasant silence. She washed it all down with her bottle of water, wincing every time she shifted in the chair.

"I'm sorry you had to have a disease that makes you hurt all the time," he told her quietly.

"Life happens," she said. "I learned to live with it a long time ago."

He frowned. "You aren't that old."

"I'm twenty-four," she reminded him. "But I've had it since I was about nine."

"Nine years old!" he exclaimed.

"Some children are born with it," she replied. "Arthritis isn't just a disease of old people. There's a little boy, five, who goes to the same rheumatologist I do. He's got osteoarthritis and he has to take doses of ibuprofen just like I do."

Mikey winced. "What a hell of a life."

She nodded. "At least I've had it long enough to know how to cope with bad days and flares. It's much harder for a child."

"I can only imagine."

"Why are you up so late?" she wondered.

He moved crackers around on the plate, next to his opened soft drink. "You mentioned that I was worried about putting people in danger by living here," he said, recalling her uncanny perception.

She nodded. "You're in some kind of trouble, aren't you, and your cousin's trying to help."

"That's about the size of it." He leaned back with his soft drink in his hand. He looked gorgeous with his black, wavy hair tousled and his robe open.

He chuckled at her expression. "Your eyes tell

me everything you're thinking, Bernie," he said softly. "You can't imagine how flattered I am by it."

"Really?" she asked, surprised.

He stared at her quietly. "I'm a bad man," he said after a minute, and he scowled. "Getting mixed up with me is unwise."

She just looked at him and sighed. "I never had much sense."

It took a minute for that to register. He burst out laughing. "Oh. Is that it?"

She grinned. "That's it."

"Then, what the hell. I've got all sorts of people looking out for me. That means they'll be looking out for you and everybody in the boardinghouse, too."

"Okay," she said, smiling.

He cocked his head. "Do you like chocolate cake?" he asked suddenly.

Her eyebrows arched. "Well, yes. It's my favorite."

"Mandy made me one and I couldn't eat it," he said with a grimace. "I get migraine headaches, real bad ones. Chocolate's a trigger."

"My dad used to get them," she replied. She

frowned. "Isn't anything aged a trigger? I mean, like cheese?"

He looked at her and then at the plate of cheese and let out a breath. "Well, damn. I never thought about it. Every time I eat cheese I get a headache, and I never connected it!"

"Dad's neurologist said everybody's got more than one trigger, but sometimes they don't recognize them. He couldn't drink red wine or eat any dark fruit or cheese. And he loved cheese."

"How about chocolate?"

She laughed. "He never liked sweets, so it wasn't a problem."

"Do you get headaches?"

She shook her head. "I had one bad one when I was about thirteen. Never since."

"Lucky you," he told her.

"I guess so."

"Paulie says I can bring you over to the house to visit on Saturday, if you want."

Her heart skipped and ran away. "He did? Really?"

"So did Sari. There are kittens in the barn and horses to pet. I think there's a dog somewhere, too."

"Ooh, temptation," she cooed, and grinned at him.

He laughed. "I thought the kittens might do it."

She cocked her head and her eyes adored him. "The kittens would be a bonus. Spending time with you is the real draw."

He caught his breath. Amazing, the effect she had on him. He felt as if he could walk on air.

"It's like that with me, too, kid," he said softly. "I like being with you."

She felt exhilaration flow through her. "The cane doesn't put you off?"

He shrugged. "I'll get one, too. We'll look like a matched set."

Tears stung her eyes. She'd never dreamed that a man, especially a gorgeous, worldly man like this, would ever find her attractive and not be put off by her condition.

"Aw, now, don't do that," he said softly. He got up, lifted her into his arms and sat back down with her across his lap. "Don't cry. Everything's going to be all right. Honest."

She put her arms around his neck and snuggled close. "You think so?" she asked tearfully.

"Yes, I do." He rubbed her back, feeling protective.

The sound of a door opening broke the spell. But he wouldn't let Bernie up even when Mrs. Brown came into the kitchen.

"Oh, dear," she said, taking in Bernie's tears and Mikey comforting her. "Pain got you up, didn't it?"

"Yes. I came to get a bottle of water so I could take one of those horrible pills, but I have to eat something first. I hope you don't mind..."

"Bosh," Mrs. Brown said. "That's why I keep snacky foods and soft drinks in the fridge."

"The cheese is really good," Mikey said.

"It's hoop cheese," Mrs. Brown told him with a grin. "I get them to order me a wheel of it at the grocery store and I slice it and bag it up. I like it, too. I got peckish so I thought I'd get myself a snack. Is it bad, Bernie?" she added.

Bernie nodded. "I'm sorry if I woke you."

"I don't sleep much," Mrs. Brown said quietly. "You didn't bother me at all."

Bernie got off Mikey's lap reluctantly. "Thanks for the comfort," she said, wiping her eyes. "I don't feel sorry for myself, but the pain is pretty bad."

"Go to bed, honey. Don't forget your water,"

he told her. "Saturday, if you're better, we'll go see the kittens in Paulie's barn. Okay?"

Bernie's eyes lit up. "Okay."

"Want me to carry you down the hall?" he offered.

"Thanks," she said, a little self-conscious at Mrs. Brown's amused expression. "But I'm good. I hold on to the wall when I get wobbly. Good night," she added to both of them.

"Try to sleep, sweetheart," Mrs. Brown said. "If you need me, you call, okay?"

"I will. Thanks." She glanced at Mikey, flushed, smiled and went out the door.

"She's got grit," Mikey told the landlady.

"Yes, she really has," Mrs. Brown replied. "We all try to look out for her, as much as she'll let us. She's very independent."

"I noticed," he chuckled.

"You're eating cheese," she said worriedly. "Didn't you tell us that you got migraine headaches?"

"Well, yes..."

"Cheese is a trigger," she said. "Like red wine and chocolate."

He made a face. "I can't eat chocolate at all, but I never thought of cheese bringing on a headache." He laughed. "You know, I used to get headaches all the time and never knew why. It was always after I'd been out with a colleague of mine. He loved cheese, so he always had a platter of it with his dinner, wherever we ate. I nibbled on it and then almost died in the night when the pain came."

"Do you get the aura?" Mrs. Brown asked.

He grimaced. "Yeah. Flashy lights or blind in one eye until the pain hits."

"Do you have something to take for it?" she persisted.

"Just over-the-counter stuff."

"You should see a doctor and get something stronger," she told him. "They even have a drug that can prevent them, if you don't have drug allergies."

"They do?" he asked, and was really interested.

"They do." She laughed. "It's why I don't have them much anymore," she confessed. "Cheese is one of my biggest triggers. But I haven't had a migraine since back in the winter," she added.

"Maybe I should do that," he said. "They get worse as I get older."

"You're not old, Mr. Fiore," she teased.

He shrugged. "Thirty-seven," he confessed. "Really too old for Bernie..."

"Nonsense. I was fifteen years younger than my late husband, and we had a wonderful life together."

His eyebrows arched. "Did people talk about you?"

She nodded. She smiled. "We didn't care. It was nobody's business but ours." She sighed. "I'm so glad you and Bernie are friends. She's never had much in the way of companionship. She's so alone."

"Yeah, me, too," he confided. "After my grandmother died, all I had left was Paulie. He's a great guy."

"So I hear."

He got up. "Well, I'll go off to bed and hope the cheese doesn't do me in. But it was worth it," he added with a chuckle as he put his empty plate in the trash can. "Best cheese I've had in a long time."

"I'm glad you like it. And if you get the preventative, you can eat all you like of it," she laughed.

"I guess so. Sleep well."

"You, too."

* * *

But he didn't sleep well. He woke two hours later with a headache that almost brought him to tears. He walked into the bathroom, half-blind, and almost collided with Bernie, who was wetting a washcloth in the sink.

"My goodness, what's wrong?" she asked, because he was deathly pale.

"Migraine," he said roughly. "Any Excedrin in there?" he asked, indicating the medicine cabinet. "I can't find mine. I think I put it in here…"

She opened the cabinet and looked. "Yes, there is."

"Shake me out a tablet, will you, honey?"

"Oh, yes." She did and handed it to him. "You need this more than I do," she said, indicating the wet washcloth. "Come on. I'll help you back to bed."

"You should go," he said, swallowing hard.

"Why?"

"I get sick…" Before he could say anything else, he managed to make it to the commode and lost his supper, the cheese, the crackers, the soft drink and just about everything else.

When the nausea passed, he found Bernie on

her knees beside him with the wet cloth, wiping his face. She flushed the toilet.

"Better now?" she asked.

He swallowed and drew in a breath. "Yeah. I think so. Honey, you shouldn't..." he began.

"You looked after me when I was having a flare," she reminded him. "Tit for tat."

He managed a smile. "Okay."

"Come on. I'll help you back to bed."

He let her lead him back into his bedroom and help him under the covers. She put the washcloth over his eyes.

"I'll go get you something to take the tablet with. Want water or a soft drink?"

"Ginger ale, if there's any in the fridge," he said weakly, loving the comfort of her touch, the compassion in her voice. All his life, women had wanted him for his wealth, his power. This woman only wanted him. It was a revelation.

"I'll be right back."

"You shouldn't be walking," he said.

"It's just to the kitchen, and I took the big pill. It's helping. I'll be right back."

Mrs. Brown was just getting ready for breakfast in the kitchen. She turned as Bernie came in.

"Do you want some coffee, sweetheart?" the landlady asked.

"I'd love some, but Mikey has a migraine. I found his migraine medicine, but he wants ginger ale to take it with."

"There's one bottle left that's cold," the older woman said. "I'll get some more and put them in there. Is he all right?"

"He lost his supper," Bernie said. "He's really sick. I'm going to sit with him for a few minutes."

"If you need me, just call. We can get one of the Coltrain doctors to come over here and give him a shot if he needs them to. Those headaches are horrible. I used to have them before I got on the preventative."

"He should see a doctor," she said as she got the ginger ale out of the fridge.

"You make him do that," Mrs. Brown said.

Bernie flushed and laugh. "As if I could."

"Bernie," Mrs. Brown said gently, "can't you see that the man is absolutely crazy about you?"

Chapter Seven

Bernie stared at Mrs. Brown as if she'd sprouted grass in her hair. "He what?"

"He absolutely adores you," the older woman replied, smiling. "Everybody noticed, not just me."

Bernie flushed. "Well," she said, stumped for a response.

"You just go take care of your fellow," Mrs. Brown said. "I'll get breakfast ready. If he can eat anything, I'll make him whatever he likes."

"I'll tell him," Bernie replied. "Thanks."

"You come and eat whenever you like. I'll make you up a plate that you can reheat, okay?"

"Okay!"

Bernie went back to Mikey's room and closed the door. She sat down on the edge of the bed. "Still got the tablet?" she asked, because she'd handed it to him earlier.

"I got it."

"Here. It's open." She'd already taken the top off the bottle before she handed it to him. He swallowed down the tablet and handed her back the bottle. "Thanks, honey."

"No problem." She put his drink on the side table. "Will it stay down?" she worried. "Mrs. Brown said we can call one of our local doctors and they'll come give you a shot if you need it."

He swallowed. "Maybe the pill will work."

"Does it usually?"

He smiled. "No. It helps just a little. Nothing stops it."

She smoothed back his cool, wavy black hair. "You just let me know what you need. I'll get it."

His eyes adored her. "There was never a woman in my whole life who'd have taken care of me the way you just did. Well, except for my grandmother."

"I'm sure there were plenty who wanted to," she teased.

"Maybe a couple. But I'm funny about women.

Most of them are jaded and glitzy," he added, his eyes cold with memory.

"Maybe you've been looking in the wrong places for them," she said, tongue in cheek.

His black eyes twinkled at her. "Think so?"

"It's a possibility."

He lay back and closed his eyes, wincing. "Of all the things to get from cheese," he groaned. "It's my favorite food."

"You can find a new favorite one. Maybe squash," she teased. "Or okra."

"Stop! You're killing me!"

She laughed. Most of the men she worked around hated both vegetables with a passion.

"Frozen yogurt, then."

"That sounds nice."

They were quiet for a few minutes, but it was obvious that even when the tablet had time to work, it wasn't doing much.

"Pill helping at all?"

He put his hand over his eyes. "Not so much." He closed his eyes and winced. "It's just over-the-counter stuff."

"Let me call a doctor. Please."

He drew in a breath. "Okay," he said finally.

"Be right back."

* * *

She phoned Lou and Copper Coltrain's office. The nurse said she'd ask Lou to come right out. Lou was short for Louise, she was blond and sweet and she knew exactly what to do for Mikey.

"You should see a neurologist," she told him after she'd given him an injection for the pain. First, of course, she'd examined him, asked what he'd already taken for the headache and inquired about any drug allergies. He had none. "But in the meantime, I'll write you a prescription for the preventative and something for the headaches that works when you get one." She turned to Bernie. "I'll give these to you, Bernie. You get them filled today."

"I will," Bernie said, smiling at the physician. "Thanks for coming."

"You're most welcome. If you have any more issues, Mr. Fiore, you call the office, okay?"

"Yes, ma'am," he said complacently. He smiled up at her through dark-rimmed eyes. "Thanks, Doc."

"You're welcome."

"I didn't think doctors made house calls anymore," he said.

"Jacobsville's not like most small towns," she laughed. "We do what's needed." She glanced at Bernie. "I thought you might be dying, from Bernie's description. She was very upset."

He opened both eyes and stared at Bernie. "She was?" he asked softly, and smiled at her.

She flushed even more. He laughed. Lou hid a smile, said her goodbyes and left.

"Can I get you anything else?" Bernie asked.

"No, but you can give the prescriptions to Santi. I'll text him." He pulled out his cell phone and made a face. "Damn, I can't see it," he murmured.

"Just a sec." She took the phone from him, pulled up messaging and looked at Mikey. "What do you want to tell him?"

"Ask him to come over right away."

She typed it in. The response was immediate. "On my way," it read.

"He'll think I'm dying or that Cotillo got me," he chuckled.

She frowned. "Who's Cotillo?"

"A bad man. Even worse than me," he said in a husky tone. His eyes tried to focus on her face. "There's a lot you don't know about me, kid."

"Well, there's a lot you don't know about me, too," she said.

His big hand searched for hers and held it tight. "We'll learn about each other. It takes time. Right?"

She smiled. It sounded like a future. She felt herself glowing inside. "It takes time," she agreed.

He took a deep breath and closed his eyes. "I'm going to try to sleep. Santi has plenty of cash for the prescriptions."

"Okay." She got up. "If you need anything, you just call, okay?"

He smiled without opening his eyes. "Okay. Thanks, honey."

"You're very welcome."

She went out of the room, the soft words lingering, touching, making her feel valued.

There was a knock at the front door. She went to answer it. Santi was standing there.

"What's wrong with the boss?" he asked at once.

"Migraine," she said. "We had to call the doctor."

"It's a doctor you know, right?" he asked, and his broad face looked troubled.

"Oh, yes, Dr. Louise Coltrain. She came out and gave him these prescriptions. He asked you to get them filled for him at the drugstore."

He took them from her and nodded. "I'll get right on it." He grimaced. "I don't like being away from him at night, even with all those other guys watching out for him. Listen, you hear any strange noises or if anybody tries to get in the house, you text me. Got your cell phone with you?"

"Yes." She pulled it out and handed it to him.

He pulled up the contact screen and put information into it. He handed it back. "That's my cell phone number. The boss isn't twitchy, so he might pass over something that could be dangerous."

"I'll call you if anything happens here," she promised. "Thanks," she added softly.

He smiled. "You're a nice kid. I'm sorry we were rough on you when you fell in front of the car. It's just that women have tried that before in the boss's old neighborhood."

"Really?" she asked, and she was honestly surprised.

He nodded. "He's loaded, you know? Plenty of women would do anything for money."

She smiled. "I've known one or two of those myself. I like having enough to pay the bills and eat out once in a while. That's about all. Money doesn't make people happy. Very often, it does just the opposite."

"Yes, it does." He held up the prescriptions. "I'll get these filled and bring them back to you. The boss, you're sure he's okay?"

"Why don't you look in and see, before you go?" she asked, leading him down the hall. "He's had a rough night."

"I used to nurse him through these head-aches," Santi said. "They're a nightmare."

"I can see that."

She knocked briefly and opened the door. Mikey turned his head, wincing at the pain. He managed a smile.

"Hey, Santi. Had to make sure I hadn't croaked, right?" he teased.

Santi chuckled. "Something like that. You okay?"

"Getting better by the minute."

"Okay. I'll go get your meds and be right back."

"Bernie," Mikey called, when she started to go out, too. She went back in and paused by the bed. "You haven't even had breakfast, have you?" he asked.

"Well, not just yet..."

"Go eat something."

"Okay. Mrs. Brown said you can have anything you want to eat when you feel like food."

He smiled drowsily. "She's a doll. So are you. I'm not hungry yet. I think I'll just sleep for a while. Eat something."

"I will."

"Hey," he called softly when she was at the door.

She turned, her eyebrows arching.

"When I get better, suppose we take in another movie? Paulie says they've got all the latest movies on pay-per-view and DVD. And a door that locks," he added with a wicked smile.

She laughed, flushing as she remembered the last movie they'd gone to but not seen. The memory of his mouth on hers was poignant. "I'd like that," she said.

"Me, too."

"Get some rest. I'll check on you in a few minutes."

He sighed. "Sweet girl. Don't ever change."

"I'll do my best."

She went out and closed the door.

* * *

Paul came over to see about his cousin, alerted by Santi after the bodyguard had dropped off Mikey's prescriptions.

"You look rough," Paul said, sitting by his cousin's bedside. "I remember what a misery those headaches are."

"Misery is right. I lost everything I'd eaten. Bernie was right in the bathroom with me, mopping me up," he added. "What a hell of a woman. I never knew anybody like her."

"She's unique," Paul agreed. "Amazing how she keeps going. Her disability never seems to get her down."

"She has good days and bad ones."

"Don't they have shots for that condition now?"

"Yeah, they do," Mikey said. "I overheard her landlady saying what a shame it was that they were so expensive. Bernie can't afford them." His face tautened. "I can, but she'd never let me do it for her. She's proud."

"She is."

"Mikey, how well do you know Santi?" Paul asked.

Mikey's eyebrows rose. "As well as I know you," he said. "Honor's his big thing. He'd never sell me out because it would seem dishonorable to him. He takes his job seriously. Why do you ask?" he added.

"Just some gossip. They say Cotillo's got somebody close to you."

"It's got to be Mrs. Brown, then," Mikey said with twinkling dark eyes. "Right? I mean, she's the obvious choice. Friendly, sweet, just the sort to set you up for a hit."

Paul chuckled. "Okay. I see what you mean. Just the same, we're checking out everybody who lives here. Just in case."

"That's not a bad idea. You still got Billings somewhere with a sniper kit?"

Paul nodded. "I don't think he ever sleeps. He seems to get by on catnaps, but we have an alternate in place anyway."

Mikey drew in a breath and laughed huskily. "These damned headaches. I didn't know there was a way to prevent them. Doc prescribed something, along with a prescription to take when the pain gets bad." He grimaced. "I hate drugs, you know? But this is a sort of pain that makes you want to hit your head with a hammer just to make it stop throbbing."

"Grandmama used to get them," Paul recalled. "They were bad."

"So are mine. Imagine a woman who doesn't run for the hills when a man's losing the contents of his stomach," he said. "Bernie didn't leave me for a minute, not until after the doctor came."

"I hear you did pretty much the same for her the day you met, when she fell in front of the car."

"Yeah," Mikey's mouth pulled down. "I thought it was a trick. You know how women used to come on to me. One even pretended to fall down a flight of stairs. I didn't know Bernie from an apple. I assumed she liked the looks of the limo and wanted a ride. Bad call." He drew in a breath. "She asked us to look for her cane, and we didn't believe her. Santi found it. I felt like a dog."

"Your past isn't full of guileless women," Paul said with a grin. "Understandable mistake."

"I guess." He put a hand to his head. "At least the throbbing has stopped. That doctor's pretty good. Nice looking woman. She married to the redheaded doctor?"

"Copper Coltrain," Paul agreed. "There was

a mismatch. She worked with him for almost a year, and he hated her guts for something her father did years ago. It wasn't until she started to leave the practice that he got his ducks in a row. It was a rocky romance."

Mikey just sighed. "Mine's not rocky at all," he said. "You know, I never thought about having a family before. Little girls are sweet."

"Yeah." Paul didn't say any more. He and his former wife had a little girl. His wife and the child were gunned down by one of Paul's enemies, in revenge for his arrest and conviction. It was a sad memory.

"Sorry," Mikey said, wincing. "I forgot."

"I try to," Paul said. "I mean, I'm happier than I ever dreamed I could be, with Sari. But there are times when I think of my little girl…" He broke off.

"We all have bad memories, Paulie," Mikey said. "Mine aren't as bad as yours. I'm sorry for what happened to you. But the guy paid for it," he added coldly.

Paul glanced at him. "Yeah, one of the marshals in Jersey said he thought you might have had something to do with that."

Mikey just pursed his lips. "Who, me? I go out of my way to be nice to people."

"Yeah, but you know people who don't."

Mikey chuckled. "Lots of them."

"Have you told her?" he asked, his head jerking toward the door.

Mikey knew who he meant. He leaned back against the pillows. "I don't know how. At first, I didn't think there was a reason I needed to tell her. Now, I'm scared of what she'll think of me."

"She's a sweet woman."

"Sweet, and innocent. She doesn't see wickedness. She always looks for the best in people. Even in me. I'm not what she thinks I am. But how do I tell her what my life has been like? How do I do that, and keep her?"

"You underestimate how she feels about you, Mikey," Paul said. "You don't love or hate people for their actions mostly. You care about them because of what they are, deep inside. Bernie knows you aren't as bad as you think you are."

"I hope you're right. It hasn't been a long time, but if I lose her, it will be like having an arm torn off, you know?"

"I do know. That's how I feel about Sari."

"She's a winner."

He smiled. "I agree. Hey, if you're not better Saturday, you can bring Bernie over for lunch Sunday, you'll be welcome. You can take her walking around the property, maybe even catch that movie you went to see at the drive-in. It wasn't a new one, because it's on pay-per-view now."

"That sounds nice," Mikey replied. "I hope this stupid headache goes away before then," he added. "They usually last two or three days."

"I remember. You take your meds. Maybe they'll cut this one short."

"I hope so. Thanks for the cousinly visit," he added. "Anything more from Carrera?"

Paul shook his head. "He's got Tony in a safe place, he says, and not to worry."

"I'm in a safer place," Mikey chuckled. "Little bitty town in the middle of nowhere, with half the retired mercs in the country. Lucky me."

Paul grinned. "I'll second that. Ask Bernie over Sunday."

"I will. Thanks."

"No problem. See you later."

"Yeah."

* * *

Bernie was delighted with the invitation. It did take Mikey a few days to get over the headache, but he was fine Sunday afternoon. "Are you sure they don't mind?" she asked.

"They wouldn't invite you if they minded, honey," he told her as they sped toward Paul and Sari's house. "You warm enough?"

"I'm fine," she said, huddling down in her warm berber coat. "It's chilly tonight."

"Imagine that, chilly in south Texas," he teased. "Now if you want to see chilly, you have to come to Jersey. We know about cold weather."

"I guess you get a lot of snow."

"We used to get more, when Paulie and I were kids. We had some great snowball battles in the neighborhood. These older boys would lie in wait for us and pelt us with frozen snowballs every chance they got. So Paulie and I got some ice cubes and put them inside our snowballs. Ouch! The bullies ran for their lives."

She laughed. "I'll bet they did."

"Our grandmother was so fierce that they were more afraid of her than even the big boss in the neighborhood," he recalled with a smile. "I told you about her hitting him with a salami.

Chased him all the way out the front door with it, and his people didn't dare laugh. It taught him a whole new respect for women."

She laughed softly. "I wish I could have met your grandmother."

"Me, too, honey. She'd have loved you." His hand reached for hers and held it tight. "She had no time for modern women with modern ideas."

She sighed. "Me, neither. I'm a throwback to another generation, I guess. My dad pretty much raised me after we came back here." Her heart felt like lead in her chest. She hated remembering why they'd come to Jacobsville.

"What's wrong?" he asked, sensitive to her mood.

She grimaced. "Things I can't talk about. Bad things."

"Honey, I could write you a book on bad things," he commented. He drew in a breath. "One of these days we have to have a long talk about my past, and it isn't going to be nice."

"It won't matter," she said quietly. "The person you were isn't the man you are today."

"That's not as true as I wish it was," he replied.

"I can't believe you'd do anything terrible."

DIANA PALMER

But he had. Really terrible things. They hadn't bothered him much until now. This sweet, kind woman beside him didn't have any idea about what sort of evil lived in his real world, the world she'd never seen.

"Listen, you read books?" he asked.

"Oh, yes. It's how I get through bad nights, when the pain overpowers the medicines I take for it."

"There's this book—I'll give you the title. It's about a man who paints houses."

"A painter?" she asked.

His fingers contracted. "It's a different sort of painting. If you read the book, you'll begin to get some idea of the sort of world I live in." His face tautened. "It's a hard life. Dog eat dog, and I mean that literally. The man I work for is hiding out from a man even worse than he is. What I know, what I've seen, can clear him. The feds just have to keep me alive long enough until the trial comes up." He turned and glanced at her. "It's a business. Like regular business, in a way. It's just that somebody wants what you have and thinks up ways to get it, most of them illegal and deadly."

She frowned. "I don't understand."

"How could you? Raised in a tiny little town, surrounded by law-abiding citizens, most of whom love you." His face hardened. "In my whole damned life, my grandmother was the only person who really loved me."

Her heart almost stopped. She loved him. And she'd only just realized it. She was faintly disconcerted by a revelation that should have occurred to her much sooner. "There's your cousin Paul," she said after a minute.

"Yeah, Paulie. We're fond of each other. He'd do anything he could to help me. In fact, he already is. But that's not the same way I felt about my grandmother."

"I don't remember mine very well," she said tightly.

He glanced at her. "Bad memories?"

She swallowed. "They don't get much worse."

His fingers linked into hers. "Can you tell me about it?"

She hesitated. He was insinuating that his life had been a little outside the law. Perhaps he might understand better than most men what it had been like for her, for her family.

"I want to," she said. "Can it wait until later?"

He laughed. "It can wait." He was flattered

that she wanted to trust him with something that was obviously a secret, something she kept hidden. It was an indication of feelings she was beginning to have for him. He was beginning to have the same sort for her. If she had something traumatic in her past, it might help her relate to his own life.

Then he stopped and considered what he'd be letting her in for, after the trial, when he went back to Jersey, back to the old life. He'd pledged his loyalty, his life, to the crime family he belonged to. Betraying that code, that omertà, would get him killed. Not that he had any plans to turn his people in to the feds. In fact, even Tony was working with the feds right now, to ward off the takeover by Cotillo. But that was a temporary truce. Nobody in Tony's employ was going to rat out anybody to the feds, least of all Mikey. That would get you killed quick.

On the other hand, if he wanted a life with the sweet woman at his side, and he was beginning to, how could he drag her into the shadows with him?

It would be her choice in the end. But she was sheltered and disabled. Not that his people would be bad to her, oh, no. Even the women would welcome her like a relative. His underlings would treat her like royalty. So it wouldn't be bad from that standpoint. But the rackets Tony and Mikey were mixed up in were illegal. They specialized in online gambling, in numbers running, in casinos in Vegas. One of Mikey's properties was a casino, in fact. He'd told Bernie that it was a hotel. It was a hotel, but it wasn't in Jersey. It was in Las Vegas, and big-name entertainers came regularly to appear there. He ran it like a legal business, but he did do things off the books that could land him in jail. Bernie was such a gentle, trusting soul. She liked the country, the outdoors, little animals. Mikey liked bright lights and casinos. It was going to be a difficult adjustment, if she was even willing to make it.

"You're brooding," she accused, watching the expressions cross his handsome face.

He laughed self-consciously. "I'm brooding." He turned his head for a minute and caught her eyes. "Sorry. I have things on my mind." He made a face. "Paulie said they've got somebody close to me."

"They?"

"The guy who's after Tony and me," he explained. He chuckled. "I told him it was probably Mrs. Brown. You can tell she's just the kind of person who would set a man up," he added with a grin.

She burst out laughing. "Oh, that's wicked."

"I'm a wicked man, honey," he said, and he wasn't kidding.

She frowned. "He doesn't have any idea who it is?" she added.

"Not yet. He's checking people out."

"I'd check out that Jessie person in my office," she muttered. "She's one of the most horrible people I've ever known. She's always cutting at the other women in the office. Poor Glory has high blood pressure. It can be dangerous, you know, and she has a small child. Jessie makes all sorts of unpleasant remarks to her about the medicines she takes, even about the way she dresses."

"Your boss should get that woman out of the office," he commented.

"He'd like to, but he's the DA. He has to have a legitimate reason to let her go or she could take him to court. He'd like her to leave, too. She messes up appointments all the time, another reason Glory's so stressed."

His fingers stroked hers. "We all have our crosses, don't we, kid?"

She nodded. "Nobody gets through life without a few traumas." She sighed. "It's really sad, you know. She's so beautiful. How can a person who looks like that be such a pain to be around?"

"You never know what sort of background people come from," he said simply. "A lot of times, kids turn out bad because of the way they were raised. You know, I only saw my dad a few times in my whole life. My mother died of a heart attack when she was just in her twenties, not too long after she had me. Her mother, my grandmother, took me in. Paulie's mom bit the dust about the same time, so he ended up with our grandmother, too." He grimaced. "Paulie's dad was even worse than mine. He took some licks when the old man was home. Fortunately, it wasn't often."

"Did your fathers work in some sort of away job, like construction?" she asked innocently.

"They worked for the big bosses. They went where they were told, and did what they were told." He smiled sadly. "That's the life, kid. You pledge to obey and you do it. There's a code of honor. We call it omertà. It means you pledge your loyalty to a don and you never forget it. You sell out your colleagues, you meet with a quick and sad end."

Her heart jumped. "But you're going to testify against a man who's a, what did you call him, a don?"

His fingers contracted comfortingly around hers. "That's a different thing," he said. "This guy Cotillo is trying to muscle in on territory that doesn't belong to him. The other families are as much against him as Tony's is."

She frowned. "Tony's your family? Is he a relation?"

He chuckled. "Tony's a character," he said. "No, we're not related, but we'd die for each other. So in that sense, yeah, I guess you could say he's family. The feds are protecting him. Me, too. What we know can put Cotillo away for a very long time. The families are working toward that end, even making a temporary truce with the feds to keep them from prying too closely into our business."

She blinked. "You talk about federal people as if they're the enemy," she said. "But your cousin works for a federal agency."

"It's just a figure of speech, honey," he said, backtracking. "We're all grateful for their help. Nobody wants a guy like Cotillo in charge in Jersey. He's a weasel. First chance he got, he'd start lining up other families for elimination. They know that. So the feds are sort of the lesser of the two evils."

"I see."

"You don't, but you will," he promised. He sighed. "I just hope it isn't all going to be too much for you, Bernie. You've lived a sheltered life."

"Actually, I haven't. Not so much."

"Oh?"

"Well, I haven't lived in a commune or had lovers, or anything like that. But I'm anything but sheltered. I'll tell you," she added. "I promise."

He smiled. "I'll tell you, too."

"That's a deal."

Chapter Eight

They were heading down the long driveway to Graylings when his fingers contracted around hers. "No secrets from now on," he said. "I'll tell you about my life today and you can tell me about yours."

"It might matter..." she said worriedly.

"It won't." He sounded very positive. "Nothing you tell me will change anything." One side of his sensuous mouth pulled down. "On the other hand, what I have to tell you, well, that may change a lot of things," he added heavily, and he was regretting things in his past that might drive her out of his life. It was a terrible thought. She was already part of him.

"Whatever sort of trouble you're in, I'll stand by you," she said.

He wanted to pull her over into his lap and kiss the breath out of her for saying that, but he had to restrain himself. His fingers worked sensuously into hers, caressing them. "I never thought I'd get mixed up with a girl from a little town in Texas," he said, chuckling. "I feel just like Carrera must have."

"Carrera?" she asked. "Oh, yes, Delia's husband." She smiled. "Delia had a bad time of it. Her mother turned out to be a woman she'd always thought of as her sister, and her father turned out to be her mother's husband. She saved Mr. Carrera's life in the Bahamas, but she lost her baby. She came home and she was so miserable. It hurt me to see her when I had to go to the dry cleaner's." She sighed. "But then Mr. Carrera showed up with some sort of quilt he'd made for her, and the next thing we knew, they were getting married."

"Yeah, he quilts," he said with a soft laugh. "The guy looks like a wise guy. He's big and rough and he intimidates most people. The quilting habit gave him a lot of heat until he started throwing punches. Now nobody laughs at it. He wins international competitions with his designs, too."

She nodded. "They have one of his quilts in our library, on permanent display. It's a Bow Tie quilt. They say he has one just like it in a casino he owns. Gosh, imagine owning a casino! Those are the richest, flashiest places on earth!"

He hadn't told her that his hotel in Vegas was also a casino. "You ever been in one?" he asked.

"When I was small, my parents took me to the Bahamas on a cruise one year, on summer vacation. I wasn't allowed inside, but they drove me by one over on Paradise Island. It was fascinating to me, even as a child."

His fingers contracted. "Suppose I told you that the hotel I own is actually a casino," he said slowly, "and it's in Las Vegas?"

Her eyes widened. "You own a casino in Las Vegas?" she exclaimed. "Wow!"

He laughed, surprised at her easy acceptance. "I run it legit, too," he added. "No fixes, no hidden switches, no cheating. Drives the feds nuts, because they can't find anything to pin on me there."

"The feds?" she asked.

He drew in a breath. "I told you, I'm a bad

man." He felt guilty about it, dirty. His fingers caressed hers as they neared Graylings, the huge mansion where his cousin lived with the heir to the Grayling racehorse stables.

Her fingers curled trustingly around his. "And I told you that the past doesn't matter," she said stubbornly. Her heart was running wild. "Not at all. I don't care how bad you've been."

His own heart stopped and then ran away. His teeth clenched. "I don't even think you're real, Bernie," he whispered. "I think I dreamed you."

She flushed and smiled. "Thanks."

He glanced in the rearview mirror. "What I'd give for just five minutes alone with you right now," he said tautly. "Fat chance," he added as he noticed the sedan tailing casually behind them.

She felt all aglow inside. She wanted that, too. Maybe they could find a quiet place to be alone, even for just a few minutes. She wanted to kiss him until her mouth hurt.

He pulled into the long driveway and up to the house, which was all aglow with light. It was a huge two-story mansion with exquisite woodwork and a long, wide porch. The front door opened as Mikey helped her out of the car, retaining her hand in his as they approached the house.

"Paisano," Paul greeted him in Italian.

"Salve! Come stai?" Mikey replied, and let go of Bernie's hand long enough to hug his cousin.

"Sto bene, grazie, e tu?" Paul replied.

"Va bene," Mikey responded with a grin. *"Cosi, cosi. Non mi posso lamentare."*

"Benissimo!"

"English, English," Sari Fiore chided. "Bernie doesn't understand Italian," she laughed.

"Just greetings, honey," Mikey told her, and brought her hand to his lips. "I'll teach you some nice Italian words the minute we get some time together."

She grinned. "Okay."

"Come on in," Paul added as two feds got out of the sedan that had trailed Mikey's car. "McLeod, do you and Agent Murdock want coffee?"

"I'd love some," McLeod said, and glanced at Murdock. "As long as that guy doesn't offer to make it," he added firmly.

Murdock, a good-natured man, just chuckled. "I get stuck with making it at our office. People pour it in the ficus tree."

"Yeah, the poor damned thing shivers all the time," Paul commented on the way to the kitchen. "I think it's on the verge of a nervous breakdown. Hey, Mandy, can you make us a pot of coffee?" he called to the woman working to clean up the kitchen counters.

"Of course I can!" she exclaimed, and grinned. "Hey, Mikey! Hello, Bernie. Nice to see you both."

"Nice to see you, too, Mandy," Mikey replied, and kissed her cheek. "I miss your cooking. Not that Mrs. Johnson isn't good."

"I know she is," Mandy replied. She gave Mikey and Bernie a secret smile when she saw them holding hands.

Mikey noticed, but he didn't let go, even when they sat down together at the long kitchen table with Paul and the two feds.

"Okay," Mikey said. "What's up? You guys tailed us the whole way here," he added to McLeod.

"Cotillo sent one of his boys down here after you," McLeod replied quietly, watching Mikey's face harden. "We caught him at the courthouse yesterday."

Mikey blinked. "How?"

"We have facial identification software," McLeod said simply. "I used it. He's got wants and warrants outstanding in Jersey. Our guys took him into custody and they're delivering him right back to the authorities there."

US Marshals, that was, Mikey knew without being told. He let out a breath. "I guess I'd better be more careful about taking Bernie out to public places."

Her fingers, unseen, contracted around his.

"Not at all," Agent Murdock said. "As long as they're pretty public. Drive-ins aren't a good idea. Too much opportunity for covert work."

Mikey sighed. "I guess so. Damn."

"It's okay," Bernie said. "We can sit in Mrs. Johnson's parlor anytime we like, and talk or watch television," she reminded him.

He smiled at her. "You're a rare girl, Bernie."

She flushed and laughed. "Not so much."

Mikey glanced at the government agents. "So why was he at the courthouse?" he asked.

"We think he was looking for a contact there. But he came after quitting time, so we didn't have the opportunity to find out. When we questioned him," McLeod added, "he said he was looking for San Antonio and got lost. He was just looking for directions."

"Oh, that sounds very sincere," Mikey said sardonically.

"Yeah, considering that he flew into the San Antonio airport," Paul added drily.

"Here's coffee," Mandy said. "And how about some nice pound cake? I made a chocolate one!"

Mikey made a face. "Gosh, I'd love that, but I'm just getting over a really bad migraine. Chocolate's one of my triggers," he reminded her.

"I'm sorry," Mandy said. She patted him on the shoulder. "But I've got a nice cherry pie?" she teased.

He chuckled. "I'll take that. Thanks. You know, she nursed me through the headache, sickness and all," he added, looking at Bernie with evident affection. "She never left me, and even called a doctor out to the boardinghouse to treat me. She's quite a girl."

Bernie's face flamed because everybody was looking at her.

"Yes, she is," Sari said, smiling. "At work, she's always the first one there and the last one to leave, and she never minds staying over if we need her." She made a face. "It's not the same with that new woman the boss hired. Jessie. She's constantly late and she makes clients uncomfortable. She made a real play for one of the wealthy married local ranchers, and the boss gave her warning." She sighed. "I wish she'd do something he could fire her for. Nobody likes her."

"She's an odd fit for a small town," Bernie said. "She's overly sophisticated."

"We have a few overly sophisticated people, like the police chief's wife, but she's nice," Mandy broke in, putting a platter of sliced pound cake, saucers and utensils on the table, along with a saucer containing a slice of cherry pie for Mikey.

"This looks delicious. Thanks, honey," he told the housekeeper and grinned at her.

"You're welcome. Go ahead, people, dig in. We don't stand on ceremony here."

"No, we don't," Sari said, smiling warmly at her husband.

"Oh, that's good coffee," Paul said with a long sigh. "I just hate trying to drink it at work," he added with a pointed glare at Murdock.

Murdock made a face. "Not my fault. My

mother always drank tea. She never taught me how to make coffee and I never drink it."

"No wonder it tastes so bad," Paul teased.

Murdock sighed. "There have been threats, you know," he said complacently. "In fact, ASAC Jon Blackhawk's brother, McKuen Kilraven, was openly talking about men in ninja suits and a pickup truck and a big sack."

"You'd never fit in a sack, Murdock," Paul chuckled. "Besides, Kilraven's too occupied with their new daughter to do any such thing. That's two kids now. He and Winnie are over the moon."

"She still working 911 dispatch down here?" Murdock asked.

Paul shook his head. "She's got her hands full with two preschoolers. Kilraven's still with the company, but he's mostly administrative these days. No more hanging out of helicopters by one leg wrapped in camo netting while he fires at enemy agents."

"You're kidding!" Bernie gasped.

"Oh, no, I'm not," Paul chuckled. "The man was a maniac when he was after a perp. He's calmed down somewhat since he married, but he's still good at what he does."

"He was a patrolman here, working for Chief Grier as cover on a covert federal assignment, for a while," Bernie said as she nibbled cake and sipped coffee. She laughed. "There was gossip that Chief Grier wanted to put him in a barrel, drive him to the border and send him down the Rio Grande. They did butt heads a few times over procedure."

"The chief butts heads pretty good," Paul assured her. "He's lowered the crime rate with a vengeance since he's been in charge of our local police."

"Nobody thought he'd stay here when he first came," Bernie said. "He was really tough. Then they made a movie here with the Georgia Firefly, Tippy Moore, and before any of us realized it, he was married to her."

"She's a knockout," Paul said. He slid his hand over his wife's. "I'm partial to redheads, you know," he added, grinning as he studied Sari's red, red hair pinned up over big blue eyes.

She grinned back. "Thanks, sweetheart."

"So what do we do about Cotillo and the trial and Tony Garza?" Paul asked as he finished his pie and his coffee.

"First things first," Paul said. "We've got tails

on Cotillo and his men, with interagency cooperation. Cotillo's killed a lot of people trying to forge new alliances and take over territory. He's made enemies."

"The killings are going to get him in trouble," Mikey said. "The big guys don't like that. It invites the feds in. They want problems solved with dialog, not automatic weapons."

"Well, they do kill people who rat them out," Paul replied solemnly.

Mikey nodded. "Omertà," he agreed. "Loyalty is life itself in the outfit. The number-one sin is selling out your people to the feds. Nobody likes a rat. They get put down and sometimes their whole families do as well, as a warning." He ground his teeth together when he saw his cousin's face. That had happened to Paul. His first family had been gunned down when Paul locked up one of the minor bosses and shut down a lucrative illegal operation. The man had gotten even in the worst possible way.

"I'm sorry," Mikey told his cousin. "Truly sorry. I should never have brought that up."

Paul's face relaxed. "It was a long time ago. Still stings," he said, and his eyes were filled with horrible memories.

"Just the same, I'm sorry."

Paul smiled. "We're family. Don't sweat it."

Mikey sighed. "You're the only family I've got. Well, except for Tony's family." He glanced at the feds. "I hope you guys understand that I'm only cooperating because Tony's being falsely accused. I'm not selling out my people. Not for anything."

"We know that, Mikey," Paul said quietly. "Nobody's asking you to rat out your colleagues."

Mikey sipped coffee, not looking at them. "I took a blood oath," he said very quietly. "I made a solemn promise. I swore to it, like you'd make a vow in church. I won't break it. Not if they lock me up forever."

"We only lock up people when we can prove they've broken the law," Paul assured him. He leaned closer. "So make sure we can't prove anything on you," he chuckled.

Mikey laughed. "I don't do that stuff anymore. I have a legit casino and I run it like a legit business."

"I know that," Paul replied. "You're not as bad as you make out, Mikey. You saved Merrie's life," he added, referring to Sari's younger sister. Both women had been targeted by an enemy of their late father, victims of professional hit men. Mikey's input had helped save both of them. "In fact, you helped save Sari's, as well."

"I just made a few calls," Mikey replied.

"Well, those few calls helped us catch all the perps," Paul replied.

Mikey grinned. "I like Baby Doll," he said, referring to Merrie. "How's she doing?"

"She and Ren are expecting again," Sari said with a wide grin. "She's over the moon."

"She still painting?" Mikey asked.

"Oh, yes. She never gives that hobby up," Sari told him.

He glanced at Bernie with real hunger. "I'd love her to do a portrait of Bernie for me," he said.

"You know she'd be happy to!" Sari said. She glanced at Bernie, who was flushed and beaming. "Bernie, do you have a few photos of yourself that we could send her?"

Bernie grimaced. "Well, no, not a lot. I don't have anybody to take pictures of me…"

While she was speaking, Mikey took out his expensive cell phone and snapped photos of her from all angles. He showed them to her in his photo app.

"You're really good at this," she said, surprised as she looked at herself in the pictures. She looked happy, mysterious, almost pretty. She laughed. "These don't even really look like me!"

"They do. You don't laugh a lot," he replied. His face tightened. "I love it when you laugh, Bernie," he added. "You're beautiful when you're happy."

She felt her heart almost bursting. He thought she was beautiful. He wanted a painting of her. She could have floated up to the ceiling, she was so lighthearted.

"Thanks," she whispered.

He wrinkled his nose at her and grinned. "We'll have to wait until that movie we were watching comes out on pay-per-view and we can watch it together."

"I don't have pay-per-view," she said morosely.

"We do," Sari said, and grinned. "You can watch it in the library. In fact, we already have it. The drive-in is showing it, but it's not a first-run movie. Wouldn't you like to see the rest of it?"

Mikey pursed his lips. "Would I! It's a great movie."

"It is, but I'd need tissues," Bernie confessed. "One reviewer said it would twist your heart open."

"You can have tissues and more coffee," Sari said. "Mandy, can you do refills and find a box of tissues for Bernie?"

"You bet!" Mandy said, and went to get both.

The government agents left shortly after. Mikey took Bernie into the luxurious study with its plush couch and chairs and the expensive media center, with a fifty-five-inch television screen.

"Wow," Bernie said as Mikey closed the door behind them. "This is awesome."

"They've refurnished it since old man Grayling died," he told her as he went to turn on the television and set up the movie. "In fact, they've redone the whole house. It has some bad memories for Sari and her sister."

"I remember hearing about how badly their father treated them," Bernie said. "He must have been a horrible father."

"From what I hear, he was." He grimaced. "Mine was pretty bad, too."

"My dad was a sweet, kind man," Bernie

said sadly. "He died much too young. He lived through a lot of trauma. I think it affects people, you know? Affects their health."

"Maybe so."

He turned on the movie and brought the controller back as he dropped down onto the plush couch beside Bernie. He put the controller on the coffee table and turned to Bernie.

"Gee, look, we're all alone," he said with a grin, "and there are no cars around us."

"Isn't that fascinating?" she laughed.

"Oh, you bet." He pulled her onto his lap, letting her head fall back on his shoulder. "And I have some really interesting ideas about what we could do while the movie runs."

Her arms looped around his neck and her eyes riveted to his wide, sensuous, chiseled mouth. "You do?" she whispered.

He drew her close and bent his head, smiling. "Oh, yes. Very, very interesting."

As he spoke, his mouth slowly covered hers. She sighed and sank against his big, muscular body, letting him take her weight while he kissed her.

"I could get used to this," he whispered.

She smiled under his lips. "Me, too."

He nibbled her upper lip and traced under it with just the tip of his tongue, loving the way she reacted to him. She wasn't coy or reticent. She met him halfway. If those long, soulful sighs were any indication, she loved what he was doing to her.

He shifted her and his fingers ran gently up and down her rib cage, setting fires, making her hungry. His mouth grew slowly insistent. She twisted against him, hungry and burning with new needs.

His big hand slid under the sweater she was wearing and teased around her breast while he kissed her slowly.

She moaned and twisted up toward that maddening hand whose touch was making her wild for more.

He smiled against her soft lips because he knew that. His thumb slowly trespassed under the lacy cotton cup and against her firm breast. She gasped under his mouth, but she didn't try to stop him. He loved that. His mouth opened on hers, deepening the kiss, diverting her while his hand went to the hooks that held the bra in place and snapped them open. His hand, warm and strong, moved slowly back around, teasing just under her breast. He could hear her breathing change, feel the need in her grow, as it grew in him.

"Oh, baby," he murmured as his mouth grew hard on hers and his big hand tenderly swallowed her breast up whole, his palm rubbing gently at the hard little nub he found.

She caught her breath and moaned.

"This is sweet," he ground out. "Oh, God, it's sweet like sugar candy…"

He moved, turning her so that she was lying under him, full length, on the plush couch. He was on his side, his elbow taking his weight as his hand moved the bra out of his way so that he could touch her more easily.

Her body arched, helpless, as she reacted to the intimate tracing of his hand. She couldn't even pretend not to want it. She was aching, throbbing with hungers she'd never felt in her life. A faint whimper escaped the mouth that his was devouring.

"Yes," he whispered huskily. "It's not enough, is it? Try not to cry out," he added as he slid the sweater and bra up under her chin. "They might hear us…"

What he was saying didn't make sense until

his mouth lowered, and she felt it cover and consume her whole breast, taking it slowly into the moist, warm darkness, his tongue sliding over the nipple and making her throb from head to toe.

She had to stifle a cry. She sobbed under the expert touch of his mouth, shivering, arching as she pleaded for something more, something to ease the ache that was slowly consuming her.

He began to suckle her, hungrier than he could ever remember being with a woman. She sobbed as if he was hurting her, but he knew he wasn't. His long, powerful leg inserted itself between both of hers in the slacks she was wearing and began to move sensuously, making the hunger even worse.

He rolled over onto her completely, hesitating just long enough to open the buttons of his shirt and pull it apart over the thick hair that covered his muscular chest. When he went down against her, it was bare skin against bare skin, something she'd never felt.

Her arms went under the shirt, around him, her hands digging into his bare back. Odd how it felt there, she thought dimly, because there was a definite depression, a coin-shaped one. But he was moving on her and she felt the power and heat of him, the sudden surge of his body that told her graphically how capable he was.

His mouth ground into hers. He groaned as he pushed between her long legs and right against the heart of her in that soft fork of her body. She lifted up, shivering, and he moved roughly on her, feeling the passion burn him alive.

But his mind froze the passion as he realized how innocent she was. This was wrong. He could live with it, he could love it, but it would shame her, make her feel soiled. He couldn't do that to her. He couldn't, even if it was agony to stop.

He rolled over, shivering, and pulled her hard against his side. "Don't move," he whispered unsteadily. "Just lie still. Please, honey. Help me. I hurt like hell!"

She managed that, just. She was on fire and he'd stopped. Why had he stopped? She wanted him so desperately, just as desperately as he wanted her.

But sanity slowly returned. Was this what she really wanted, to have sex with a man on a sofa in a room with an unlocked door, a man to whom she had no real ties except physical ones? She was religious. She didn't believe in sex before marriage. But she wanted Mikey. She wanted him so badly that she'd have given in right here, without a single protest. In fact, she'd done that. But he'd stopped. She could feel how difficult it had been for him to do that. His body was shaking with unfulfilled needs. Now she felt guilty that she'd let it go so far. How would she have felt afterward? She didn't even know how to protect herself. What if she'd become pregnant? How would she live with that in a small town where everybody knew her, and knew that the only man she'd kept company with in recent years was the one lying so stiffly beside her right now? It would be no secret who the father was. Mikey had a casino in Las Vegas. He was a big-city man. It was highly unlikely that he'd throw all that up to live in a little town like Jacobsville with a woman who might end up an invalid in a very few years.

Besides that, he had a past, and bad men were after him because of a man he worked with, who was hiding from assassins. This was a terrible time to start an affair. In fact, she had to admit she wasn't the sort of woman who could even have an affair. It just wasn't like her, despite her aching hunger for Mikey and the violent attachment that she felt to him.

He was breathing easier now. He stretched and laughed softly when he felt her breasts against his bare rib cage.

"Well, that was a damned near thing," he whispered as he turned over, rolled her onto her back, and looked at her pretty firm pink breasts with their hard, dusky crowns. He touched them very gently. "I didn't want to stop."

"We're on a sofa," she began, flushing.

"Honey, all I had to do was push your pants down and go into you," he whispered blatantly, smiling at her expression. "It wouldn't have taken three minutes, as hot as I was. That's how easy it would have been. You didn't realize, did you?"

She caught her breath. "Not really," she confessed. "I haven't ever..."

"I noticed." He bent and brushed his mouth over her bare breasts. "God, woman, you're so beautiful," he whispered. "I'll dream of you every night of my life after this!"

"You will?" She thought how comfortable she was with him, how easily they'd slipped into intimacy. It felt so right. She wasn't even embarrassed.

He chuckled. "Yes, I will." He lifted his head and drew in a breath. "When all this is over, you and I are going to sit down and have a very serious talk." He brushed back her damp, disheveled hair. "Very serious."

She smiled slowly, her heart lifting. "Okay."

He laughed. "Everything's so easy with you, Bernie," he said, touching her cheek gently. "You never make waves, do you?"

"Not much, no."

"I love that about you," he said. "I feel at ease with you. Safe."

"I feel that way with you, too."

His big hand brushed tenderly over her breasts. "I guess we should put our clothes back on and watch the movie," he said with a sigh.

She nodded.

He pulled her up beside him, but before she could pull her sweater and bra back down, he turned her into his lap and pulled her inside his shirt, shivering as he felt her bare skin rub gently over his. His arms contracted hungrily and he held her, rocking her, in a blistering silence of passion.

"You'd do it with me, wouldn't you?" he whispered at her ear.

"Yes," she replied in a husky, shaky little voice.

"I don't even have anything to use," he confessed gruffly. He held her even closer. "You know what? I don't think I'd mind."

"You wouldn't?"

His hand went to the base of her spine, and he rubbed her against the hardness of him, holding her there firmly. "I like babies," he whispered.

She shivered. "Oh, Mikey," she sobbed, and her arms tightened.

He shivered, too. "Oh, God, I've got to get up and lock the door," he groaned. "On the sofa, on the damned carpet, against a wall—I have to have you, right now!"

"Yes," she whimpered, pushing closer. "Yes!"

He eased her away from him, his eyes blazing as he looked at her breasts. "I'll lock the door..." he said.

Just then, footsteps sounded down the wood floor of the hall and there was a sudden knock at the door.

"How's the movie going?" Sari called.

Mikey and Bernie looked at each other in a moment of shocked embarrassment while they waited for that doorknob to turn…

Chapter Nine

"Just a sec!" Mikey called in a strained, deep voice.

There was a muffled laugh from the door. "Mandy's got more coffee. Come on out when your movie finishes."

"We will. Thanks!" he called back.

The footsteps withdrew.

He let out the breath he'd been holding. Bernie sat beside him as if in a daze, her top still up around her neck, her breasts pressed hard into the thick hair on Mikey's broad chest. He looked down at her with wonder.

"I guess the jig would have been up if Sari had opened that door," he laughed.

She smiled dreamily up at him. "I guess."

He drew in a hard breath. "I suppose we'd better stop while we're ahead." He drew back and looked down at her bare breasts with fascination. "Over the years, I've seen a lot of women undressed," he murmured. "But none of them were half as beautiful as you are, honey." He stroked her soft, firm breast and leaned down, putting his lips reverently to it. "I'll live on this my whole life."

Her heart skipped. She just looked at him with everything she felt for him in her green eyes. His jaw clenched. He still wanted her, now more than ever. But he managed some control as he pulled down the bra and fastened it, then drew the sweater down over her waist.

She smiled and fastened the buttons of his shirt. He looked rumpled and his hair was mussed from her hands in it. She loved the way he looked. He was a little flushed, too, and his dark eyes danced as they met hers.

"You'd like Vegas," he said. "For visits, anyway, it's an exciting place. Plenty of music and neon lights. An oasis in the desert."

She put her hands on his chest, over the buttoned shirt. "I don't guess you'd like a little

Texas town that draws the sidewalks in at dusk," she said without meeting his eyes.

"I'd like wherever you called home, Bernie," he said solemnly. "We come from different places. But that doesn't mean both of us can't adapt to something else, even if it's just for a little while." He bent and kissed her very softly. "I didn't want to stop. You go to my head like whiskey. It was like sailing on the clouds."

She laughed and pressed close. "For me, too."

His arms contracted, holding her close and rocking her. "We'd better finish watching the movie. There may be a quiz after."

She laughed with pure delight. "Okay."

He drew her gently down beside him and clasped her hand tight in his. They watched the screen until the credits came on. Mikey turned off the entertainment center and drew Bernie along with him out the door and into the kitchen.

Paul and Sari looked up as they came into the room. Both were grinning.

"Yeah, we got a little friendly," Mikey said defensively. "It was me, mostly."

"It was me, too," she said, and smiled up at him.

"You don't need to excuse anything to us,"

Paul chuckled. "We've only been married three years."

"He means, we're still on our honeymoon," Sari teased. "So how about that coffee?"

"Sounds lovely," Bernie said, and stars were in the eyes she turned toward Mikey, who looked like a cat who'd just eaten a canary.

That expression went along with Bernie to work the following Monday, where Jessie saw it and grew sarcastic and insulting.

"We all heard about you and Mikey going over to his cousin's place. Some mansion," Jessie drawled sarcastically, glancing at Sari as she paused by Bernie's desk. "Got your eyes on that nice rich fish, don't you? But do you think a little hick like you could land a man that sophisticated?"

Bernie's face flamed, but she didn't back down. "Backgrounds don't make much difference when people have feelings for one another," she said.

"As if he'd have feelings for you," Jessie said with a laugh. "I don't know him personally, but I know about him. He's had women who were movie stars, and debutantes and millionaires' daughters. He's not likely to take up with a woman who's looking at a wheelchair a few years down the road."

"That's enough," Sari said icily, standing up. "One more word and Mr. Kemp is going to get an earful."

Jessie knew when to quit. She shrugged. "Just stating facts, that's all."

"Ooh, somebody's so jealous she can't stand it," Olivia drawled with an amused look at Jessie. "What's the matter, sweetie, did he slap you down over at the courthouse and you're getting even?"

Jessie actually flushed. 'He did not," she spit. "I could have him if I wanted him."

"Do be my guest and try," Olivia taunted. "We heard that you made him sick."

Jessie was almost vibrating by now. She started to speak just as Mr. Kemp's door opened and he came out. She went quickly to her desk with a forced smile at the boss and pretended to work.

Kemp, no fool, looked from Bernie's flushed face to Sari's angry one and drew a conclusion. He didn't say a word, but the look he gave an oblivious Jessie wasn't one that would have encouraged her about her longevity in this office.

Glory Ramirez came in the door, a little fatigued. "Court is bound over until tomorrow," she told Mr. Kemp. Glory was an assistant DA, like Sari.

"Does it look like the jury will convict?" Sari asked.

Glory made a face. "Who knows what a jury will do?" she asked with a sigh. "I hope I'm good enough to put this guy away. He lured a fourteen-year-old girl in with promises of true love and she fell for it. He's thirty-five," she added coldly.

"What a mess," Sari said.

"It's worse than that. She's pregnant," Glory said.

"Oh, that's no problem," Jessie laughed. "She can just go to a clinic and have them take it out."

"She and her people are deeply religious," Glory replied. "Not everybody thinks of termination as birth control, Jessie."

There was a whip in her voice. The other women knew why. Glory had lost her first baby after a horrible fight with her husband when they were first married, before they really knew much about each other. It had taken her two years to get pregnant again. She and Rodrigo had one child, a boy, and Glory's precarious health made another unlikely. Her blood pressure was extremely high and she'd already had angioplasty for a blocked artery that had caused a mild heart attack.

"You people take everything so seriously," Jessie muttered.

"Babies are serious business," Mr. Kemp broke in. Everybody except Jessie knew that he'd been in love and engaged, and his fiancée had died after a local woman spiked her drink with a drug. The fiancée had been pregnant at the time, and the child died with her.

"Babies are a nuisance. They cry and keep everybody upset, and you never get your waistline back again. I'd never want one," Jessie said.

"I would," Bernie said on a long, happy sigh.

"Good luck with that, in your physical condition," Jessie said sarcastically.

"If I could have a child, with my blood pressure, there's no reason Bernie couldn't have one with her limitations."

Bernie smiled at her. "Thanks."

"Not a chance I'd take," Jessie muttered.

"Thank you for your input, Miss Tennison, and how about that call I asked you to make half an hour ago to the DA in Bexar County on the Ramsey matter?" Kemp asked shortly.

Jessie flustered. "Oh. Sorry. I forgot. I'll get him for you right now, Mr. Kemp!"

Kemp gave her an angry glance, smiled at the other women and went back into his office.

Bernie went to lunch at Barbara's Café and there was Mikey, holding down a table for them. He got up as she joined him, after she'd given her order and paid for it.

"I could have gotten the tab, honey," he said.

"I can pay for my own stuff," she teased. "But thanks for the thought."

His hand slid over hers and held it tight. "You don't look so good. Bad morning?"

"Sort of," she said. "But it's improving already," she added with a loving glance at his handsome face.

He grinned. "That's better. I like it when you're happy."

"I usually am." She didn't mention the confrontation with Jessie or the woman's harsh words. She pushed them to the back of her mind while she and Mikey had nice pieces of roast beef with perfect mashed potatoes and gravy and home-cooked green beans.

"This is so good," she sighed. "I love to cook, but it's hard for me to stand for long periods of time. Still, I used to do it when I lived at home with my parents."

"We were going to talk last night," he mused.

She flushed.

He laughed sensuously. "We didn't do a whole lot of talking, though, did we, baby," he whispered. "It's hard to think of things like that when I'm with you. I just go nuts when I touch you."

"I go nuts, too," she whispered back, and her face colored even more as she looked at his mouth and recalled the havoc it could create suckling at her breast. She caught her breath just with the memory of how it had felt.

"Oh, this won't do," Mikey said, and shifted uncomfortably. "We'd better not think too much about last night. Especially in a roomful of people."

She laughed softly.

He laughed, too.

"What sweet memories we're making, honey," he murmured as he forced himself to go back to his roast beef. "And we'll make plenty more, I promise you."

"You still have your shadow, I see," she replied under her breath, glancing out the front window at the black sedan parked there.

"They're being careful. After all, one guy almost got by them." He made a face. "It makes me wish I'd made fewer enemies along the way. This isn't the first time I've had somebody come after me over territory."

She was looking at him with open curiosity.

"What is it?" he asked.

"Nothing much. Just… Well, there's a coin-shaped depression in your back," she began. "I felt it last night."

"Noticed, did you?" He wasn't offended. He just smiled. "Yeah, I caught a bullet there when I was overseas in the Middle East. Punctured my lung and almost killed me, but I survived."

"I'm so glad you did," she said demurely, and she was unspeakably grateful that it had happened in a combat zone and not as a result of conflict with gangsters. He spoke of that world as if he knew it very well. Certainly he had to, if he was mixed up with a Mafia don whom he was protecting. It made her just a little uneasy.

She didn't know much about organized crime. What she'd seen in movies and read in books was unlikely to be a mirror of the real thing. That word Mikey had used, *omertà*, she'd seen it in print somewhere. She couldn't recall where. She was going to do a search on Google when she got home that night, just to see if she could find the connection. No need to tell Mikey. She looked at him with hungry eyes that she couldn't help. He was becoming the most important thing in her life.

But what if Jessie was right? Mikey was rich and sophisticated. Yes, he liked going out with her and kissing her, but that wasn't a future. She knew some gangsters married, but most of them seemed to just live together. Or so she thought. And she couldn't do that.

It would break her heart if Mikey didn't feel the same way she did. If he was only playing with her, she was going to die.

"Hey, what's wrong?" he asked. "You look tragic."

She forced a smile. "It's been a long morning, that's all," she said brightly. "Lots of people breaking the law. Of course, that's not a bad thing for us."

"Not at all." He looked up and his dark eyes sparked.

Bernie followed his gaze and there was Jessie, just picking up a salad and coffee at the checkout. It was on a tray, which meant she wasn't leaving.

"The bubonic plague has arrived," Mikey muttered.

"Well, hi there, Bernie. I didn't know you were coming here for lunch. And Mikey, how's it going with you?" she added, almost purring.

He looked up at her with cold eyes and took a minute to answer. "We're having a private conversation, if you don't mind."

Jessie shrugged. "Well, excuse me, I'm sure," she drawled. She went to a table nearby, at the window, and put down her food.

Bernie was crestfallen. She'd hoped to have a nice quiet lunch with Mikey, but Jessie was already staring at them. Cooking up plots. Bernie was certain that the woman was searching for ways to split her from Mikey, because Mikey was rich and Jessie wanted him.

"Don't look like that," Mikey said, smiling at her. "She's trying to upset you. Don't let her."

"She really likes you," Bernie said, almost choking on the words.

"It isn't mutual."

The way he looked at her sent all her fears flying away. She smiled slowly. So did he. The rest of the world faded away until there were just the two of them.

They didn't look in Jessie's direction at all. She glared at both of them the whole time. She didn't stop even when they were walking out of the café.

"If looks could kill," Bernie said on a heavy sigh when they were back on the street.

"Why doesn't Kemp fire her?" he asked abruptly.

"I think he'd like to, but he has to have a reason that will hold up in court."

"Lawyers," he muttered.

She laughed. "You sound like one of the men we prosecuted for theft. He was sure that lawyers were all bound for a fiery end."

His hand caught hers. "I've gone my rounds with prosecutors," he mused as they walked toward her office.

"You have?" she asked, curious.

He looked down at her solemnly. "We really are going to have to have a talk," he told her. "There are things about me that you need to know."

She drew in a long breath. "There are things about me you need to know, too."

"Come over for lunch Sunday," he invited. "Paulie said Sari was going to ask you, anyway. We can walk down through the woods and talk without people watching us all the time."

"Would you be safe if we did that?" she worried. "I mean, snipers love deserted places, don't they?"

He chuckled. "The one who's watching me surely does," he pointed out.

"Oh! I forgot."

He grinned. "I'm glad. I don't want you upset. I can take care of myself, honey. I've been in worse jams than this. I'll tell you about it, Sunday." He paused and turned toward her. "You think you can live with my past. I'm not sure you can. But I'll leave the decision up to you."

"You undervalue yourself," she said, searching his dark eyes. "I said it wouldn't matter. I meant it."

He smiled and touched her cheek gently. "You

think it wouldn't," he said sadly. "That may not be the case."

"You can tell me Sunday."

"And there you both are again," Jessie said from behind them.

"Yeah," Mikey said, glaring at her.

She made a face and went past them into the office, slamming the door behind her.

"Sore loser," he muttered after her.

Bernie smiled. It made her feel good that Mikey preferred her to the beautiful woman who'd just gone past them. She felt valued.

"Idiot," he whispered. "You're worth ten of a woman like that." His head jerked toward the office. "She's anybody's. She'll play up to a man for what he's got, nothing else. Women like that are after hard cash, not love."

"I don't care about money," Bernie said.

"I know that. It's one of your best traits, and you've got a lot of them."

"Me?" she laughed. "I'm just ordinary." She drew in a breath. "You know, I have flares in the winter," she began. "I spend a lot of time in bed…"

He put his forefinger over her lips. "That won't matter, either. You nursed me through one of the worst headaches I've ever had. If you get down, I'll take care of you," he added huskily.

Tears stung her eyes. She lowered them to his broad chest.

"Don't cry," he whispered. "People will think I'm being mean to you."

She laughed. "Sorry. It's just that I've never really had anybody take care of me, not since my father died."

"I don't want to be your dad," he pointed out. He frowned. "You know, Bernie, I'm a lot older than you."

"Bosh," she mused, looking up into his face. "You'll never be old. Not to me."

His breath caught in his throat. He looked around. Cars everywhere. People on the sidewalks. Her boss, coming toward them.

"Oh, damn," he said under his breath.

Her eyebrows arched. "What?"

"Bernie, I want to kiss you so badly that it hurts and we're surrounded by people. Damned people!"

She grinned up at him. "There's Sunday," she teased.

He pursed his lips. His dark eyes twinkled. "Yeah. There's Sunday."

"Lunchtime's almost over, Bernie," Kemp teased as he came up beside them. "Back to boring routine."

"It's never boring, Mr. Kemp," she said, and meant it. "Tedious and maddening, but never boring!"

He grinned, nodded to Mikey, and went inside the building.

"I'd better go in. When?" she asked. "Sunday, I mean."

"About eleven suit you?"

She nodded. "That sounds great."

"I won't see you for a couple of days," he said. "I've got some people to see up in San Antonio. Santi and I have a room reserved for it. But I'll be here to pick you up Sunday, okay? And tell Mrs. Brown not to rent out my room while I'm gone!"

"I will, but she never would. She thinks you're terrific. So do the other boarders." She lowered her eyes to his chest. "So do I."

He bent and brushed a kiss over her forehead. "I think you're terrific, too, kid," he whispered. "Now go to work before I wrestle you down in the grass over there and do what I'm aching to do!"

Her breath caught. "It's in public view!"

"So would we be, and they'd be snapping pictures for the local paper, too," he assured her. "See you Sunday, honey. Be careful. Don't go out at night for any reason at all. You're being watched, but don't take chances. I couldn't live if anything happened to you." He touched her cheek and walked away before she could get the words out that she'd wanted to say.

No matter, she told herself. She could recite them on Sunday.

Jessie was wary of Sari and Glory, so she kept her hot words to herself. But just before quitting time, she stopped by Bernie when the other women were getting their coats and leaned close.

"You think he's hooked? You just wait," she threatened softly. "There's never been a man I couldn't get!"

And before Bernie could say a word, she was out the door and gone.

Bernie was agonizing over what she was going to have to tell Mikey on Sunday. She knew that he had a past, and she was sure she could live with whatever it was. But she wasn't so sure that he could live, not only with her disability issues, but with what had happened in her family. It was so horrible that she never spoke of it. Only a few people in Jacobsville knew. Her father was a good man, a kind man, who was wonderful to his daughter. But her grandfather had been a different story. He'd been notorious, in fact, and the story was so gruesome that it was fodder for the tabloids for the better part of a month.

None of that was Bernie's fault. She'd only been involved because he was part of her family, but it stung just the same. She felt dirty because of it. There had been survivors who were outraged. Her father had been targeted by one. Only the quick arrival of the sheriff's department had saved Bernie and her dad, because the man had been armed. She couldn't even blame him. The grief must have been horrible. But her father was no more responsible for it than Bernie was. It was just that the survivors couldn't get to the people responsible, so they went after the people who were left.

That had eventually blown over. Tempers cooled, people went back to church and remembered that part of their religious faith was the very difficult tenet of forgiveness for even the most horrible crimes. Bernie and her dad moved from Floresville back to Jacobsville, and distance helped. But that didn't mean that Bernie might not be a target in the future from some other relative who was frustrated by not having a means of vengeance.

She'd have to tell Mikey that. She'd also have to make him understand about her illness. There was no cure for rheumatoid arthritis. There were many treatments, most of which worked, but the most useful were beyond Bernie's pocket. Even with them, she would still have flares, days when she couldn't work at all. And because the drugs required worked at lowering her immune system to fight the RA, she was more disposed to illness than healthy people. She had bad lungs and often had respiratory infections. Mikey had to understand that just an occasional flare was the least of her health issues.

If he still wanted her after all that, well, it would make him a man in a million. Her family's notoriety was going to make things more complicated.

But it might work out, she told herself. They might actually be able to make it work, if they could keep Jessie at bay. She was an odd sort of person, very narcissistic and pretty horrible. She didn't feel compassion and she had an acid tongue. What in the world was she doing in a small town like Jacobsville when she was obviously more suited to big cities? It was a puzzle.

There was a cold rain on Friday afternoon just as Bernie was getting ready to go home. She hadn't worn a raincoat or brought an umbrella, and it was pouring outside. Even in south Texas, it could get pretty cold in autumn.

"Let me drop you off at your boardinghouse, Bernie," Sari offered. "You'll get soaked going home and you'll be sick."

"Yes, you have to stay well or Mikey won't be able to take you anyplace, will he, sweetie?" Jessie purred as she passed them outside, her umbrella raised.

"One day," Sari said with venom, and glared at the other woman.

Jessie made a harrumphing sound in her throat and went on down the street to where her car was parked. Strangely, it was an expensive foreign one. How could she afford that on what she made as a stenographer and receptionist for the local DA, Sari wondered.

"You should have a car," Sari chided gently as the limousine driver started off down the street with his two passengers in back.

"They break down," Bernie said with a smile. "I can't afford to run one. And I can mostly walk to work, except when I'm having flares. Then I get a cab."

"You can always ride with me," Sari said. "Anytime you need to."

"Thanks," Bernie said. "But I do okay."

Sari laughed and shook her head. "Honestly, you're the hardest person to do anything for."

"I guess so. Sorry."

"It's not a bad trait. Jessie would do anything for someone with money," she added harshly. "That woman makes my blood boil."

"Mikey can't stand her," Bernie said with a wicked little smile.

Sari laughed. "So he said. I guess he's seen that sort so much in his life that he hasn't got any interest in them anymore."

"He said that he was a bad man," Bernie mentioned.

"Some bad, some good, like all of us."

Bernie looked at her warmly. "I told him it wouldn't matter, whatever he'd done."

"That's like you," Sari replied. She studied the other woman quietly. "He'll tell you the truth. I know about it from Paul. He and Mikey both had hard lives as children. They grew up with people who weren't good role models. Mikey went the wrong way. I think he's trying to leave that behind him now. But..." She hesitated, noticing how Bernie hung on every word. "But he'll have to tell you the rest. And you'll have to make a choice." She paused. She didn't want to say it. "That choice may be harder than you think right now."

Bernie drew in a long breath. "It's too late for choices," she said softly. "He's my whole world, Sari. He's...everything."

Sari smiled. "Paul is mine. I understand. It's just... Well, Mikey will explain it to you," she finished.

Bernie studied her hands, poised on her purse in her lap. "He's mixed up somehow with organized crime, I think," she said without noting Sari's sudden alertness. "I watched *The Godfather*, so I sort of know about that stuff."

She didn't know anything, not a thing, about

the harshness and the blood and the savagery with which Mikey's associates did and could act. Sari didn't want to enlighten her, though. It was going to be up to Mikey. If Bernie truly loved him, they'd find a way to make it work.

"Paul says he's never seen Mikey so happy," Sari said, instead of voicing her thoughts.

Bernie beamed. "I've never been so happy, not in all my life." She looked at Sari. "You know all about my family, about what happened. Will Mikey be able to handle it? I mean, there are people who went after Daddy, when he was alive, because of what my grandfather did."

"Nobody's ever come after you, and nobody ever will. If they even try, we'll sic Mr. Kemp on them. He'll handle it. Okay?"

Bernie let out the breath she'd been holding. "Okay."

"And Mikey's the last person who'll blame you for something someone in your family did," she added.

"I was notorious for a while," Bernie said hesitantly.

"Only for a while, and never after you moved here with your dad," Sari added.

"I suppose so." She lowered her face. "I don't want Mikey to be ashamed of me."

"As if that would ever happen! Honestly, Bernie!" she laughed. "He's crazy about you. It won't matter."

Bernie smiled. "Okay."

"And the past doesn't matter. For either one of you."

"If I stay sick all the time, it may," Bernie voiced her other fear. "I've got a weak immune system already, and the medicines I have to take for RA make it even weaker. I get sick a lot, especially in cold weather."

"It won't matter," she said firmly. "Besides, Mikey could afford those outrageously expensive medicines that they think might help you," she added with a smile.

"As if I'd let him do that," Bernie began.

"Under certain circumstances, you would," Sari drawled, and laughed at the expression on her coworker's face. "Life is sweet. You're just finding that out."

"It's never been sweeter, in fact."

"So live one day at a time," Sari counseled, "and let tomorrow take care of itself."

"That sounds easy. It's not."

"Nothing is easy. But we get by. Right?"

"Right."

"And if Jessie makes one more snide remark about how unhealthy you are, I'm going to encourage Olivia to pour coffee on her head!"

"Oh, don't suggest that—Olivia would do it on a dare," Bernie laughed uproariously.

"I heard about the coffee incident after I got back from vacation this summer," Sari said mischievously. "Nobody had made coffee. Agent Murdock came to see the boss on a case, and he made coffee just for himself and turned off the pot. Olivia went to get herself a cup. It was barely lukewarm by then, but she thought she'd drink it anyway. She took a sip, spat it out, glared at Murdock, who was flushed by then, and she poured the whole carafe right over his head and his suit. Lucky it wasn't hot!"

"Mr. Kemp came out of his office to usher Agent Murdock in," Bernie recalled, laughing so hard she almost choked. "And when he saw Olivia with the empty pot and the full cup in Agent Murdock's hand, he put his hand over his mouth and went right back into his office and closed the door. I swear, he laughed for five minutes."

"What did Agent Murdock do?"

Bernie whistled. "He got up, in the ruins of his suit, stared at Olivia for a minute, and then poured the contents of his own coffee cup over her head."

"And?" Sari prompted.

"He walked out the door in a huff and she went home to change. We're still laughing about it. Except that when Agent Murdock comes through the door, they both pretend that the other one is invisible. It makes things interesting."

Sari just grinned.

Chapter Ten

Sunday morning, Mikey came by to pick up Bernie at Mrs. Brown's boardinghouse. He was preoccupied at first, frowning.

"What's wrong?" she asked gently. "Can I help?"

He turned toward her and smiled slowly, oblivious to Santi's quick and amused glance in the rearview mirror from the front seat. "There's that sweet compassion that I've hardly had in my whole life," he said. "You really are one in a million, kid."

She flushed. "So are you. But can I help?"

"You can listen, when we get to Paulie's house," he said. He glanced in the front seat.

"And you can have the day off until I call you to take us home, Santi," he added with a grin. "You might go take in a movie."

"Not a bad idea, boss," Santi said with a big smile. "Thanks!"

He shrugged. "I'm not a bad guy."

Santi made a sarcastic noise, but Mikey ignored him. They got out at the front door of Paul's house, and Santi raised a hand and waved as he drove off.

Mikey held Bernie's hand tight in his and put his finger on the doorbell.

Before he could push it, the door opened. Sari and Paul welcomed them in.

"We have lunch," Sari announced. "Mandy made a macaroni and ginger and chicken salad, and sliced some fruit to go with it."

"That sounds wonderful," Bernie said.

"It does. Nobody cooks like Mandy," Mikey said.

"I heard that," Mandy called from the kitchen. "Come on in. I've almost got everything on the table."

She did. The place settings were immaculate, like the white linen napkins. Mikey pulled out a chair for Bernie and then one for himself.

Mandy came back in with a basket of blueberry muffins and put them on the table. "Who wants coffee?"

Every hand went up.

Mandy laughed. "That's what I figured," she mused. "Coming right up."

Bernie was a little self-conscious at first. She wasn't used to mansions and elaborate dining room place settings, and this was her first real meal with the Fiores. But the conversation and Mikey's attention thawed her out in no time at all.

"This is delicious," Bernie commented as she savored a bite of the chicken dish.

"We like it as a light meal," Sari said. "Neither of us likes anything heavy in the middle of the day. Or in the evening, for that matter."

"No wonder you're both so slender," Bernie teased.

"People in law enforcement have to be fast," Paul chuckled. "I had to run down a counterfeiter just last week," he added. "If I overeat, I lose my edge."

Mikey grinned at him. "Not likely," he commented. "You do okay, cousin."

"Sari says Jessie is giving you two a hard time," Paul noted.

Mikey's lip pulled down. "She's persistent, I'll give her that. But she has the appeal of a skunk on acid. Know what I mean?"

Paul laughed. "I do."

"Besides," Mikey said, his eyes on Bernie, "I have other interests."

Bernie beamed and almost spilled her coffee. Her heart was going so fast that it shook her blouse. Mikey noticed that and flashed her a wicked smile.

After lunch, Mikey took Bernie's hand and led her down the wooded path that eventually ended at the stables where the Grayling race-horses lived in luxury.

"I love it here," Bernie said, looking around at the leafless trees next to tall fir trees that were still green. "Fir trees are awesome."

"Yeah, they are," he agreed. "Out west, we've got Colorado blue spruce that go right up into the sky."

"Are they really blue, or is that just a description that stuck?"

"They're really blue," he replied. He stopped

walking and turned to her. "Next time I go to Vegas, you can come with me. We'll go by way of Wyoming and have a look at Yellowstone and Old Faithful. It's a sight you'll never forget."

She hesitated.

He noticed that. "I have plans," he said softly. "First, I have to take the heat off Tony and get him out of the mess he's in. He's family, you see?" he asked, scowling. "It's loyalty. You take a solemn vow. You fulfill it. If you don't, there are terrible penalties. Nobody ever sells out anybody in his family. If he does, the penalty is unspeakable." He didn't add that he'd participated in such retribution. He had to confess as much as he could to her, but there were things he had to keep to himself.

She looked up at him with her heart in her eyes. "It won't matter," she said stubbornly.

He touched her cheek with the tips of his fingers. "Bernie, I've been involved with the mob since I was old enough to carry a piece. I've done things…" He hesitated. It had never really bothered him before. Now it was hard to reconcile what he'd done with what he wanted to do now. He drew in a breath. "You've watched *The Godfather* movies, haven't you?"

"Oh, yes. They're great movies," she said.

"You remember about the horse's head being in bed with the producer who wouldn't give the outfit's singer a job?"

She nodded.

"And the way Michael's older brother was murdered, a hit organized by a rival family?"

She felt cold chills down her spine. "Yes," she said huskily. "I remember that, too."

"Well, that was glossed-over stuff," he said flatly. "Family hits are just plain gore. You don't know what happened to Paulie, do you?"

She just shook her head.

"He had a wife and a little girl, before he came down here to work for old man Grayling as a security expert," he said. "Paulie was the only person in our whole family who went straight. He worked with the FBI in Jersey, and he shut down one of the minor crime bosses. He felt great about it. But when he went home that night, his wife and his little girl had been done with a shotgun."

Bernie put a hand to her mouth. "Oh, the poor man!" she exclaimed, shocked.

"He took years getting over it," he said. "Eventually, he fell in love with Sari, but he got cold feet and made some excuse to quit. It was three years before he came back. In the meantime, Sari's father had beaten the girls to within an inch of their lives. Sari blamed Paul and had nothing to do with him when he worked out of the FBI office in San Antonio. But she was in a hurricane down in the Bahamas. Paul thought she was dead, but he and Mandy went to bring her home. She turned up alive and they were married the same week. Paulie never got over losing his family, though. He blamed himself for pushing the crime boss too hard and going after his whole organization."

"What happened to the man who killed his first family?" she asked.

His face grew hard. "I knew a guy who was inside," he said shortly. "I took care of it."

She felt the blood drain out of her face. "You…?"

"I took care of it," he repeated quietly. "Yes. I have that kind of power. I worked my way up through the organization for years, to get to where I am now. I own one of the biggest casinos in Vegas and I'm filthy rich. I was arrested once on a murder charge, but I had witnesses swear I was nowhere near the scene of the crime. They had no real evidence, so they dropped the case."

She moved to a big oak tree and leaned back against it. This was news she hadn't anticipated, and it was shocking. She looked up into cold dark eyes.

"I'm so sorry, honey. I didn't want to have to confess how bad a man I am. But you had to know," he said. Inside, he was churning like storm clouds. He hadn't wanted to tell her these things, but he couldn't offer her a future without making her aware of the past. "There's more," he told her. "A lot more. But this is enough for now."

Her lips parted on a long breath. She looked at him helplessly. She loved him. He was a criminal. He would probably never give up that life. He'd told her graphically what the family he belonged to would do if they were betrayed.

"Omertà," she whispered heavily.

He moved closer. "Yeah. Omertà," he replied. "It's the code we live by. Or die by, if we betray anybody in our family. They don't just kill you. They kill everybody you love. It's like erasing your whole life."

She leaned her head back against the hard bark

of the tree and just looked at him. She didn't understand what he wanted from her, why he was telling her something so personal.

"So that's the secret I keep," he said. "It's bad. It's horrible. But it's a part of my life that you have to understand if we go forward together. So. What secrets are you keeping?" he added in a tender voice.

She took a deep breath. "My grandfather owned a little store over in Floresville. He and my grandmother ran it. We noticed that Granddaddy was forgetful, and sometimes he had rages, when he just went wild over something he saw on television, or something a politician said. We overlooked it because we thought it was just the product of normal aging."

He moved closer. "But it wasn't?"

"It wasn't. One day, he was listening to what a politician said about the economy and new regulations that were going to go into effect. Granddaddy started yelling that those people needed to be killed, slaughtered."

She hesitated, then plowed ahead without looking at him. "Maybe he would have calmed down, but the mayor was in his store buying some hardware, and he and Granddaddy got

into an argument about politics. They were completely opposite in their views. The mayor tried
to calm my grandfather down, and he thought
he had. My grandmother chided him for being
so violent over just stupid politics. She said he
needed to lie down for a while. Granddaddy
didn't argue with her. He went out from behind
the counter without a word. My grandmother
was relieved, she thought he was over his anger.
Not five minutes later, he came back into the
front of the store with an automatic pistol." She
swallowed hard. "He killed my grandmother
and the mayor, and then he turned the gun on
three customers and killed them, too. The survivors screamed and ran out of the store. A local
policeman heard the screams and went into the
store with his pistol drawn. Granddaddy shot
him dead the minute he walked into the store.
The police called in the SWAT team from San
Antonio. Granddaddy was holed up in the store,
and he wouldn't come out and give up his gun."
She sighed. "Long story short, the SWAT team
went in and shot my grandfather. He died on the
way to the hospital. My mother was so ashamed
and sick at what her father had done, so grieved
at the loss of her mother and the forthcoming

fury of the townspeople, that she locked herself in the bathroom and slashed her own throat with a razor blade. We thought she was taking a bath." Her eyes closed. "By the time we realized something was wrong and Daddy got the door open, it was much too late. She died."

"Oh, God," he said. "You poor kid!"

She bit her lower lip. "Daddy sold the house and moved us here. It was horrible, the aftermath. We were hated by so many people who lost loved ones that day. I didn't blame them, you know, but Daddy and I had nothing to do with what happened. Nothing at all."

He moved forward and pulled her into his arms, folding her close, rocking her while she cried. "And I thought I'd had a hard life," he whispered at her ear. "Baby, I wish I'd known you then. Nobody would ever have hurt you!"

She pressed close, resting her wet cheek over his heart. "I thought you might not want anything else to do with me when you knew about what happened."

"Dopey girl," he murmured, and laughed softly. "I'm hooked. Haven't you noticed? Who do I hang around with all the time? Who do

I take to movies and into rooms where we do naughty things together?"

She laughed through her tears. "Me, I guess."

"You." He drew in a long, slow breath. His arms tightened. "I pledged allegiance to Tony. I have to fulfill my vows. I can't let him die, whatever I have to do to save him."

"Family is more important than your own life, isn't it?"

"Yes." His breath was warm at her ear. "I'm mixed up in this in a bad way. I can't make commitments right now. But when it's over, when I clear Tony…"

She didn't move. Her eyes closed. "I told you," she whispered. "I meant it. It won't matter."

"God!" His mouth moved over hers and he kissed her with subdued passion, with pure hunger. He hadn't imagined that she could live with the things he'd done, that she could still want him after she knew them. She was an extraordinary woman. "Bernie," he said unsteadily, "you're the very breath in my body!"

She couldn't even find words to express what she felt, so she kissed him with her whole heart, her arms stealing up around his neck, her mouth answering his with the same hungry passion that he was showing her.

He groaned and his hands ran up and down her sides, his thumbs pressing under her breasts.

"Ahem."

Mikey lifted his head and stared at Bernie blankly. "What did you say?"

"I didn't say anything," she began.

"Ahem." It came again. Mikey frowned and felt around his lapel. There was a device that had been placed there in San Antonio. He glowered at it.

"Yes?" Mikey asked abruptly.

"I have a bead on you and quite frankly if you don't break that up, I'm going to have to leave you defenseless and go get several drinks of hard liquor."

Mikey's teeth ground together. "Damn it, Billings," he muttered.

"A lot of drinks," Billings continued. "Maybe a whole damned fifth. It's been a long dry spell and I have to watch you. Get it? Watch you."

Mikey drew a long breath and stared at Bernie with amused regret. "Okay. We'll go look at the horses."

"Good idea. Blakely's in there. You can drive

him nuts!" There was a click and the device went silent.

Bernie was flushed and embarrassed.

"Hey," Mikey said, pushing back the unruly long, blond hair from her face. "Billings is right. This isn't the time or place."

"Did he hear all we said?" she worried.

"Not likely. He doesn't eavesdrop. I guess we were getting pretty heated, huh?" He laughed. "Okay. Let's behave." He caught her fingers and entangled them with his. "Let's go look at the pretty horses."

She laughed. Life was sweet. He didn't mind her past. She didn't mind his. This was a relationship with a future. She'd never been so certain of anything.

They wandered through the stables. There was a man in charge of the thoroughbreds. He explained them to Bernie.

"They're descended from three stallions imported into England in the seventeenth and eighteenth centuries, the beginning of their line. We won the Kentucky Derby with this fellow," he said, smiling as he approached the big stall where the racehorse lived. "He has his own pasture and he's at stud. We get fabulous amounts of money from his colts. He's a grand old fellow."

Bernie looked at him with awe. He was grand, elegant and handsome, and he knew it, too. "He's gorgeous," she said.

The stable manager chuckled. "We think so, too. He has a colt that was born just two months ago. It's down here."

He led them down the paved aisle to another stall, where a handsome young thoroughbred was playing with a big ball.

"Horses play?" Bernie exclaimed.

The manager laughed. "Of course. They're like puppies or toddlers at this age. When they hit adolescence, or the horse equivalent, that's when the problems start. Right now, they're just children and it's a whole new world for them."

Bernie just watched the colt play, fascinated. "I've never been around horses much," she confessed. "We had a small ranch in Floresville where my people had a few head of beef cattle. There were a few horses for the cowboys, but I never rode one. I was afraid of them."

"Never let a horse know that," the manager told her. "They'll take advantage."

"I'm not likely to be put on a horse anytime soon," she assured him.

"If you ever did want to ride, we have a fifteen-year-old gelding, very gentle, who would be perfect for you. If you ever did," he added.

Mikey chuckled and pressed her fingers with his. "There may come a day," he said with a gentle smile at Bernie, who returned it.

"There may," she said.

They went back to the house.

"You're back soon," Sari commented.

"Yeah," Mikey said with a rueful smile. "Billings is a wet blanket."

"Chet Billings? You saw him?" she asked.

"No. We heard him. He's got this device on me," he added, indicating the electronic thing on his lapel.

"Oh. He talked to you?"

"He threatened to get drunk is what he did." Mikey looked at Bernie and sighed. "I guess there's no real privacy left on earth."

"Yes, there is. The conservatory is very nice, very quiet and it has a door. However," she added mischievously, "not being stupid, I'll call you when supper is ready and I'll probably open the door to do it."

Mikey sighed. "Speak loudly, okay?" he teased.

Sari laughed. "Very loudly." She gave them a knowing look and went back into the kitchen, where she and Mandy were sharing coffee. "Do you want coffee?" she called over her shoulder.

"Later," Mikey said. "When supper's ready. Thanks, Sari," he added.

"I wasn't always married," Sari replied, and grinned.

Mikey took off the lapel pen, put it on a table in the hall and drew Bernie into the room with him. He closed the door behind him and, as an afterthought, locked it.

"Just so you know," he said as he pulled her gently into his arms, "we're big on innocence. Some people might call us reactionary, but we respect our women and we don't dishonor them. You get what I mean?"

He was telling her that he wouldn't let it go too far. She smiled. "I guess you know all about me."

His mouth brushed hers. "I know that you're

an innocent, Bernie," he whispered. "It excites me and maddens me, all at once."

"Maddens you?"

"Obstacles are frustrating," he mused. He kissed her with slow, hungry brushes of his mouth, feeling hers follow it helplessly. "But we'll muddle through. When things get too hot, and they might, all you have to do is remind me that I promised not to let things go too far."

She laughed. "Okay."

He smiled as he kissed her again. "You make me hungry for things I never wanted before," he murmured as he maneuvered her onto the cushy sofa and came down beside her. "A home, a family, roots," he whispered. He had her blouse off and her bra unsnapped in seconds. "Belonging," he murmured as his mouth opened over her taut nipple and suddenly suckled her, hard.

She came right off the sofa, a tiny, shocked cry pulsing out of her throat, a sound she'd never heard from it before.

"Shh," he whispered gruffly. "They'll hear."

She bit her lower lip and pulled his head closer, her fingers spearing through his thick, wavy black hair as his mouth made magic on her body.

"Glory!" she moaned. "Mikey, do it harder," she whispered frantically. "Harder!"

"I'll hurt you," he groaned.

"No. You won't. Please…!"

He took all of her firm breast into his mouth and his tongue worked on the nipple until she was writhing wildly under the sudden heavy press of his body.

One big hand was under her hip, grinding her against the growing hardness of him, letting her feel his need. It was desperate.

She felt guilty. She was inciting him, and they couldn't be intimate. She remembered suddenly what he'd told her about heavy petting, that he could have the clothes out of the way and be inside her in less time than it would take to react.

She thought about feeling him inside her, and she shivered with the sudden need.

Her nails bit into the back of his head as she held it closer, arching so that he could feed more easily on her breast. She shivered rhythmically as he suckled her, harder and harder. All at once she arched and sobbed and felt a shaft of pleasure pierce her that was beyond anything she'd ever dreamed. She convulsed, shuddered, flew up into the clouds and exploded.

Then she cried, embarrassed. He cuddled her close, denying his starved body the release it begged for. "It's all right," he whispered. "It's natural, baby. It's all right."

"It really is? Natural, I mean?" she whispered brokenly.

He laughed softly. "That only happens to one woman in a hundred," he said. "Maybe one in a thousand. I've never seen it happen to a woman I was with." His mouth brushed over hers. "God, what a thrill it was! You've never felt it, have you?"

"Not...until now," she managed.

He drew in a rough breath. "I'm better than I thought I was," he teased.

She laughed. "You're better than I thought you were, and that's saying something."

He lifted his head and looked down at her bare breasts. "You know that you belong to me, don't you?" he asked, and met her eyes with his. They were solemn. "You're mine, Bernie."

She melted into the sofa under the hard, sweet pressure of his body. "Yes. I know it."

He moved over her, his body pressing her down. He fought his shirt out of the way so that his muscular hair-roughened chest was rubbing against her bare breasts. He shivered.

She did, too. "If you want to," she said unsteadily, "I will."

"Right here?" he asked huskily.

"Right here."

"You don't know how much I want to," he bit off.

She moved her hips just a tiny bit. "Oh, yes, I do," she said, feeling him swell even more.

"Baby," he whispered. He moved between her legs and pushed up, so that he was intimately pressed against the heart of her.

She sobbed, because it was beyond anything she'd felt before. Her legs moved apart, inviting him.

"It would have to be quick," he said gruffly. "Very quick. And it will probably hurt."

"I don't...care," she said unsteadily.

He kissed her softly, and his hand went under the band of her slacks, under her briefs. She caught his wrist, embarrassed.

He lifted his head. "You have to let me do this," he whispered, his voice shaken. "I have to know how careful I need to be with you. Okay?"

She bit her lip. "I've never..."

"I know that. But you belong to me."

She let her body relax, let the hardness of him fit against her so that it was heaven to feel. "Yes," she said, her voice tender, her eyes wide and rapt on his taut face.

His hand smoothed over her belly and he thought of a baby who would look like her or like himself. He had something to use, but he didn't want to use it. And he didn't want to take her here in a rush, the way he'd taken women in his youth. She would need time, lots of time, and he couldn't give it to her if they went too far.

His fingers moved down. She hesitated and tightened as he suddenly began to probe where she was most a woman. She bit her lip hard enough to draw blood as he explored her intimately. Even loving him as she did, it was hard to give up control to another person.

He whispered, almost groaning as he drew his fingers back and smoothed them over her stomach, "It will hurt like hell, and I'm not sure I could even get through the barrier, you understand?"

"Oh!" She winced.

"Sorry." He rolled over onto his side and pulled her into his arms, grinding her breasts into his chest. "No, I'm sorry. I never meant to take it this far." His arms contracted. "God, Bernie, I want to get you pregnant so badly…!"

He kissed her shocked mouth and groaned again as he pushed her hips closer to his. "I want you. I want to go inside you, so deep, so hard, that you'll shoot up like a rocket!"

She flushed under the pressure of his hard mouth, moaning as she felt him move her rhythmically against his hips. "I'm so sorry…"

He managed a husky laugh. "Think of it as a chastity belt. It will keep me in line until we can make things legal."

She hid her face against his throat. Make it legal. Could he mean that he wanted to marry her? She was so entranced that she didn't even hear footsteps in the hall.

Neither did Mikey, who was kissing her as if he couldn't manage to stop.

The hard, insistent knock on the door and the rattling of the locked doorknob broke them apart.

"Supper!" Sari called.

Mikey laughed. "Okay! We'll be right there."

"I have a master key, you know. It fits all the locks," Sari threatened.

Bernie went beet-red. Mikey just chuckled. "We're behaving, starting right now!"

There was a laugh outside the door. "Fair warning. Five minutes and I unlock the door."

"Got it!" Mikey called.

Footsteps retreated.

Mikey took one long, last look at Bernie's half-nude body and groaned. "I hate dressing you," he muttered, as he refastened her bra and pulled her blouse down.

"I hate dressing you, too," she teased as she buttoned his shirt again. "I love the way you look undressed."

"Yeah. I feel exactly the same way about you."

"You're not upset by what I told you?" she asked, worried.

He cocked his head and stared at her. "I've done things almost as bad as your grandfather," he said flatly. "I can't sit in judgment on somebody else. Not my business. But now that you know what my business is," he added quietly, "you have to decide if you can live with it. There's no way I'll give it up. I can't. It's for life."

She was beginning to realize that even though he ran an honest gaming hotel in Las Vegas, he was firmly entrenched with a group that routinely broke the law. He could go to prison in certain circumstances. She'd have to be in the company of people who thought of crime as a way of life, an occupation. She'd be the outsider. Would the women in his organization hate her? And what about the women he'd had before her? Would they be around? Would they be like Jessie and make her life miserable?

"Deep thoughts, huh?" he asked quietly.

"Very deep." She drew in a breath. "Mikey, I'm not like you. I don't even jaywalk. My great-grandfather was a United States Marshal. I have a cousin who's a Texas Ranger. Law enforcement runs through my whole family."

"I see," he said heavily. "You don't think you could handle it."

"No!" She went close to him. "I'd be the outsider. The freak. They wouldn't accept me."

"Baloney," he mused. He smiled as he tangled his fingers in her hair. "You have no idea how much they'd accept you. They'd go places with you, protect you if you needed protection. They'd sit with you when you were sick, when you have flares. It's another whole world, baby. One you've never seen. It's violent, yes. But the people are just like anybody else. The women are a close-knit group, because there's always some danger involved that the men have to handle." He winced at her expression. "I don't know any other way of life, Bernie," he concluded. "I can't change what I am, what I do." He shrugged. "I don't want to. If that's selfish, I'm selfish."

She pressed herself close to him, sliding her arms around him. "I can try," she whispered.

His heart jumped. It lifted as if a dark cloud had dissipated in the sunlight. His arms tightened around her. "That's all I ask," he said. "That's all I want."

She smiled and closed her eyes.

There was a click and the door opened. Sari looked in with pursed lips when they turned toward her. She chuckled. "I warned you," she said, lifting the key to show them. "Supper."

Mikey grinned. "We're right behind you."

"Yes," Bernie agreed.

Mikey linked her fingers with his and the two of them looked, to Sari, like two halves of a whole. She had no doubt that there would be a wedding in the future.

Bernie clung to his hand and smiled. She looked up at Mikey with wonder, with adoration.

He saw that look and it made him feel a foot taller. His fingers contracted gently around hers. She tightened her own grip. She'd never known such wonder, such joy. It spilled out around her like sunshine. She smiled. So did Mikey. They both knew where this was leading, now more than ever.

Chapter Eleven

Supper was as uproarious as lunch had been. Paul had a dozen stories of things that had happened to him in the course of his duties. Foremost among those stories was the one he'd heard from Sari about agent Murdock. He recited it for Mikey and chuckled at his cousin's amusement.

"I like Olivia," Mikey said. "She seems very nice."

"She is," Bernie agreed. "Mr. Kemp hired her so that there would be another paralegal in the office on the days I can't work," she added, and felt uncomfortable talking about her limitations.

"You do very well, considering your obstacles," Sari told her. "We don't think of you as handicapped, you know," she added. "You have a disability. Lots of people have them. Look at poor Glory. She had dangerously high blood pressure and a light heart attack. But she overcame that to work here, where she and her husband and little boy live."

"I'd love a little boy," Mikey said, glancing at Bernie, who flushed. "Or a little girl. I'll bet little girls are sweet."

Bernie laughed. "I was never sweet," she teased. "I got into so much trouble when I was small. The worst time was when I climbed into the corncrib and couldn't get out, and a king snake decided to come in with me. He was huge. Over six feet long. I was terrified. But he didn't strike at me or even threaten me. He just stretched out on the corn and looked at me."

"Probably hunting rodents," Sari remarked. "They love corn."

"Probably," Bernie agreed. "All in all, he was a very polite snake. He didn't even seem bothered when Daddy came to find me and lifted me out of the corncrib."

"He might also have just eaten a few rats and was feeling lazy," Paul chuckled.

"Equally possible," Bernie laughed.

"Well, I've got briefs to read," Sari said.

"And I've got cases to work," Paul added as they both got to their feet. "You two can watch movies or just sit in the conservatory and watch the plants grow. You're both always welcome. Anytime."

"Thanks, Paul," Bernie said.

Mikey echoed the sentiment.

They were left with Mandy, who started to clear away the dishes. "You two want coffee?" she asked with a warm smile.

"Not for me," Mikey said. "I don't sleep good. It keeps me awake."

"Me, too," Bernie said.

Mikey stood up and helped Bernie out of her chair. "I think we'll go watch Sari's plants grow for a while, if you don't mind."

"Help yourselves," she said with a knowing grin.

Mikey led Bernie into the conservatory and locked the door.

"Nobody's likely to try it, but who knows?" Mikey teased. He took Bernie into his arms and kissed her hungrily. "Dessert," he whispered. "Sweeter than cake."

"Sweeter than honey," she agreed on a moan.

He picked her up and sat down with her in his lap, kissing her all the while.

She didn't protest his hands under her blouse. He was so familiar to her now, so dear, that she welcomed anything he did.

He knew that, and it kept him honest. He didn't want to take advantage of an attraction she couldn't help. She was very innocent. It made his head spin, that lack of sophistication. He loved it.

He eased her blouse and bra down to her waist and unbuttoned his shirt, pulling her hungrily inside it.

"Oh, glory," she choked when she felt thick, soft hair and warm muscles against her bare breasts. Her face sank into his throat while he caressed her.

"We're good together," he whispered. "Better than I dreamed. God, I want you!"

Her arms tightened around his neck. "I want you, too," she whispered back.

His hands smoothed over her hard-tipped breasts. "We've talked around it," he said after a minute. "But not any particulars." His hands moved her away and he looked at her breasts with possession and appreciation. "You're beautiful like this, Bernie. It makes me hungry just to hold you. But this goes to my head like whiskey."

She arched backward, her body demanding, hungry, ignoring her mind's attempt to be sensible.

"This what you want, sweetheart?" he whispered, and his mouth swallowed up one small, taut breast almost whole.

She moaned and shivered.

"I thought so." His voice was rough, but his mouth was tender as he worked at the hard nipple slowly, tenderly, with a growing suction that very soon made her go stiff and then suddenly burst with pleasure that made her whole body convulse in his arms.

"God, I love this," he groaned against her breast. "I love that I can make you go off like a rocket when I suckle you!"

Her nails dug into him. It was a little embarrassing, but she was too exhausted with pleasure, with satisfaction, to protest. She shivered and clung to him in the aftermath. "I never felt anything like it in my whole life," she said brokenly. "It embarrasses me..."

His arms contracted. "Don't you dare be

ashamed of something so beautiful," he whispered at her ear. "No two people ever belonged to each other more than we do right this minute, Bernie."

She swallowed, hard. "Do you feel that, too?"

He chuckled and turned her just a little, so that her hips were pressed to that part of him that was male and very hard. "Do you feel this?"

"Mikey!" she protested.

"A man can't fake that, honey," he said at her ear. "It's as honest as the way you react when I put my mouth on you." He drew back and looked down at her with pure possession. "There's nobody in the world like you."

She reached up and touched his cheek. "Or like you," she said solemnly.

He bent his dark head and smoothed his mouth over her breast tenderly. He drew in a breath. "We need to talk."

"We are."

"We need to talk when we're both dressed," he said with a droll smile.

"Oh."

He put her clothes back on and buttoned his shirt. When they were calmer, he drew her onto the love seat and sat holding her hand.

"Bernie, I'm not proud of what I'm about to tell you. But there's more about me that you need to know." He drew in a breath. "My family has belonged to what's known to outsiders as La Cosa Nostra for three generations. My father died working for them. I've been with Tony Garza since I was sixteen. I don't know any other way of life."

"You mean, you work outside the law," she said very calmly.

"That's exactly what I mean." He studied her face. She was a little pale, but she wasn't trying to get away from him. "We're like normal people. We pay our taxes, go to church, work for charitable causes, all that stuff. We just earn our living in ways that aren't conventional."

"I told you that I watched *The Godfather* movies," she said.

He brushed her disheveled hair back from her face. "That was a sanitized version of what really goes on," he said after a minute. "I won't, I can't, tell you how brutal it can be. You don't ever quit. And you don't rat out your associates. There are deadly penalties for that. Remember what I told you about Paulie's family?"

She just nodded. Her eyes were sketching his hard face as if she were painting it.

"I could go to jail one day," he persisted. "I could die."

"A meteor could land on the boardinghouse and take us all out," she said matter-of-factly. "Nobody is ever guaranteed even one more day."

He just looked at her.

"I'm not Italian," she said. "Would that make me an outsider?"

He smiled slowly. "The wives come from all sorts of backgrounds," he said, and noticed her flush at the word. "Some are American. Some are Italian and Spanish, even Polish. But they have one thing in common and that's family. We all belong to each other. If you shared that life with me," he said, "you'd be part of it. You'd never be an outsider. And if anything happened, anything at all, you'd be taken care of as long as you live. That's how it works."

She bit her lower lip. She drew in a breath. "Mikey, I won't get any better," she began. "There's no cure for what I have. They can control it with medicine, although I can't afford the kind that might make it easier. But they can't stop it. Eventually, I'll end up with twisted hands and feet, and even if I can walk with a cane at

first, there's a good chance that one day I'll be in a wheelchair." She said it without a plea for pity. She just stated it as a fact.

He tilted her chin up. "I can live with your limitations. Can you live with my profession?"

She just nodded. She didn't say a word. She didn't have to.

He wrapped her up in his arms and just rocked her slowly, his face in her throat. They sat that way for a long time until there was a brief tap and the sound of a key in the lock.

Sari peered around the door and burst out laughing. "And I was afraid I'd have to run for my life when I opened this door..."

Mikey and Bernie both laughed.

Mikey got up and drew her up beside him. "We were talking about the future," he said, smiling. "It looks pretty sweet."

"Pretty sweet, indeed," Bernie said with a long sigh as she looked up at him.

"I'd better get her home," Mikey said. "She has to work tomorrow."

"I know. So do I," Sari wailed.

"There, there," Bernie comforted her. "But there's always next weekend!"

They all laughed.

* * *

Mikey took her back to the boardinghouse and left her at her door with a discreet kiss on her forehead because Mrs. Brown was lurking.

"It was a lovely day. Thank you," Bernie said.

"It was one of many to come," he replied. He smiled at her with his heart in his eyes. "See you in the morning, kid. Sweet dreams."

"Oh, they'll be sweet, all right," she whispered, and then flushed.

He wrinkled his nose at her and winked.

She watched him all the way down the hall before she went back into her room and closed the door.

Work was difficult. Bernie's happiness lit her up like a Christmas tree, and it showed. Olivia teased her. But Jessie watched and smoldered. She was furious that a plain little country girl like Bernie, one who was likely to end up living on disability, had attracted a man who could buy half a county with pocket change. Mikey was sophisticated, handsome and loaded. Jessie wanted him, and she couldn't get to first base. He avoided her like the plague when he was in town.

There had to be some way she could get him out of Bernie's life so that she had a chance with him. Being rude and unpleasant didn't do any good. But if she could play one of them against the other while pretending to turn over a new leaf... Well, that was a promising idea. She began to plot ways to accomplish it.

Her first step was to stop being abrasive to the other women in the office. She toned down her bad attitude and took on her share of the work instead of avoiding it. She offered to bring coffee to Olivia and Bernie when they were swamped with paperwork, and she even brought lunch back for them once.

Everyone was surprised, even Mr. Kemp, who actually praised Jessie for her changed attitude.

Nothing had changed at all except that Jessie was playing a new game. But she smiled and did her best to look humble. She even apologized for the way she'd behaved before. It was hard being a city girl in a small Texas town, she explained to the other women. She'd always had to fight to get ahead, where she'd come from, and it was difficult to stop. But she wanted to fit in. She was going to try harder. The other women in the office, suspecting nothing, warmed to her.

And Jessie just smiled to herself. So far so good, she thought. She even lost her fear of being fired, which she couldn't afford just now. She had a job to do. So she smiled and answered the phone and stopped flirting with rich men.

Bernie mentioned the changed attitude to Mikey on one of their dates, and he laughed. Bernie, he commented, was rubbing off on the other woman. He was happy to see it. So the next time he came across Jessie in the courthouse, where he'd gone with Paul to talk to a judge, he smiled and was pleasant to her.

Several days later, there was a complication. Bernie was walking back to the boardinghouse from work, after refusing a ride from Glory, and a car ran off the road, up onto the curb, and missed her by a few feet.

It sped away while she was getting back onto her feet. She was badly shaken. She picked up her pocketbook and her cane, and stood shivering while she tried to catch her breath. Had it been a car that just lost control, or was it deliberate? She worried the question all the way home.

She'd have told Mikey, but he was out of town on business. He'd mentioned at the boardinghouse that he had to meet with one of the deputy marshals in San Antonio, but he'd be back in time for a date they'd arranged for Saturday. He and Bernie had planned a sightseeing trip to San Antonio because they had plenty of chaperones. Bernie had always wanted to go through the Alamo, but there had never been time since she'd been an adult. Now she looked forward to seeing that part of Texas history with the love of her life.

Mikey picked her up in the limo, with Santi at the wheel, just after she got off work at one o'clock on Saturday. She was wearing a beige sweater and skirt with flats and a cane that matched her outfit.

"Color coordination, huh?" Mikey teased as he helped her into the back seat and climbed in beside her.

"I like things to match," she teased.

He indicated the beige suit he was wearing with a white shirt and a brown paisley tie. "And so we do," he laughed.

She grinned. "We do, indeed."

"I wanted to see the Alamo when I was here last time, when Merrie was in trouble. But I never had the time. You Texans are pretty proud of it, aren't you?"

She nodded. "We really are."

He sighed. "I don't know much about history, even in Jersey," he commented. "Well, maybe one sort of history, but it's not told in polite company," he chuckled.

"I won't ask," she returned, smiling up at him.

"You haven't carried the cane lately, until today," he pointed out. "Having a flare?"

"Well, not really. I had a fall the other day on my way home from work."

He scowled. "A fall?"

She nodded. She bit her lower lip. She hadn't wanted to mention it. "A driver lost control of his car and it came up on the curb where I was walking. It missed me by several feet," she added.

"What sort of car?" he asked with barely concealed anger.

She blinked. "That's the thing, I really didn't have time to notice. I fell and, while I was getting up, it sped away."

"Big car, small?"

She frowned. "Medium."

"What color?"

She tried to remember what it had looked like. "I think it was dark. Not black, but not a colored car, like blue or red or anything."

He looked troubled. He pulled out his cell phone and texted a message to someone. She couldn't tell who.

"I don't think it was deliberate, Mikey," she added softly. "I mean, it didn't come right at me."

"Warnings don't," he said curtly. He typed some more.

Her heart jumped. He was thinking it might be his enemy. But she was thinking it might be an enemy of her family, someone who'd tracked down the one surviving member and tried to avenge a loved one. It wouldn't be the first time it had happened. That worried her.

He put down the phone. "I wish you'd told me sooner," he said. His big hand reached out and touched her long hair lightly. "I couldn't bear it if anything happened to you, Bernie."

She beamed.

He caught her hand in his and held it tight. He leaned back against the seat, clearly concerned. "I sent a text to Paulie. Did you tell Sari about it?"

"No," she said. "She's been in court all week and then she had to go and depose a witness in an assault case she's prosecuting. And honestly, we've been pretty busy at work all week, too."

He was weighing it in his mind. He knew Cotillo was after him, that the man could also target Bernie. But it wasn't the way Cotillo did business. He'd already sent a cleaner after Mikey. That was how he handled threats. Aiming a car at a woman and missing her by several feet, that wasn't the way a man used to violence did business.

Bernie's hand in his tightened. "Maybe it was just an accident," she said. "People do lose control of their cars for all sorts of reasons."

"Yeah. They do. But it's suspicious."

She leaned her head on his shoulder and laughed. "That's you. Suspicious."

He kissed the top of her head. "I've spent my whole life being suspicious. It's why I'm still alive, kid," he teased.

"I suppose so." She looked up into his eyes. "It could be somebody from my own past, from my family's past, still hunting vengeance, you know. Daddy was almost killed once for it."

"How many years ago was that?" he asked.

"Well, quite a few," she recalled.

"It's more likely that it's somebody connected to me," he said. "But in any case, the feds will hash it out." He slid an arm around her shoulders. "Your coworker Jessie has changed," he commented. "Even Paulie said Sari's talking about it." He glanced down at her. "Is she pretending?"

She laughed. "You really are suspicious. She said that it was hard to come from the city and get used to a small town, that she was used to having to be on her guard with people."

"Did she say what city?"

She shook her head. "She came down here from San Antonio. But she's originally from somewhere up north, I think, like her friend Billie who works at the courthouse. They room together."

He frowned. He hadn't considered that the two of them were both from up north. "Have they been here a long time?"

"Not really. Jessie's only been here a few weeks. I believe she and her friend moved from San Antonio together. Billie knew somebody at the courthouse who wanted a temporary secretary after his got sick. They know the cook at Barbara's, too—he's from New Jersey."

Mikey felt his heart stop and start again. He hadn't been asking the right questions. Neither had Paulie. What if the two women and the cook were part of Cotillo's bunch? If nothing else, the timing was right. He was going to suggest to Paulie that they get somebody to keep an eye on those three as well. It was too convenient to be a coincidence.

"You're worried," she said, breaking into his thoughts.

He smiled at her. "Nothing major," he said. "Just thinking. We're going to see the Alamo. No worries for today, at least. Okay?"

She grinned. "Okay!"

They walked around the old fort like tourists, holding hands and watching leaves drift down out of the trees.

"It's going to be Halloween next week," he pointed out.

She grinned at him. "Are we going trick-or-treating, then?"

He burst out laughing. "Oh, that would be one for the books, wouldn't it?"

"I used to go when I was a little girl," she recalled. "Mom and Dad would drive me up to some of the nice neighborhoods in San Antonio door-to-door so that I could get candy. We had only a couple of close neighbors, and they didn't celebrate it at all."

"Paulie and I went with a bunch of the guys from our neighborhood," Mikey recalled. "This one house, a little old lady always invited us in for hot chocolate. It was a hoot. She'd been a Hollywood agent in her younger days. She could tell some stories!"

"I'll bet!"

"I imagine kids in Jacobsville have a great time at Halloween. And the other holidays."

"They do. Christmas is the best time, though. They stretch garlands of holly and lights all over the streets and across them. There are Christmas trees everywhere, and the local toy store has trains running in the window." She sighed. "It's just magic."

He chuckled. His hand tightened on hers. "Grandma always made Christmas special for me and Paulie," he said. "Of course, we had to go with her to midnight mass every Christmas Eve and it went on for a couple of hours. You know how kids are. We squirmed and suffered, but we didn't dare complain. She was scary for a tiny little old lady," he added.

She smiled. "I know what you mean." Her eyes were sad. "My grandmother was so sweet. She was always baking for people who had family die and sitting with sick people. She was wonderful. My grandfather was violent and dangerous. Daddy said he'd been in trouble with the law a lot when he was a young man. But I never thought he'd do something so terrible."

"Listen, kid, lots of people do terrible things they never planned. Kids get on drugs and kill people. Old people get dementia and kill people. Alcoholics get behind the wheels of cars and kill people. I don't think most of them go out with the idea that they'll do harm. It just happens."

"I've never used drugs," she said.

He laughed softly. "Why am I not surprised?"

She leaned her head against his arm. "I'm predictable."

"Very. I love it," he whispered.

She drew in a long breath. "I've never been so happy in my whole life."

"Neither have I, baby," he said gently.

She looked up at him and he looked back, and the world vanished.

It took a car horn out in the street to snap them back to reality, and they both laughed.

They walked through the dark halls of the Alamo, paused at the door to the Long Barracks, looked at the graffiti on the walls where the last stand had been held. They were solemn as they filed into the gift shop for souvenirs.

"It's a sad history," she commented.

"Most history's sad," he returned. "Life is violent."

"I suppose it is."

"What would you like?" he teased, indicating the gifts in the glass display case. "Come on. Be daring. Pick out something outrageous."

She looked up at him, searching his dark eyes. She looked down into the shelves and when the saleslady came over, she indicated a pretty inlaid turquoise ring."

Mikey's hand tightened on hers. "Yes," he said under his breath.

The saleslady handed it to her and she started to try it on her right hand, but Mikey stopped her and slid it onto her left ring finger, his eyes holding hers. It was a perfect fit.

"We'll take it," Mikey said.

The saleslady took the credit card he handed her while Bernie touched the pretty ring.

"You can think of it as an engagement ring until we can do the thing right," he whispered at her forehead.

She caught her breath and fought tears as she looked up into hungry dark eyes.

"An engagement ring?" she asked.

"I can't let you go," he said quietly. "I'd have no life left. Whatever happens."

She bit her lower lip. "Whatever happens, Mikey," she whispered huskily.

And just that simply, they were engaged.

Mrs. Brown cried when she saw the ring and heard the story. "It's a lovely ring!" she said.

"Not a diamond just yet," Mikey chuckled, "but it's standing in for one. I have to text Paulie and tell him." He bent and kissed Bernie's cheek. "I have to go up to San Antonio tomorrow, but we'll do this again next weekend, okay?"

"Okay," she said softly.

"I'll see you at breakfast in the morning, honey. You sleep well."

She reached up and kissed his own cheek. "You, too."

He laughed. "I doubt I'll sleep a wink." He grinned, smiled at Mrs. Brown, and went along to his room.

"Congratulations," Mrs. Brown said.

Bernie hugged her. "I'm so happy!" she exclaimed. And then the tears did, finally, fall.

Bernie showed her ring off at work. Olivia was overjoyed, so was Glory. And when Sari saw it, she just hugged Bernie.

"He's never been the sort of man who wanted to settle down and get serious about anyone," Sari told Bernie. "But I can see why he wants that with you."

"Me and my limitations," Bernie said with a sigh. "He could have any woman he wanted, you know. Somebody young and beautiful and, well, whole."

"Oh, you'll be fine," Jessie said, and she even smiled. "Men don't think about obstacles, you know. They just plow right ahead when they want something. Congrats," she added.

"Thanks," Bernie replied.

Jessie noticed that nobody thought she was the least bit insincere. Which worked to her advantage.

Later in the day, Billie alerted her to the fact that Mikey was at the courthouse with his cousin Paul, talking to a man in a black suit.

"I'm going to lunch early so I'll be here when all of you leave, is that all right?" Jessie asked them.

"Sure," Glory said.

"I won't be long," she added, and smiled again. They were so gullible, she thought smugly as she left. Nobody suspected a thing.

Mikey was by himself while Paul and the man in the suit went into an office nearby. Jessie walked up to him.

"Hi," she said breezily. "How's it going? We heard about the engagement. Congratulations!"

He grinned. "Thanks."

She sighed. "I know you'll be happy with her." She made a face. "It's just, she was talking about your past, you know? I couldn't help but overhear."

He felt his face go taut. "About my past?"

"She's such a straight arrow," she continued. "It's not surprising that she'd be upset when she knew your family had ties to organized crime. She said she gave her word and she'd keep it, but she didn't know how she was going to live with a man who was accused of murder, a man who lived with other men who killed people without guilt." She smiled sadly. "I'm really sorry. I guess I shouldn't have mentioned it..."

"No, it's okay," he said. "Really."

"She'd never tell you herself," Jessie added. "She's so sweet." She grimaced. "It will be hard for her to get used to another way of life. But, hey, she's young. She'll adjust, right?"

"Right," he said, but he didn't look convinced.

She glanced at her watch. "Oops, I'll be late getting back. I dropped by to see what Billie wanted for lunch. I'm bringing it to her." She smiled at him. "I've got two uncles who worked for a local crime boss in New York," she said. She shrugged. "I don't have a problem with it. But some people, you know, they don't quite understand the life. See you."

"Yeah. See you."

She walked toward Billie's office, feeling proud. She'd just put the first stick in the spokes of his relationship with Bernie. She had him off balance. Now it was just a matter of keeping him that way for some people she and Billie knew.

The next step was to talk to Bernie and make a similar confession to her about Mikey. Funny how easy it was to make them believe things about each other. But she knew people like Mikey. He'd never ask Bernie directly if she'd said such things because he wouldn't really want to know. He'd be afraid to hurt her feelings by accusing her of it, and of course she'd deny it— because it wasn't true. But he'd have doubts. Big doubts. Jessie was going to make them even bigger.

Chapter Twelve

Mikey went back to San Antonio with Paulie to talk to the feds, and he was morose. Could Bernie feel that way about his lifestyle and not be willing to tell him? She'd certainly been shocked when he'd told her about the man who'd killed Paulie's family. Well, he hadn't confessed that he'd ordered the hit—although he had. What he'd told her was enough to shock her, even without that. Had he been too truthful? Maybe he should have waited until they knew each other much better before he confessed just how full of violence and turmoil his life had been.

"Sari ever have a problem with your past?" he asked his cousin, who was driving them in a

Bucar, the designation of a bureau vehicle used by the FBI.

Paul frowned. "Well, she wasn't overjoyed, if that's what you mean. She's an assistant district attorney, you know. A real straight arrow. I guess it bothered her some, but she loved me enough not to let it matter. Why? Is Bernie having second thoughts? She told Sari the two of you just got engaged."

"We did. But I told her a lot of it," Mikey said quietly. "She's got violence in her own past, something tragic. But hers was the result of an unbalanced relative. I'm not unbalanced. I've been a bad boy, Paulie. I'm not sure she can make a life with me, the way she is."

"You should talk to her."

"And say what? That I'll change? That I'll go straight and sell out my family? Fat chance, and you know why. You get in this racket for life. Nobody gets out except feet first."

"Marcus Carrera did," he was reminded.

"Yeah, Carrera. Well, he was a big fish and people were scared to death of him. Sure he got out. He always made his own rules. I'm not Carrera. I'm a small fry, compared to him."

"You own a casino in Vegas," Paul reminded

him drily. "You drive a Rolls back home. You've got millions in overseas banks. And people are scared of you, too, kiddo."

"No kidding?"

"No kidding."

One corner of his mouth pulled down. "Well, that won't matter much if I turn my back on the outfit."

"Sadly, no, it won't. Hey, there's always the witness protection program," Paul teased.

"I noticed how well that worked out for the guy who squealed on the big bosses. He got hit right in protective custody, now, didn't he?" Mikey chuckled.

"He did."

"You don't get out. Hell, I don't want to get out," Mikey muttered. "It's the only life I've ever known, from the time we were kids. I like being part of a big family. I like the style and the cachet."

"Will Bernie like it? She's more of a butterflies and wildflowers girl than she is a showgirl."

"Yeah. I know that. But she's so sweet, Paulie," he replied heavily. "She's the sweetest human being I've ever known. And I don't think I can give her up, unless she wants me to. Even then, I don't know how I'd go on without her. It's only been a few weeks and I'm lonely when I'm not with her."

"It was that way with me when I was mooning over Sari and thinking how hopeless it all was. She was worth two hundred million, and I worked for wages."

"You're still working for wages," Mikey pointed out.

"I'm not a sit-at-home type of guy. I love my job." He glanced at Mikey. "So what are you going to do?"

"Rock along until I'm sure she can cope. Then I'm getting her to the nearest justice of the peace before she changes her mind," he chuckled.

Bernie, meanwhile, was still basking in the glory of her first proposal and looking forward to years of happiness with Mikey.

The others were getting ready to go to lunch. Bernie got to her feet a little unsteadily and picked up her cane.

"Rough day, huh?" Jessie asked in a gentle tone.

"Just a little," Bernie confessed. "I had a bad

fall on my way home the other day. A car went out of control and almost hit me."

"Gosh, here in Jacobsville? People need to learn to drive!" Jessie muttered.

"Just what I was thinking."

"Bernie, we'll wait for you outside," Glory called as they went out the door.

"Be right there," she said, reaching for her purse.

"Mikey was in the courthouse when I went to take Billie her lunch," Jessie said. She made a face. "I really shouldn't tell you what I over-heard him say to his cousin."

Bernie's heart dropped in her chest. "What?" she asked, and sounded a little breathless with worry.

Jessie sighed. "He told his cousin that he was worried about what you'd be like in a few years, because his grandmother had what you've got, and she was twisted like tree roots and almost helpless. He said that it was going to be hard to live with somebody who was sick so much. But that he'd made a promise and he was going to keep it. He said he was going to marry you be-cause he gave his word. But that it was going to be like pulling teeth. He was used to women who could keep up with the pace. He went all over the world on trips for his family, vacationed in foreign countries. He didn't know how you'd manage the travel. It was hard for a healthy woman, but you'd never keep up. He said," she added with sad eyes, "that he'd rushed in because he was infatuated with you, and then it was too late to turn back after he'd thought about the difficulties."

"I see." Bernie's heart was beating like a drum. She felt sick inside.

"I knew I shouldn't have told you," Jessie groaned. "I'm sorry. But I thought you should know. I mean, he'd never tell you himself."

"Of course, he wouldn't."

"Please don't tell him I told you," Jessie pleaded. "I don't want to make an enemy of him. He gets even with people. You don't know how dangerous he is," she added. "I come from up north. I've heard things about him. He scares people. Even bad people." She laughed hollowly. "I don't want to end up floating down a river..."

Bernie felt sick inside. Even Mikey had hinted at something of the sort, that he had power in his organization. She remembered what he'd said about taking care of the man who'd killed Paul's first wife and his child. It chilled her. "No, of course I won't tell."

"Thanks. I'm truly sorry. I know you're crazy about him."

Bernie managed a smile. She didn't answer. She went out onto the street with her coworkers and pretended that nothing at all had happened. But she was devastated.

Jessie smiled to herself. She was going to reap rich rewards for her little acts of "kindness." Throwing Mikey off balance had been the first step. Now she had Bernie doubting. The next thing was going to happen just as they'd planned it. And soon.

They spent all too much time in the Jacobs County courthouse, Mikey was thinking as he waited for Paulie to come out of an office where he was comparing notes with a contact in the probate judge's office.

He was staring at a plaque on the wall, denoting the building of the courthouse almost sixty years ago, and the names of the men on the county commission who'd authorized the construction. Farther down the wall were portraits of judges, many long gone. He was bored out of his mind.

"Fancy seeing you here again," Jessie said with a smile. She was carrying a box with food and a cup of coffee in it. "I came to bring lunch to poor Billie. She hurt her foot and she can't walk far."

"How're you doing?" he asked, and smiled, because she really did seem to have changed in the past week or so.

She shrugged. "Can't complain. It's just hard to get used to these Texans," she laughed. "They aren't like people up north."

"Nobody's like people up north. Where you from?"

She hesitated. "Upstate New York originally. You?"

"Jersey," he said. He grinned. "Doesn't the accent give it away?"

"It does, sort of." She cocked her head and studied him. "I've heard of your family. You were an underboss to Tony Garza, weren't you? Shame about him. He was a decent guy."

"He still is," Mikey said.

"I'm truly sorry that Bernie has such a hard time with your lifestyle..." She stopped and gritted her teeth. "Didn't mean to say that," she added quickly.

He scowled. "What did you mean?"

"Well, it's just," she hesitated. "Bernie doesn't understand the world you come from and she's afraid of it."

He felt his heart sinking. "She told you that?" he asked suspiciously.

"Of course not. She'd never talk to me about you," she said. "I told you about it before, re- member? I heard her talking to Olivia, the other paralegal in our office. She said she was crazy about you, but that she wasn't sure she could cope with the way you made your living. She said she'd never fit in with a bunch of, well, criminals."

He could barely get words out. The pain went all the way through him. He'd wondered about the way Bernie accepted what he was, that she said it wouldn't matter. But she was a girl who'd never cheated in anything. She had a tragic past that predisposed her to loving the police. After all, they'd saved her and her father from a po- tential killer after the tragedy her grandfather had caused.

Apparently he hadn't been thinking straight at

all. Rather, he'd been thinking with his heart instead of his brain. Bernie wasn't like him. They had different backgrounds, and she didn't understand the forces that honed his family into a criminal element over the years. The scandals of the Kennedy era, the unmasking of the five families, the scattering of bosses had been a wholesale offensive against organized crime. And it had largely succeeded. There were still bosses like Tony, who commanded power, but there was no more real commission that met and decided on who got hit, who had which territory, which politicians to support. Now the bosses were largely autonomous until they crossed the line. Nobody liked drawing attention to the outfit that was left, and people who did it got punished. Mostly, the days of wiping out a man's relatives to make a point were over. But there were still renegades who paid insults back with blood. Cotillo was one of those. That would never really end so long as there were power-mad people in the loop.

"I'm sorry," Jessie was saying. "I shouldn't have said anything."

"It isn't anything I wasn't already thinking," he confessed.

"You live in the fast lane. Fast cars, fast women, easy money," she said. "Bernie likes band concerts in the park and watching television in her room." Her mouth twisted. "Not a good mix."

"No." He wished he could forget what she'd told him about Bernie, the other day and now. But he knew it was true. He'd seen the way Bernie had reacted when he described his life to her. She'd said she could cope, that it wouldn't matter. It would matter.

"Please don't tell Bernie I said anything to you," she said softly. "I'd hate to have her mad at me now that we're getting along so well."

"I won't mention it to her," he said absently, and he was thinking that there was no way he could discuss it with Bernie without putting her on the defensive, making her ashamed of her feelings. He couldn't blame her. His lifestyle would be hard for any woman unless she came from a similar background. He'd been living in a dream. It was a sweet dream. But it wasn't real.

"I'd better get Billie's lunch to her. Nice seeing you." She walked away with a smile. It wouldn't do to lay it on with a trowel.

Paul came out of the probate judge's office with a worried look. He fell in beside Mikey and they walked outside. "Harvey," he said, referring to his contact inside, "told me that Billie and Jessie at Sari's office came down here at the same time. It's a little too cozy for coincidence."

"You think they're Cotillo's?" Mikey asked.

"They could be. We're going to do a thorough background search on all of them. What about that car that barely missed Bernie? Did she tell you anything about it?"

He shook his head and stuck his hands in his slacks pockets. "Only that it was a dark sedan. It happened too fast." He glanced at Paul. "Do you know about Bernie's grandfather and what he did?"

Paul nodded. "Tragic thing to happen to a child. There was a serious attempt on her father's life not long after it happened, by a member of a victim's family. He's doing time."

"She said it might have been somebody like that, trying to scare her." Mikey frowned. "It's not Cotillo's style, you know? He has people hit if he has a problem with them, like he tried to hit Tony and me. He doesn't make threats."

"Neither do you," Paul mused.

"Hey, I am what I am." He strolled along beside Paul. "I've been having second thoughts about this engagement," he confessed.

"What?" Paul stopped in the middle of the sidewalk. "But you're crazy about Bernie. She's crazy about you!"

Mikey took a breath and smiled cynically. "She likes small towns and band concerts, Paulie. She's never been in trouble with the law in her life. How's she going to like jetsetting, mixing with celebrities and crooks, wearing designer clothes, traveling around the world with me when I've got people to meet? How's she going to feel if I ever get arrested for something?"

Paul took a deep breath of his own. "I don't know. I don't live in that world. I never did."

"Well, I do. I have to." He grimaced. "And there's her health to consider. I remember our grandmother. She got twisted like a tree in a hurricane. She was in bed most of the time at the end. She got upset and she had flares, remember that? Bernie would be stressed-out all the time. It would affect her health."

"You've done a lot of thinking," Paul said. He wasn't saying anything, but his tone was full of curiosity and suspicion.

"Yeah. She's the sweetest woman I've ever known. I'd like her to stay that way. Involved with me for life? It would…kill something in her."

Paul didn't speak. He knew that Mikey's lifestyle involved stress. But he'd never seen Mikey involved with any woman to the extent he was involved with Bernie. He thought that love would resolve all those issues. Mikey clearly didn't.

"What are you going to do?" Paul asked.

"Ease off. Just a little at a time, so it doesn't look like I'm shooting her out of my life." He smiled sadly. "I want her to be happy. I can't give her the sort of life she deserves."

"You, being unselfish. Call the journalists," Paul drawled.

Mikey chuckled. "Out of character, isn't it?" he agreed.

Paul threw an arm around him. "Not anymore, it isn't, cuz," he said quietly. "But I'm sorry for both of you."

"Me, too," Mikey said. His eyes were solemn. "Me, too."

Mikey and Bernie were subdued at supper at Mrs. Brown's. Neither spoke much although they went through the motions of participating in the conversation.

But afterward, when Bernie started toward her room, Mikey stopped her.

"Listen," he began quietly, "I've been thinking—"

"Me, too," she interrupted.

She looked as uncomfortable as he did.

He shoved his hands into his pockets and felt his heart breaking inside him. He wanted to say something, but what could he say? His life wasn't butterflies and roses. And, realistically, she wasn't the sort of woman who could adjust to partying and casinos and jet travel and organized crime. It was impossible, but he hadn't realized it until Jessie told him what Bernie had said.

He looked down at her tenderly. She was so unworldly. It would be like her not to want to hurt his feelings or make him feel bad about what his world was like.

She was thinking the same thing about him, that he didn't want to hurt her feelings by admitting that he couldn't live with a woman who might be an invalid one day, a woman who could barely keep up with him on a slow walk in the woods. He needed somebody vibrant and healthy, who could thrive in his company, not a woman who would limit his activities.

"It might be an idea to cool it, just for a little while," Mikey said finally. "I've got people working on that car that almost hit you. We'll find out who it was."

"Probably somebody drunk who misjudged the curb," she replied with a faint smile. "It's a small town. Odd things happen here."

His dark eyes seemed even darker as they searched her light ones. "I've never enjoyed anything more than this time with you."

"Me, either," she confessed, and tried not to show that she was dying inside.

"But we need to give each other a little space. Just for now," he added quickly so it didn't sound like he was trying to dump her. He couldn't bear to hurt her feelings.

She nodded. "It's a good idea." She fingered the ring that stood in place of an engagement ring. She started to take it off.

His big hand went over both of hers. "No," he said, and sounded choked. "You keep that. You keep it forever. Think of me when you wear it."

She looked up, fighting tears. "I'll never forget you. No matter what."

"Yeah. It's like that with me, too." He hesitated. "Santi doesn't like having me apart from him at night, the way things are going."

Her eyes widened with worry. "They haven't sent somebody else after you...?" she asked almost frantically.

He almost bit his lip through. That soft concern made him hate himself. "No," he lied quickly. Some quick thinking by Paulie and the feds had saved him, already. "It's just that he thinks a bodyguard should stay with the boss, and he can't live in the room with me here. So... well, I'm moving over to the motel, and Santi and I can have adjoining rooms."

Her heart sank. She'd gotten used to seeing him at the table when they had meals, in the hallway, everywhere. "That's probably a good idea," she said softly. She looked up. "You take care of yourself, okay?"

His big hand touched her cheek. "You do that, too. Don't go out alone after dark. Be aware of your surroundings."

"I always do that. Well, almost always," she

TEXAS PROUD

amended. "But the car came out of nowhere. I didn't even hear it coming."

That wasn't surprising. Most newer model cars had quiet engines. It still bothered him that it didn't sound like an accident. Paul was checking. If there was anything sinister, he'd find it.

"So," Mikey said. "I'll see you around."

She forced a smile. "Yes. Well, goodbye."

She went into her room, resisting the urge to look behind her. She closed the door and let the tears fall silently. It was the biggest pain of her life, almost as bad as knowing what her grandfather had done, losing her sweet grandmother and the community where she'd grown up. It was like losing a loved one.

Outside the door, Mikey was feeling something similar. But he had to do it. If he stayed here, seeing her every day, he'd go nuts. He couldn't keep away from her, not unless he distanced himself from her. It was the hardest thing he'd ever done in his life. It was the only thing he could do. Bernie couldn't live with the man he was. He didn't blame her. It was just that she was the only woman he'd ever wanted to live with him.

He let out a weary breath and went into his room to pack.

* * *

"You moved out of the boardinghouse," Paul remarked a week later, when Mikey was having supper with him and Sari while Mandy bustled around in the kitchen making a cake.

"Yeah," Mikey said. He moved his cup around in the saucer. "Santi kept harping on it. He said he couldn't protect me if he was several blocks away. I finally listened."

Paul, remembering an earlier conversation, knew what the truth was. Mikey was distancing himself from Bernie, removing temptation.

Sari glanced at Mikey's lowered head and started to speak, but a sharp jerk of the head from Paul silenced her. Instead, she started talking about a reality show she and Paul had been watching lately.

After Mikey went back to his motel, Sari questioned Paul about his odd behavior.

"He's doing it for her own good," Paul said on a sigh. "He thinks she couldn't cope with his lifestyle. You know, Isabel, it's not the same life as this one. Not at all. He's in constant company with people who break the law. He travels in high social circles just the same, rubs elbows with movie stars and politicians and gamblers.

He couldn't settle down here if his life depended on it—well, except briefly, like he's having to do now. But Bernie would never fit into that sort of world."

Sari met his eyes and nodded sadly. "But she was so happy," she said softly. "Bright as the sun. She almost radiated with it. And now she's so quiet we hardly know she's around. She never jokes and smiles anymore."

"Neither does my cousin," Paul said. He pulled her close. "You and I came from different worlds, but we worked it out, because we loved one another. You can tell how Mikey and Bernie feel about each other just by looking at them. Why couldn't they work it out, too?"

"I don't know," she said with a sigh. She laid her head against his broad chest. "What about the sudden residents? Any new intel on them?"

"Not a lot," he confessed. "Jessie and her friend Billie are both from New York originally. They do have mob ties, but not to Cotillo or Tony Garza. Their connections aren't apparent, but we're trying to run them down. There's still a family that operates in New York, even covertly, but it's fragmented and the boss is in prison."

"He can still run it from prison. It's not even hard."

"True. He has an underboss holding power for him. Jessie may have something to do with him. That wouldn't necessarily mean she or the boss favored Cotillo. He's an outsider and he does a bloody business. You know how well that goes over in mob circles. They don't like attention. Cotillo's getting them a lot of it."

"Wouldn't it be lovely if somebody in one of the old outfit families decided to take Cotillo out of the equation?" she asked on a sigh. "Shame on me. I work for the court system. I should be ashamed."

"Yes, you bad girl." He kissed her hungrily. "You need to be severely reprimanded. Come right over here and I'll do my best."

She laughed as he tugged her down onto the bed. "Oh, this is a reprimand I'm going to love," she teased.

He chuckled as he started to remove her gown. "You bet, you're going to love it!"

The driver of the car that almost hit Bernie was a local businessman who'd had three drinks too many out at Shea's Bar and misjudged the curb, just as Bernie had figured. He turned himself in to Cash Grier with many apologies and Cash got him into rehab.

Bernie listened to Cash's explanation in the office a couple of weeks after Mikey had moved out of the boardinghouse.

"I thought it was something like that," she said quietly. "I mean, if people in organized crime want to hurt you, they just kill you, don't they?"

"More or less." They were alone in the office. It was just after lunch and the other women hadn't returned. "What about you and Mikey? I thought that was going to be permanent."

She flushed. "I'm not healthy," she said. "His grandmother had what I've got. She was an invalid, bedridden, when she was old. I'm likely to end up in that condition a lot sooner." She fought down panic at the thought that she might not even be able to work. She was far too proud to ask for government relief, even though she might one day be forced into it.

"There are new drugs," he pointed out.

She smiled sadly. "Chief Grier, the sort you're talking about costs over a thousand dollars a month. They do have programs to help people afford them, but it isn't that much of a reduction."

He grimaced.

"I get by. My rheumatologist has me on a regimen of medicines that mostly take care of the pain. I have flares, days when I can't get out of bed, and I have to use a cane from time to time. But there are lots of people worse off. Look at Glory in my office, and what she had to go through in her life. She still limps from time to time because her hip was broken long ago and it has arthritis in it, and her blood pressure is controlled but still subject to spikes. She lives with it. I live with my problems."

"But you don't think Mikey could?" he fished, his eyes piercing hers.

She toyed with a pen on her desk. "He was overheard telling his cousin that he wasn't sure that he could." She looked up. "Don't you dare repeat that, ever. It would hurt his feelings. He can't help what he thinks. He lives with glitzy people, rides in limousines, travels all over the world. I'm lucky if I can get from work to my boardinghouse without falling over my feet. How would I fit into that sort of lifestyle? I'd be a sparrow among peacocks, if you see what I mean."

He did see. But she was a sweet, kind woman. "If he loves you, it won't matter."

"That's the thing, though," she continued. "He said it would be better if we sort of let things cool off. And he's probably right. He has enough problems right now. They won't kill him, will they?" she asked, and looked agonized by the thought.

"He has powerful friends," he replied. "Marcus Carrera is one of them. Carrera runs a legitimate operation in the Bahamas, but he wasn't always a good guy, and his reputation still strikes fear in people who knew him back in the day." He chuckled. "He's got Tony Garza so surrounded by experienced mercs that only a suicidal maniac would try to get to him."

"Sari said that Mr. Garza gave her sister away at her wedding to that Wyoming rancher," Bernie said.

"He did. He's not what he seems." He cocked his head and studied her. "Neither is Mikey. His reputation is fearsome. But he's not as bad as people think he is."

"He was arrested once, though," she said.

He nodded. "And charged with attempted murder. But the charges were dropped," he reminded her. "Nobody's ever been able to bring him to trial on a major crime. For a man who operates outside the law, he's amazingly conventional."

She smiled sadly. "He's amazing, period," she said softly. "I'll never forget him." As she spoke, she twisted the turquoise-and-silver ring he'd given her. She wore it on her right hand, though, not her left. She didn't want it to get back to him that she considered herself engaged, not when he was backing away.

Cash muttered something about men being fools, smiled, and left her.

"What in the hell is wrong with you?" Cash asked Mikey when he saw him with Paul at Barbara's Café one day at lunch.

Mikey's eyebrows raised. "Excuse me?"

"You have almost as much money in foreign banks as I do," Cash said as he joined them for coffee and pie. "You could easily afford the newest treatments for rheumatoid arthritis, whatever they cost."

Mikey stared at him. "I don't have arthritis."

"Bernie does."

Mikey averted his eyes. "I know."

"She wouldn't let him, though," Paul said, and

he was giving Cash expression cues that asked him to cool it. "She's too proud."

"Besides that, we're not... Well, we're not an item anymore," Mikey added. "She has her life, I have mine."

"Yes, but she..." Cash continued, ignoring Paul.

Before he could finish the sentence, Jessie came in the door, spotted Mikey and came right to the table, smiling.

"Don't forget, you're taking me to Don Alfonso's for supper, right?" she asked.

Mikey chuckled. "You bet, doll. Santi and I will pick you up about five."

"I thought maybe you could drive us both and leave Santi at home," she said with a husky laugh.

"Sorry. Santi drives, I don't."

"Well, okay. It doesn't matter. I'll be ready on time. Hi, Chief Grier. Mr. Fiore," she added, a little unsettled when Paul just glared at her without speaking. "See you later."

She went to the counter to pick up her order. Paul glared at Mikey with much more venom than he'd shown the gorgeous, well-dressed woman waiting for her order.

"She doesn't mind riding around with a criminal," Mikey said sarcastically. "She loves casinos and fancy restaurants and she's classy enough to take to ritzy gatherings. So?"

"You're about to ruin your life," Paul said curtly. "What if Bernie finds out? Jessie works in the office with her, for God's sake!"

"I told you," Mikey said, averting his eyes. "Bernie and I are no longer an item. I can date any woman I like. Jessie's not so bad."

But Paul was thinking that Jessie was every bit as bad as she seemed. She was rubbing Bernie's nose in the fact that she had Mikey's attention. Not only that, she was pressuring Mikey to be alone with her, without Santi. That was suspicious. Very suspicious. He glanced at a taciturn Cash Grier and had the impression that the police chief was thinking the same thing.

"I need a night on the town, anyway," Mikey said as he finished his pie and washed it down with coffee. "I've been vegetating down here in cowboy town."

"You watch your step," Paul said shortly. "Don't forget that Cotillo may have people here that we don't even know about."

"Surely you don't think Jessie's one of them?"

Mikey drawled. "You checked her out and found no connections to any of Cotillo's people."

"Yeah, I checked out our last limo driver, too, and he almost got Merrie killed because the perp had connections I didn't ferret out," he was reminded.

"I can handle myself," Mikey reminded him curtly.

"You'd better have a concealed carry permit if you walk around with a weapon in my town," Cash told him humorously, but with a cold glint in his eyes.

"I got one the second day I was in town, for your information," Mikey said smugly. "I know you, Grier. No way I'm stepping out of line around here!"

Cash just chuckled.

Paul cornered him after Grier left, while they were waiting on the sidewalk for Santi to collect Mikey.

"This is going to ruin any chance you have of getting back together with Bernie," he told his cousin. "You know that, right?"

Mikey's eyes were hollow with pain. "She

can't live with a crook, Paulie," he said shortly. "That's what she said."

Paul's lower jaw fell. "She said that to you?"

"Of course, she didn't say it to me! She wouldn't hurt my feelings for anything. But she was overheard saying it," he added, and flushed, remembering who'd told him. "There's Santi. I gotta go. See you around, cuz."

"Watch your back!" Paul called after him.

Mikey waved and climbed into the limo.

Paul stood watching it pull away from the curb. Something Mikey had said piqued his curiosity. He was going to speak to Sari about it when he got home.

Chapter Thirteen

Sari was going over a brief when Paul walked into the study and closed the door.

"What's up?" she asked, because he looked worried.

"Did Bernie say anything to you about having an issue with Mikey's background?" he asked curiously.

"No," she replied. She grimaced. "But she doesn't really discuss Mikey with me," she added. "I guess she thinks I might tell him what she said." She put down the pencil she was using to edit the document she was working on. "Why?"

"He said she told somebody that she couldn't

live with a man who made his living outside the law, with a criminal," he replied. "Would she tell somebody at work something so personal?" he persisted.

She frowned. "Well, I don't really think so. Bernie's a very private person. She's not the kind to blurt out intimate details of her life to people she works with. It's not the way she is. And there's not really anybody else she might tell, either. She has no close friends."

"That's what I thought. Mikey has the impression that she can't live with his past."

"I know that's not true," Sari said gently. "She loves him."

One side of his mouth pulled down. "I tried to tell him that. He wouldn't listen. He's destroying any chance that he could get back together with Bernie."

"How?"

"He's taking your coworker Jessie out on the town in San Antonio tonight," he said through his teeth.

"Oh, no!"

"I tried to warn him. It will ruin everything. But he wouldn't listen. He's convinced that he's so bad, only a bad woman would ever want him."

"What an idiot. Even if he is your cousin."

"Hey, no argument from me. I said the same thing, to his face."

"It will kill Bernie if she finds out."

He laughed coldly. "If? Jessie will tell the world tomorrow. I don't doubt she'll embroider it into something even more than it is."

"Jessie." Sari made a rough sound. "She was our worst nightmare for weeks. Then overnight she turned into a caring, worrying coworker who did everything she could to make things easier for us."

"And all an act," Paul said. "I can see right through her. I wish Mikey could."

"I didn't. Neither did Bernie or Glory or Olivia," Sari said.

"I've spent my life with people who bend the truth. I'm good at recognizing phonies."

"Poor Bernie."

"Poor Mikey, when he finally realizes he's been had," Paul said flatly. "I'm checking out an acquaintance of Jessie's in Upstate New York. I have a suspicion that she didn't just happen down here with her friend Billie."

"What about the cook from New Jersey who's working in Barbara's Café?"

He laughed. "I'll tell you about that," he said. "It's a hoot." And he did tell her.

"Now, this is my kind of place," Jessie said as they were seated in the five-star restaurant.

"Mine, too," Mikey said, but without any real enthusiasm. He studied the gorgeous woman across from him with only vague interest. She was wearing a couture cocktail dress with diamond earrings, necklace, bracelet and several rings. All diamonds. The best quality and set in 18 karat gold. He knew, because he'd spent a fortune on them for various women over the years. He was curious about how she afforded that kind of jewelry on a receptionist's salary.

Even as he had the thought, he felt cold chills inside. He was carrying. He had a snub .38 in a pancake holster behind his back, and a hidden gun in an ankle holster. He never went anywhere without being armed. Would he need to be? Santi was at the next table, apparently oblivious, but watching.

Odd, how he suddenly remembered that if the family ordered a hit on you, they sent your best friend to do it. He was warned that if he didn't, somebody else would, and he'd end up as dead as the intended victim. His blood ran cold as he stared at Santi.

But his bodyguard just grinned at him and went to work on a huge plate of spaghetti. He was getting paranoid, Mikey considered, just like his old man.

He remembered his father with loathing. The man had been a dirty jobs soldier for the underboss in New Jersey, the one who'd preceded Tony Garza. Mikey's dad had killed men over and over again, never felt the least remorse, and spent his life at a local bar where the outfit hung out. Mikey rarely saw him, and if he ever did, his father treated him like a disease. He hated Mikey and made no secret of the fact that he thought the kid was some other man's son. Mikey's mother, long dead, had an affair, he'd told the boy one day, and Mikey was the result. It was to get even with him for something he'd done to her. So Mikey had no real family at all until his maternal grandmother, Paulie's grandmother, too, took both boys in and raised them. The old lady was Greek. She still spoke the old language. Mikey and Paulie had been schooled in Italian by the other kids and the families they associated with, but their grandmother taught them Greek, as well. Mikey could even read in it. Not a lot of people knew that. He kept his intelligence hidden; it gave him an advantage if his colleagues thought he was stupid.

"How was it you heard what Bernie said in the office?" he asked out of the blue.

Jessie's hand, which was holding her wineglass, jerked, but she recovered quickly. "Oh, she and Olivia didn't know I was there," she replied. "I'd just come out of Mr. Kemp's office and they were in the hallway."

"I see." He didn't know Bernie well, but it seemed unlike her to confide something so personal to an office worker, even one she was close to. She was, like him, a very private person.

"This place is nice," she said, changing the subject. She smiled at him alluringly. "You know, I have the use of a friend's apartment here in town," Her voice changed to a throaty purr. "We could be all alone there."

Mikey just stared at her. His dark eyes were cold, as cold as they'd ever been when he had another man at gunpoint. "Really?"

His glare disconcerted her. "You know, Bernie won't change her mind, and she'll never tell you what she really thinks of you," she said.

He cocked his head. "You're trying too hard."

"Excuse me?"

He just laughed, but it had a hollow sound. He was just beginning to believe he'd been had. And he was out with this jeweled barracuda, who would go back to the office Monday and tell Bernie all about this date, probably with some embroidering. He took a big sip of his Chianti and cursed himself silently through the rest of the meal.

"Oh, it was the most wonderful date!" Jessie enthused to the other women, including Bernie, the following Monday. "Mikey made me feel like a princess! And we went to this apartment a friend loans me..." She stopped when Bernie's face went white. "I'm so sorry, that was cruel," she added in a conciliatory tone. "But you know how he feels about you, honey."

"She knows what you told her," Olivia replied, her eyes narrow and suspicious.

"Odd, how you knew something so personal," Sari added her own comment to the discussion. "I mean, Mikey isn't the sort to discuss personal things with Paul, even in private, and Paul's the only person he's really close to."

Jessie looked uncomfortable. "It was just a comment he made—he didn't seem to think it was very personal."

Mr. Kemp's door flew open and he looked livid. "Miss Tennison!"

Jessie actually jumped. "Yes, sir?"

"Come into my office, please," he said icily.

Jessie collected herself quickly and forced a smile. "Yes, sir, at once." She jumped up and headed toward him without looking back.

"Don't you believe her," Sari told Bernie firmly. "Mikey never told Paul anything about you, not ever, in private. He would never blurt out something like that in a public place."

Bernie wasn't comforted. She forced a smile. "I could never keep up with him, don't you see?" she asked softly. "He lives in the fast lane. Some days, I can't even get out of bed. He'd get tired of it. I don't like bars and flashy places. I've never even owned an evening gown." She cocked her head and smiled at Sari. "The people in his circle would think he'd lost his mind if they ever got a look at me, and you know it."

Sari wasn't convinced. "Bernie, if somebody loves you, things like disabilities and things they've done in the past—none of it matters at all."

Bernie's green eyes were sad. "I believed that, once. But he took her out on the town," she added, indicating the door behind which Jessie was closeted with Mr. Kemp. "And he slept with her. It's over. I'm going to get on with my life. It's obvious that he's gotten on with his."

And she went back to work.

Jessie came out of Mr. Kemp's office with an absolute snarl on her face. "I'm fired," she said icily. "Just because I told that old man on the phone that Mr. Kemp didn't want to talk to him and not to go to court because I thought it was canceled that day!"

"What old man?" Olivia asked.

"Oh, some rancher named Regan."

Olivia's eyebrows arched. "Ted Regan?"

"Yes, I think that was it," Jessie muttered. She started pulling things out of desk drawers.

"Old man Regan," Sari told her, "is worth millions. He owns the second biggest ranch in Jacobs County, and properties all over the country. He's also a prime witness in a case we're prosecuting." She pursed her lips. "Or he was. I'm assuming Mr. Kemp lost the case, if you told Ted not to show up. Judge Drew was presiding and he didn't want to try the case to begin with."

Jessie just ground her teeth. "Well, it doesn't matter now, I'm fired," she muttered. She looked up and noted the pleased expressions on all the faces except Bernie's. Bernie wouldn't even look at her. "It's just as well," she commented. "I've done what I came to do. Aren't you the gullible bunch? I put on an act and all of you bought it. You pitiful little small-town people, you'll never know what life is all about."

"It's about family," Glory Ramirez said.

"It's all about family," Sari agreed. "Something you'll never understand."

"The only family I care about is the one I take orders from," Jessie muttered absently, and then looked up and flushed as she realized what she'd said. "My dad, I mean," she corrected, "and he's not from some little Texas town!"

But Sari picked up on what she'd said at once and hid her suspicions. She went back to work, ignoring Jessie.

"Well, so long," Jessie said as she carried the cardboard box with her things in it to the door. She turned and stared at Bernie. "I'll tell Mikey you said hello, Bernie," she purred. "After all, we're going to be seeing a lot of each other. I know his world and I love it. Unlike you, I don't mind being seen with him and his criminal friends," she drawled sarcastically.

Bernie felt shocked. "What do you mean?"

Jessie had slipped again. She shrugged. "Nothing at all. Goodbye."

She went out the door and closed it behind her.

Bernie didn't say a word. She brooded, though. Mikey was already involved with that vicious woman, but perhaps he liked that sort of person. Maybe he was frustrated because he'd wanted Bernie and she wasn't the sort to sleep around. But it still hurt to think of him in bed with Jessie. It hurt terribly.

"She was lying," Sari said gently.

Bernie looked up. Her eyes were sad and wise. "No, she wasn't," she said quietly. "And like I said, it doesn't matter. We were mismatched from the start. Opposites attract, don't they say, but the divorce rate for marriages like that is pretty dismal. I'd better get back to work."

Sari didn't say any more, but she was livid.

* * *

"Mikey did what?" Paul Fiore asked at supper, his fork poised in midair.

"He slept with Jessie," Sari said angrily.

He whistled, aware of Mandy's curious stare. "Well, damn, that's the end of it all."

"I know." Sari picked at her food. "Jessie was poison. I'm glad Mr. Kemp fired her. It was all an act, that sweetness and light attitude."

"No surprise, there."

"She let something slip when we were talking about families and how they mattered," Sari continued. "She said the only family she cared about was the one she took orders from."

Paul dropped the fork. "Families. Like Cotillo's."

"Maybe," Sari replied, watching him retrieve the utensil from the floor and carry it to the sink before he got another and returned to the table. "Don't you have somebody checking her out?"

"I do. I'll call him after we finish eating. Damn the luck! If she's involved with Cotillo, then her friend Billie may be, too. It's been right under our noses."

"What about that cook at Barbara's?" Mandy asked as she refilled coffee cups. She made a face at Sari. "And you should be drinking milk, not caffeine!"

Sari flushed. "Mandy…"

Mandy was grinning.

Paul, caught unaware, looked at Mandy's twinkling eyes and his own darted to his wife, looking flushed and guilty.

"Okay, spit it out," he told Sari. "What's going on that I don't know about?"

She cleared her throat and glared at Mandy. "I was going to tell you later."

"Tell me now," he persisted.

She drew in a breath. "I'm pregnant."

Paul sat very still for just a minute, then he rose, picked her up in his arms, and kissed her and kissed her, whooping in between at the top of his lungs.

Mandy pursed her lips. "Well," she said to nobody in particular, "I guess it's no secret that he's happy about it."

Bernie went home to a lonely apartment, her heart down in her shoes. Mikey was sleeping with that rat, Jessie. Mikey was a rat, too, she told herself. He'd taken her in, pretended to care about her, then backed off because she had an incurable disease.

If he'd been that concerned about her illness, why hadn't he stopped seeing her in the beginning? Why had he spent almost every day with her? Why had he bought her a ring and then asked her to marry him?

None of it made sense, unless he'd truly thought he could make it work and then decided he couldn't live with her limitations. She felt miserable. She couldn't help what was wrong with her. She couldn't cure it. Maybe she could have adjusted to travel, to his friends, to flashy places, if she'd been given the chance. But what did it matter now? She would never get over the fact that he'd promised to marry her and then cheated on her with another woman. She had too much pride.

"Are you out of your mind?" Paul demanded of Mikey the next day when they were having a quick lunch at the house.

Mikey blinked. "Excuse me?"

"Sleeping with Jessie. My God!"

Mikey's lips fell open. "Sleeping… Good

Lord, do I look crazy to you? I wouldn't touch her with a pole!"

"You took her out on the town, didn't you?" he persisted.

Mikey grimaced. "I was feeling pretty low. I needed to feel like a man again."

"Great job."

"Bernie didn't want me!" he burst out. "She said she couldn't live with a man who'd been a criminal most of his life!"

"She told you this, huh?" Paul asked.

Mikey sighed. "No. She'd never want to hurt my feelings like that. She told somebody else and she was overheard."

"Let me guess—by Jessie."

Mikey scowled. "What?"

"Jessie told Bernie that you went with her to an apartment in San Antonio."

Mikey grimaced. He could only imagine how much that had hurt Bernie. He was hurting from her rejection, but it wounded him to think he'd caused her even more pain.

"She let something else slip. She has a 'family' that she takes orders from."

Mikey lost color. "Hell!"

"I've got a man digging hard into her past.

He's hit a couple of dead ends, but he thinks he's onto something. I should have an answer today," Paul told him.

"You think she's on Cotillo's payroll."

"I think she might be," Paul replied. "Think about it. She and Billie are as out of place here as roaches in a ritzy hotel. So why are they here? Maybe to watch you and report on your movements to a third party."

"Like a cleaner," Mikey said, referring to a contract killer.

"Maybe. It depends on which family she has ties to. Cotillo's not the only man in the game. He has enemies. She's from New York. Cotillo's moving on Tony Garza in Jersey. Suppose another boss has Cotillo in his sights and wants to know if you're protected before he orders a hit."

Mikey toyed with his coffee cup. "That's a possibility."

"Cotillo's drawn a lot of attention to himself and to the outfit in general with this takeover thing. He's harking back to the mob wars in the past, which were bloody and public and ended in the congressional hearings that tore the Five Families apart. They can't really afford to make themselves too visible even today. Cotillo's a threat to them as well as to you and Tony. They might decide to act."

"If Jessie was lining up a hit, she had a perfect opportunity while we were at the restaurant," Mikey said. "Santi was at another table. Of course, I was watching the door. I know how hits go down."

"Which is why I don't think her boss is Cotillo."

Mikey drew in a long breath. "That might be." He looked into the coffee cup at the thick black liquid. "Bernie will never forgive me. I don't guess it matters. She didn't want me to begin with."

"Or so Jessie told you. She likes rich men. Kemp already called her down about it at least once. Of course, he fired her this morning."

"What?"

"She mouthed off to Ted Regan, of all people, and told him court had been canceled. Since she was calling from the DA's office, he believed her. He didn't show up and the case was thrown out of court. Kemp was livid."

"I guess so. She'll get another job, I guess."

"She and Billie left town late this afternoon," Paul replied. "I got that from Mandy. She knows everything that goes on in this town. But I'm sure Jessie will keep in touch with you," he added sarcastically. "I mean, since you're dating her and all."

"You don't understand," he burst out. "I lost everything! Bernie couldn't live with what I am, and I don't know how I'm going to live without her! Jessie kept asking if we could get a meal somewhere and I said yes. I know I shouldn't have done it. I was so damned low I didn't care about how it would look."

"Jessie is poison," Paul said. "I'd bet real money that she told Bernie some tale about you, as well, to the tune of your not being able to live with a woman who might be an invalid later on."

Mikey was very still. He just stared at his cousin.

"Think about it. She told you that Bernie hated your past. Maybe she told Bernie that you hated her disease."

"Dear God," Mikey said huskily, and buried his face in his hands. "Oh, God, what am I going to do?"

"Talk to Bernie."

Mikey removed his hands from his face and drank the coffee. "Sure. I'm going to walk into the office, and she's going to throw me out head-first, or the verbal equivalent. She thinks I slept with damned Jessie. She'll hate me."

"Sari hated me, too, when I first came back here." Paul grinned. "Remember what I did when she wouldn't speak to me?"

"Everybody in Jacobsville remembers," Mikey chuckled. "They even talked about it at the boardinghouse and it was three years ago."

"Whatever works," he commented pointedly.

Mikey drew in a breath. "I'll think about it."

"Meanwhile, I have news."

"About Cotillo?"

Paul chuckled. "Not yet. About Sari."

Mikey's eyebrows arched.

"She's pregnant," Paul said, and smiled from ear to ear.

"Damn, that's great! Absolutely great!" Mikey burst out. "I'm happy for you."

"It's the nicest surprise," Paul confessed. "We've been trying for a long time, but, well, nothing happened and I thought maybe we couldn't have kids. It wouldn't have mattered. I love her so much. I'd rather have her and no kids than the biggest family in the country with any other woman."

"I know how that feels." Mikey put his cup down. "I wanted them with Bernie. Never with anybody else. Even with her limitations, she could carry a child. I asked a doctor." He flushed. "There are medicines she can't afford that I could have bought for her, and they would have helped. She could have private duty nurses, anything she needed. I'd have...taken care of her." He stopped, choking up.

"It isn't too late."

Mikey looked up, with the saddest expression Paul had ever seen. "Yes, it is, Paulie. It's too late. And I did it to myself, by not telling her what Jessie said and giving her a chance to tell me what she felt."

"We all make mistakes."

"Even you aren't in my class, cousin," Mikey said. He leaned back in the chair. "At least you're having that happy ending people dream about," he added with an affectionate smile. "You got lucky."

"I wish you had, too."

Mikey shrugged. "Let's just hope that Cotillo doesn't."

They were prophetic words. A day later, the story broke on all the major news networks. A

New Jersey mob figure named Anthony Cotillo was found dead in his apartment of apparently natural causes. A friend said that the man had no apparent health problems and that it came as a shock to his associates.

"Can they detect an air embolism?" Mikey mused. "It doesn't matter—they'll have people in the coroner's office to make sure that doesn't go into the report."

Paul sighed. "Well, it's a novel way to take care of an interloper without getting the government all stirred up," he agreed. "No mess, no blood trail, no nothing. But I wonder who hit him?"

Mikey smiled. "Marcus Carrera has many friends from the old days," he pointed out. "Some of them owe him really big favors."

Paul's eyebrows arched.

"Really big," Mikey emphasized. And he smiled.

Tony Garza came home to New Jersey amid promises from an obscure New York outfit family that the loose association of bosses, the one that had existed since the Five Families were scattered by pressure from the feds, had no problem with him. They assured him that no more problems were expected, and that they had several people making sure of it. The message was clear—Carrera might not be a mob figure any longer, since he'd gone straight, but he was still a power to contend with in the States. A lot of people were afraid of him. Tony was going to be safe.

"So I guess I'll go home now," Mikey said sadly, when he was having supper with Paul and Sari. "I'll come back for the christening, though," he teased.

"Wrong church," Paul teased. "We're Methodist. Although, Reverend Blair does have a sort of christening ceremony, but not like the one you're thinking of."

"We can pretend. I'll come anyway." He toyed with his food. "So I guess Jessie and Billie worked for the New York boss."

"I guess so," Paul said.

"Carrera was a terror when he was younger," Mikey remarked with a smile. "You could just say his name ten years ago and people would start running for the door."

"It shocked everybody when he went legit," Paul said. "Even the feds. Now he's got a wife and two sons and he's the happiest man on earth."

"Families are nice," Mikey said absently.

"You should get married and have one," Sari said firmly.

"Chance would be a fine thing."

"You never know," she replied. "Strange things happen when you least expect them."

He smiled at her. "They do, don't they? What do you guys want, a boy or a girl?"

"Either," Paul said.

"Both," Sari said, and grinned.

"No twins on our side of the family, cousin," he told Paul.

"But there are loads on my side," Sari laughed. "Distant cousins, but at least three sets of twins among them."

"Son of a gun! You could have your whole family in one year."

Paul laughed. "Who knows?" he teased, and he looked at his wife with eyes that absolutely ate her. She looked back at him the same way.

Mikey felt more alone than he ever had in his whole life. Much more, although he was happy for his cousin. But he was leaving town. His heart would stay here, with that sad little woman who lived in Mrs. Brown's boardinghouse. She'd never forgive him for Jessie. He knew it without asking. It was the worst mistake of his life, and he couldn't fix it. Nobody could.

He packed his bags and Santi packed his. His heart was breaking. Bernie was the light of his life and he was leaving her behind. He hadn't felt so low since the death of his grandmother, and the murder of Paulie's wife and little girl. He felt the grief like a living thing.

"Where we going, boss," Santi asked. "Vegas or Jersey?"

"Vegas," Mikey said without missing a beat. "I need a diversion. A big, bright, flashy, glitzy diversion."

"Vegas is a nice place," Santi said. He grinned. "Lots of glitzy girls there."

"You're welcome to all you can find," his boss replied glumly. "You can have my share, too."

"That's nice," Santi replied.

They packed their things into the convertible. Mikey went to the office and took care of the bill. Santi was waiting just outside the door in the limousine as he came out.

Mikey put himself into the back seat and

leaned against it wearily as Santi pulled out into traffic. It was early morning, so they'd probably hit the work traffic on the way to the airport. He didn't care. Santi had been a wheelman for Mikey in earlier times. He was still a great driver.

"Do me a favor," Mikey said suddenly.

"Sure, boss. What?"

"Drive through town. Past the courthouse."

Santi didn't say anything. He just smiled.

The women who worked in Kemp's office were just filing in. There was Glory Ramirez and Sari Fiore. Olivia was ahead of them all. And there, behind them, in an old tweed coat, walking slowly with a cane, was Bernie.

"Slow down, okay?" Mikey asked, sounding half out of breath as he watched Bernie's slow progress to the door. She was hurting. It was a cold, rainy day, and he imagined she was having one of her flares.

He remembered her sitting up with him when he'd had the migraine. He remembered carrying her into the boardinghouse the day they'd met, when she had fallen in front of the car and he thought she was playing him. It seemed so long ago.

She made her way into the building, not looking behind her. She'd screwed her beautiful blond hair up into a bun. She looked tired and in pain, worn-out. He grimaced as he watched her disappear into the office. The door closed behind her.

Mikey felt the loss of connection like a blow to his chest.

"We leaving now, boss?" he asked Mikey.

There was a hesitation, only a very brief one. "Yeah," Mikey said finally. He slumped a little. "Yeah, we're leaving. Let's get to the airport."

"Sure thing," Santi said, and sped up past the office building, leaving it and Bernie behind, perhaps forever.

Chapter Fourteen

Bernie, never a late sleeper, woke very early the next morning. She couldn't get what Sari had said out of her mind. Suppose Jessie had told lies to both her and Mikey? She had been too shy to speak to him about something so intimate, and he would probably have been reluctant to say anything to Bernie about her supposed distaste for his background.

Jessie had been putting on an act. Why? The woman was patently out of place in Jacobsville, which led to a worrying conclusion. What if she was a lookout for that man who was trying to have Mikey killed? It really bothered her.

She got up and dressed, aching and barely able

to walk for the pain and stiffness. After a few minutes, she felt better, but she'd still need the cane, even on level ground. Rheumatoid arthritis flares were painful and fatiguing. She took her medicines regularly, but they'd begun to be less effective, as many drugs became over the years. She recalled the wonder shot that was used to control it, but even with a large discount, she'd never be able to afford the monthly expense. It might have made a difference in her quality of life. Days like this, cold and rainy, were agony to people who lived with arthritis.

She didn't tell the other women that she'd walked to work, because they'd have fussed. Any one of them would gladly have offered her a ride, but she wanted to be independent. It wasn't good to lean on people. Her father had always said that they had to take care of their own problems and not advertise them to the world. It was a burden that honorable people shared. She smiled, remembering the wonderful man who'd raised her. She missed him.

"You're just on time," Sari Fiore teased, smiling.

"I'm always on time," Bernie replied with

a small laugh. "I wouldn't want Mr. Kemp to fire me."

"No danger of that, as long as you don't tell Ted Regan that court's been dismissed," Olivia said, tongue in cheek.

They all laughed as they filed into the office.

Bernie was the last one inside. She almost stumbled going in, but she regained her footing quickly, holding on to the doorknob. The back of her neck tingled. Odd, she thought, that feeling. But it was probably nothing. She ignored it and went on inside the building.

Sari was pregnant. It was happy news, and the whole office went wild when they knew. Even Mr. Kemp congratulated her, grinning from ear to ear.

"You'll find that babies are addictive," he teased. "Which is why we have another one on the way, too."

"That's wonderful," Sari said, smiling. "I know Violet's over the moon. Are the twins coping with your toddler?"

"The twins?" Bernie asked curiously.

"He has two Siamese cats," Sari explained. "He made them mad one day and they tag-teamed biting his ankles and ran under heavy furniture afterward."

Mr. Kemp chuckled. "They've calmed down. Well, a little. Violet learned early that they like salmon, so she keeps cans of it handy."

They all laughed. Bernie was thinking about children. She'd wanted one so badly with Mikey. Just as well, she realized, that she'd never been intimate with him, considering the way things had turned out.

In his world of glitzy women and casinos, he probably had a procession of beautiful women at his beck and call. Including Jessie.

But she remembered that Sari had told her Mikey was no longer in danger; nor was his boss, Tony Garza. Apparently a group of bosses had decided that Cotillo was calling too much attention to certain underworld figures, and he'd been taken out of the equation. It was called "natural causes," but Sari said it wasn't at all, that the mob knew how to cause sudden death that looked natural.

That was Mikey's world. Death. Violence. Glitter. Of course, she was well out of it. Her health wouldn't have allowed her to endure the stresses of his profession, much less the strenuous lifestyle he enjoyed.

But she missed him terribly. It had sent her into days of depression when she knew he was gone. He'd left without even bothering to say goodbye. But what, she reasoned, could he have said? That he couldn't live with a disabled woman, that he preferred her sexy coworker, that Jessie was great in bed? All those things? It would have tormented her forever. No. It was better the way it had happened—a quick ending, as painless as possible. It was over.

Now all she had to do was adjust to her new reality. Maybe one day she could look back and remember a handsome, dashing man who'd taken her places and kissed her as if he'd have died for her mouth, who'd seemed to love her. Maybe she could recall just the joy of being with him, without remembering how it had ended. It would be a pretty memory, tied up with ribbon and tucked away in a scrapbook.

Mikey watched people come and go in the casino with hardly any interest at all. Beside him, Tony Garza, who was breaking his California trip with a stop in Las Vegas to see Mikey, was sipping a whiskey highball.

"They ever find out who hit Cotillo?" Mikey asked.

"No. And they never will. The New York family arranged it all. Cotillo was about to point the finger at one of their underbosses. It would have devastated the family. So they sent Jack the Mackerel and Billy Tenspot down to visit Cotillo. They had a guy in the coroner's office swear it was a natural death."

"What about Cotillo's family?" Mikey persisted.

"Running scared. It wasn't that big, and most of them tried to talk Cotillo out of biting off more than he could chew. The New York boss even spoke to him personally and told him how it was. He didn't listen."

"Terminal error," Mikey commented.

"Very." He sighed. "At least we're off the hook. I owe you, Mikey. Big-time. You ever need a favor, you know where to find me."

Mikey shrugged. "No sweat. You'd have done it for me, boss."

Tony chuckled. "Yeah. I would have." He

paused. "What's this about some Texas girl you got involved with?"

Mikey's face closed up. "Closed chapter," he said tautly.

"I got a good look at Texas women when I gave Merrie Grayling away at her wedding," he reminded Mikey. "They're good people."

"She was. But she couldn't live with my profession."

"I heard you couldn't live with her maybe being an invalid one day."

Mikey turned. His eyes glittered. "I never said that," he replied. "Never! It wouldn't have mattered to me if she couldn't even walk. I'd have carried her—" He broke off, averting his eyes.

Tony laid a big hand on his shoulder. "Jessie Tennison belongs to the New York boss. She's his mistress," he continued. "She made trouble for you because it's what she does. Nobody likes her, and one day the wife is going to complain loudly enough that the boss will have to do something about her. Something unpleasant. She's making her own sad future and she doesn't even know it."

"I won't mourn her," Mikey said.

"Your cousin said she carried tales to both of you," he said. "She lied and you both believed her."

Mikey's face hardened. "Bernie told me herself that she was always on the right side of the law."

"And you told her that it didn't matter that she might become disabled one day, yes?"

Mikey's teeth clenched. "For all the good it did me."

"It's your life, *paisan*," he continued. "But you've been moping around here like a lost soul ever since I walked in the door, when we should both be celebrating. If I were you, I'd go back to Texas and talk to the woman. Really talk to her."

Mikey grimaced. "I took Jessie out on the town. I know, it was stupid. I was feeling low because of what I'd heard, what Jessie told me that Bernie said about my past. I wanted to feel better, so I took her up to San Antonio for supper. She told Bernie I slept with her. It's a lie, but Bernie had every reason to believe her. So even if I wanted to go back and talk it out, she'd never trust me again. She'd probably shut the door in my face."

"There are these things called roses," Tony mused. "Women go nuts over them. I know my late wife did. Chocolates. Greeting cards. I went through all those things while I was courting her." His eyes were wistful with memories. "She didn't even like me at first, but I wore her down. I was a bad man, too, Mikey, and her dad was a cop, but it didn't matter. She had leukemia," he added softly. "I took care of her when she had relapses, right up until the last one that took her out. I never minded. She knew it. We loved each other. None of the small stuff mattered. Love kept us together in spite of the difficulties we faced."

Mikey hadn't said anything. He just listened. "That's a lot like me and Bernie," he said after a minute.

"Yeah. How about that?"

Mikey took a deep breath. "I'll think about it." He glanced at the boss. "Roses, huh?"

"Might send yellow ones," Tony suggested. "Isn't there some song about yellow roses and Texas?"

Mikey actually laughed. It was the first time he had since he'd left Jacobsville.

* * *

It was the middle of the afternoon when the florist brought them in. Judy, who owned the flower shop, came herself, grinning from ear to ear as she carried them straight to a shocked Bernie at her desk and placed them on it.

"Oh!" Bernie's hand went to her throat. She couldn't believe what she was seeing. There must have been three dozen yellow roses in the arrangement, along with flowers of every single color, and greenery highlighting it all.

"I know, it's closer to Thanksgiving than spring," Judy laughed, "but the man said yellow roses, so that's what you get."

"The man?" Bernie was dumbfounded. Her coworkers were grinning from ear to ear.

"Read the card," Judy suggested, indicating it on a plastic stand inside the arrangement.

Bernie pulled it out with hands that held a faint trembling. She opened the envelope. The card only said, "Miss you terribly. Can you forgive?" And it was signed "Mikey."

Tears were rolling down her cheeks. She read the card again, just to be sure that she wasn't seeing things.

"Well?" Sari prompted. "What does it say?

Who's it from? Or should we just guess?" she added with a grin.

"Mikey," Bernie said in a husky tone. "The flowers are from Mikey!"

"Doesn't he do things in a big way?" Olivia mused, studying the huge arrangement. "Amazing that your back didn't break under the weight, Judy," she teased the florist.

"I have liniment," Judy chuckled.

"They're so beautiful," Bernie said, caressing a petal on one of the roses, most of which were in bloom.

"I guess he thinks you are, too, sweetheart, because let me tell you, I could almost retire on what this arrangement cost," Judy laughed.

Bernie struggled to her feet and hugged the florist. "You always do the most beautiful arrangements, but this one is extraordinary."

"Thanks." Judy hugged her back.

Mr. Kemp came out of his office, stopped dead, and gaped at the arrangement that took up most of Bernie's desk. "Did somebody die?" he asked.

They all burst out laughing. Kemp grinned.

"Mikey, huh?" he asked Bernie, who flushed.

"I figured he'd work it out sooner or later. Okay, people, back to work."

"Yes, sir," they chorused.

Bernie and Judy moved her beautiful floral arrangement to a side table so that the desk was clear, but all day Bernie's eyes went to it, and she felt as if she could walk on clouds.

Paul and Sari Fiore drove her home so that Paul could carry the arrangement inside for her. It was very heavy.

"Right there, if you don't mind," Bernie said, indicating the cleared-off part of her chest of drawers. "It's so beautiful!"

"Good thing that Judy makes arrangements that don't have a loud scent," Sari teased, "or you'd smother in here from the fumes."

"Oh, I wouldn't even mind." Bernie sighed. "Nobody ever sent me flowers in my whole life," she added softly.

Paul and Sari exchanged glances. It was obvious that Mikey's peace offering had struck pay dirt.

He phoned Paul that night.

"Well?" he asked. "Did she donate them to

the hospital or her church?" he prompted, and sounded worried.

"No. She cried," Paul said. "Then Sari and I brought her home so I could carry them inside for her. God, Mikey, did you buy out a florist? I never knew there were that many yellow roses in the whole damned state," he added, chuckling.

"I wanted to make an impression," Mikey replied. There was a smile in his voice. "So she liked them, huh?"

"She loved them."

There was a sigh. "In that case, Santi and I might come down for a visit in a week or so. Just to get the lay of the land."

"I think that would be a very good idea," Paul replied.

Bernie was walking home late in the afternoon, wrapped in a coat against the chill, using her cane because it was rainy and her footing wasn't good.

A big, black limousine pulled up beside her and the window rolled down while her heart almost beat her to death.

"Now, don't fall under the wheels this time, okay?" said a man with a New Jersey accent.

Bernie laughed. "Hi," she said softly.

The door opened. Mikey got out, leaving Santi behind the wheel. He stuck his hands in his pockets and moved close to Bernie. His dark eyes searched her wan face in the late-afternoon dimness. They were intent, as if he was looking at something almost out of a fantasy.

"You look good," he said. "A little worn. You've lost weight, I think."

"Just a little," she confessed. Her eyes went over his lean face. "You look worn, too."

"I never slept with Jessie," he blurted out. "I like to stick to my own species."

She laughed in spite of herself.

"I did a dumb thing," he muttered. "I should have known that you wouldn't pour your heart out to somebody in a public place."

She grimaced. "I should have known the same thing about you."

He drew in a breath and smiled. "So. Suppose we start over? Hi. My name's Mikey. I sometimes break the law, but I'll try to restrict myself to jaywalking for the rest of my life if you'll take a chance on me."

Her heart leaped. "Hi. My name's Bernadette, but everybody calls me Bernie. I never break the law, but I'd take a chance on you no matter what you did for a living."

His lips parted on a husky breath. "Oh, baby," he said in a rough whisper. "God, I've missed you…!"

She would have told him the same thing, but he had her up in his arms and was kissing her as if there was no tomorrow. Her arms were around his neck, her cane was on the sidewalk somewhere getting wet. She was kissing him back.

Long minutes went by. The rain was coming down in buckets and they were both soaked. Finally Santi got out of the car and stopped beside them, coughing loudly.

Mikey drew back, shivering a little with the overwhelming hunger he felt for Bernie. He looked at Santi blankly. "What? You got a cold?"

"Boss, it's raining. Really raining. You know?"

Mikey blinked. Santi's hair was plastered to his head and face. He scowled and looked down at Bernie. Her hair was plastered to her head and face, too. He laughed out loud. "Damn. So it is! I guess we should find a dry place, huh?"

"I guess," Santi mused. He opened the car door.

"But I'm wet," Bernie wailed.

"The seats are leather, honey, they'll dry. Santi, find her cane, would you?"

"You bet!"

Santi closed the door.

"Now," Mikey murmured, drawing her close. "Where were we...?"

They were married in the courthouse, in the office of the justice of the peace. Bernie wore a winter-white coatdress and carried a bouquet of white roses. She had on a little saucy white hat that had a veil, and Mikey lifted it as he kissed her for the first time as Mrs. Michael Fiore.

Sari and Paul were their witnesses, and Tony Garza came down with his entourage for the wedding. In fact, Marcus Carrera and his Delia, and their little boys, also came to town for the event.

"I owe you a lot," Mikey told Marcus.

The big man waved away the thanks. "No sweat," he chuckled. "But if you come across a bolt of antique cloth, you know where to mail it, right?" he teased.

Mikey clapped him on the back. "You bet I do."

The honeymoon was in Jamaica, in Montego Bay, where they swam and acted like tourists. Well, at least, after the first night they were together.

"You don't need to worry about a thing," Mikey whispered to her as he undressed her very slowly and eased her under the covers.

She shivered a little at the first contact with his nude body, but he kissed her and caressed her until she didn't care what he did as long as he didn't stop.

He carried her from one breathless plateau to another, from one side of the bed to the other, for what seemed hours before he finally moved over her with intent. She was so sensitized by then that she barely felt the little flash of pain that hallmarked his slow penetration of her welcoming body.

She was aching for him, so hungry that she knew nothing, saw nothing, except his face above her as the passion grew and grew and grew and finally exploded into pleasure beyond anything she'd ever dreamed.

"Oh, my goodness," she moaned as they finally moved apart. She shifted her hips and the exquisite sensations went on and on.

He chuckled, drawing her to his side. "It's addictive."

"Very!"

He pulled her onto him and looked up into her soft eyes. "I've never missed anyone the way I missed you. I was just ashamed to even call you, after what I did."

She bent and kissed him tenderly. "We both believed lies because we were insecure."

"But no more."

"Not ever," she agreed.

"There's still the matter of the little unlawful things," he said, grimacing. "But I've got a legitimate casino now, and two of the biggest mob bosses in history in my corner. So if I want to move out into the world, so long as I don't betray any secrets, I can leave the old life behind. Not that I'll give up my house in Jersey. You'll like it," he added softly. "It's old, but it's got character."

"I'll love anywhere you live," she said simply.

"And I'll cope, however I have to." Her pale eyes met his dark ones. "I love you."

He hugged her close. "I love you, too, baby. And don't you dare think I mind about the cane and the days you have flares, or if you get sick. I can afford nurses, anything you need. But I'll take care of you myself," he added, lifting his head, and his eyes adored her. "Because you're the most important thing in the whole world."

"So are you to me," she whispered, and kissed him.

"Listen, I spoke to your doctor," he said. "Louise Coltrain said there are medicines you can inject, that will make your quality of life a hundred times better."

"Yes, but they're so expensive—"

"I could fund the treasury of a small country, honey," he interrupted. "It will be money well spent, especially when the kids come along. You won't need to try and keep up with me," he chuckled. "I'll carry you, if I need to. But you *will* need to keep up with our kids..."

She laughed with pure delight. "Are we having several?"

He grinned. "However many you want. And

I'll learn to change diapers and give bottles, just so you know."

"We can do it together," she said softly.

"We'll do everything together," he replied quietly. "As long as we live. Yes?"

She bent and kissed him hungrily. "As long as we live."

And they did.

* * * * *

LET'S TALK
Romance

For exclusive extracts, competitions
and special offers, find us online:

f facebook.com/millsandboon

⊙ @millsandboonuk

🐦 @millsandboon

Or get in touch on 0844 844 1351*

For all the latest titles coming soon,
visit millsandboon.co.uk/nextmonth

Want even more
ROMANCE?

Join our bookclub today!